STONE HEART DEEP

PAUL BASSETT DAVIES

Published in 2021
by Lightning Books Ltd
Imprint of Eye Books Ltd
29A Barrow Street
Much Wenlock
Shropshire
TF13 6EN

www.lightning-books.com

British Library Cataloguing in Publication Data
A catalogue record for this book is available from the British Library.

Printed by CPI Group (UK) Ltd, Croydon CR0 4YY

ISBN: 9781785632655

*Violence is not completely fatal
until it ceases to disturb us*
Thomas Merton

PROLOGUE

The image is blurred.

Adam crouches down a little more, and brings his face closer to the camera. His features spring into focus as he speaks: 'Is this good, Chris?'

A woman's voice: 'Just a moment.' The image sharpens. 'OK, all good.'

'Great. We only get one take for this gig.'

'Don't fuck up, then.'

Adam smiles. 'I won't, if you won't.'

'Deal. Are you ready to go?'

Adam checks his watch and turns to his right. 'OK for you, Alex?'

'I'm good,' says an unseen voice.

'Let's do it.'

'We're rolling,' Chris says.

'Sound?'

'Sound. And…action.'

Adam speaks directly into the camera. His voice is low and urgent, but steady: 'In a few minutes I'll be meeting Enver again. Having come to trust me over the last three weeks, he now believes I'm going to introduce him to Mr Jones, the man who wants to buy the fifteen-year-old Slovakian girl called Nadia. Enver thinks his new customer runs a chain of brothels, where Nadia will be pimped out to men, perhaps as many as twenty a day. In reality, "Mr Jones" is this man beside me, Alex Burnside…'

The camera pans left to take in a burly man hunched down beside Adam, squashed up against him uncomfortably in the cramped surveillance van. Alex nods curtly, and the camera pans back to Adam, who continues: '…who served with a British special forces unit before becoming a private security consultant. The men we're dealing with can be very violent. We've already seen how they treat the women and girls they smuggle into the country, including Nadia, who has been helping us with such incredible bravery. We now intend to free her, and expose Enver's operation. Let's hope everything goes to plan.'

Adam stops speaking and continues looking into camera.

'It's good for me,' Chris says, 'and…we're still rolling.'

'Let's go,' Adam says.

'Wait, let me switch audio source. OK; test it.'

Adam pats his chest, producing a loud THUD from the microphone concealed under his shirt.

'Say something,' Chris says.

'See you on the other side.'

'Good for sound. Break a leg.'

Adam and Alex turn around awkwardly, unable to stand upright. Adam opens the back doors of the van and daylight floods in.

The shot swings around. There's a glimpse of Chris's hand as she flips open a spyhole in the van's side panel and places the camera up against it. The focus and exposure are adjusted, and now Adam and Alex are walking away from the van, between two rows of big trucks. The sound is picked up by Adam's concealed microphone as the two men walk almost to the end of the canyon formed by the parked vehicles. They wait.

'Here they come,' Adam whispers. His amplified voice sounds weirdly close, given that he and Alex are a hundred yards away now, at the far end of the commercial vehicle parking lot. The ceaseless flow of traffic on an unseen motorway, somewhere nearby, sounds like the sea.

A large black BMW glides into view, swings slowly into the canyon between the trucks and stops a few yards from Adam and Alex. The front door on the passenger side opens and a man with a thin face gets out. He strides around the back of the car and opens the rear passenger door on the driver's side. A squat, shaven-headed man emerges, and raises a hand to Adam with a smile. Meanwhile the driver steps out of the car and stands motionless beside it, his hands clasped in front of him. He's big.

The squat man reaches back into the car, making a beckoning gesture with his hand, palm downwards in the European way. After a moment a girl emerges. Hair in pigtails, short skirt. She looks pale, but she seems steady enough as she stands beside the squat man. Even though she's clearly very young she's nearly as tall as him. He puts an arm around her waist and walks her to Adam. He extends his free hand.

'Adam, my friend. Good to see you again. All OK with you?'

'All good, Enver. This is my friend Mr Jones.'

Enver turns to study Alex. He nods slowly. 'Mr Jones. Shall we be on first-name terms, now we finally meet and do business?'

Alex steps forward and offers his hand. 'Charlie. Charlie Jones.'

They shake hands.

'OK, Charlie,' Enver says, 'now you meet Nadia.'

He draws the girl close, cuddling her as he speaks to her in a coaxing, avuncular tone, his lips brushing against her hair.

'Mr Charlie Jones is a fine English gentleman,' he says, 'and he will be very good to you if you are nice to him. He will buy you gifts, you know?'

Enver winks at Alex, who reaches out to take Nadia by the hand. Enver gazes at him for a long moment before he removes his arm from around Nadia's waist.

Alex gently pulls her towards him, pivoting slightly as he does so, to place himself between her and the others. The move is casual but deliberate.

'She is a good girl,' Enver says to him. 'Very clean. Fresh. No men yet.'

Alex nods, and smiles blandly. His grip on Nadia's hand is tight.

Enver turns to Adam. 'So, it's good. You have the money, my friend?'

'No.'

Enver glances around. 'Who has the money?'

'There's no money, Enver. I'm a journalist. You're being filmed.'

Enver moves closer to Adam. He speaks softly. 'What are you saying, Adam?'

'We've been filming you secretly since–'

Enver cuts him off: 'Give me the girl.'

At the sound of Enver's raised voice, his driver and the other man move forward swiftly. Adam shifts his balance and loosens his arms, ready to fight. Beside him, Alex plants himself squarely in front of Nadia, still holding her with one hand while with the other he whips a thin police-style baton from inside his coat and with a flick of his wrist extends it to its full length.

'No,' Adam says, 'Nadia stays with us.'

In a single fluid movement Enver produces a gun and raises it to point at Adam's face, very close. Adam doesn't flinch: 'This is being filmed, Enver. You'll get eight years or so, serve four, maybe get deported. Murder will get you life. Twenty years minimum.'

Enver's hand remains steady.

Adam says, 'That white van behind me? That's where the team is. They're calling the cops right now.'

Enver's eyes flick away from Adam's face and, unnervingly, he looks directly into the camera for an instant without knowing it. He returns his gaze to Adam's. He lowers the gun, takes a swift step back and shouts to his men: 'We go!'

Adam glances at the driver and the other man as they run back to the car. While he's distracted, Enver raises the gun again and whips the barrel across Adam's face.

Adam staggers but doesn't fall. Enver and his men jump back into the car, which reverses at high speed and clips the back edge of the last truck in the row as it swings around with a squeal of tyres and roars away.

Adam turns to the camera, his hand clamped over his bleeding cheek. He grins and winces at the same time. 'Tell me you got all that!'

The image freezes.

***

A thunder of applause.

I glanced back up at my own image, huge on the screen behind me. Insufferable prick. That was what part of me thought, anyway. I looked out at the audience. The ballroom was filled with fifty round tables, each seating a dozen people, some of whom were now rising to their feet, presenting the others with the choice of joining the standing ovation or seeming ungenerous. To me. The person they were all there to honour and validate. And part of me loved it.

I was aware that I cut a dashing figure, both up on the screen, where I looked tough and dishevelled – the wounded hero – and onstage, in a tuxedo that still fitted me as well as it did when I bought it, at the age of nineteen. That was two decades ago, and there was still no grey in my hair. Good posture, nice smile. I scrubbed up well, and I knew it. And part of me hated it. This isn't meant to be about me, I thought, and immediately realised how stupid that thought was. Of course it was about me. I was the one receiving the bloody award, which was currently in the hands of a tall, elegant woman of sixty standing beside me in front of a microphone.

'The footage we've just seen,' she said, 'like the rest of Adam's remarkable work, speaks far more eloquently than anything more I could hope to say. I will simply end by telling you I'm certain that my late husband would have been the first to applaud this choice. And so it is with great pleasure that I present the Simon Draper Investigative Memorial Prize to Adam Budd.'

Another explosion of applause. Those in the audience who were old hands at this game had wisely remained on their feet, to avoid repeating the awkwardness of deciding whether or not to offer another standing ovation.

The woman – Lynn Draper – handed the award to me. It was an ugly, abstract collision of metal and glass, which might charitably be interpreted as symbolising a probing, penetrative spirit, expressed as a collection of spiky protrusions. I grasped the angular lump of kitsch in my hands, and Lynn leaned in to kiss me on the cheek. She whispered, 'Simon would be proud.'

I ducked in acknowledgement, very nearly head-butting Lynn as she moved in for a kiss on my other cheek, which I wasn't expecting. We manoeuvred through the moment gracefully, and as Lynn hugged me I tried to prevent the award, which I was holding in front of me, from stabbing either of us in the belly.

Lynn stepped away, and I placed the award on the lectern in front of me. I kept one hand curled around its narrow stem, mistrusting its stability.

I leaned into the microphone and did my thing. I thanked each member of my team by name; I thanked the production company, and the BBC. I threw in the usual line about being flustered by this overwhelming honour, and hoping I hadn't forgotten to acknowledge anyone as a result, although I was pretty sure I hadn't. I paused and gazed out at the audience for a moment. The final part was important; I needed to get it right.

'The only people left to thank,' I said, 'are those I can't name in public. I'm very happy to tell you that our brave colleague, Nadia, who gave and risked so much to help us, is safe and well. But there are others – some of them helping us undercover – who are still trapped in the repugnant trade that Nadia's courage has helped to expose. This award is for her, and for them – the extraordinary people whose inspiring spirit never ceases to humble me, and who will not, I truly hope, need to remain nameless for much longer.'

I raised the award in a salute – dear god, it was heavy – and turned away. More applause, with some people cheering. I was acutely conscious of enjoying the warm glow of appreciation, even as I wanted to despise it. I wished I hadn't said that stuff about being humbled. That must have sounded so fake.

I followed a man with headphones and a clipboard to the steps at the side of the stage, and trotted down them and wove my way back towards our table, through a gauntlet of congratulations -- smiling faces, thumps on the back, handshakes.

As I neared our table I saw Maria coming towards me. I prepared myself for her embrace, but as she approached I saw concern in her expression. Without ceremony she elbowed aside a well-wisher, and grabbed my shoulder. She put her lips to my ear so she could be heard above the hubbub: 'Come with me, something's happened.'

She took my hand and began to lead me towards the back of the auditorium, past our own table. I stopped her before we reached the doors.

'What is it?'

Maria held up my mobile phone. I'd left it with her when I went to the stage, having discovered that it spoiled the cut of my evening clothes when it was in my pocket.

'It's your mother,' she said.

I looked at her in astonishment. 'On the phone?'

Maria shook her head. She showed me the message on the screen.

I stared at it for a long time. 'Oh god,' I said, 'she's gone.'

The noise in the room around me became an abstract background, swelling and diminishing like waves crashing on a shoreline.

ONE

I gazed down into the swirling grey sea, keeping a firm grip on the railing as the tiny ferry bucked and plunged through the waves. The conditions had been described to me as bracing, rather than rough. If they were rough, I'd been told, I wouldn't have been allowed on the deck.

Another burst of spray hit my face. I raised my head to shake it off, and for a moment I visualised Maria standing beside me at the rail, her dark hair being whipped by the wind, chin raised defiantly. Would she have enjoyed being out here? I had to admit I didn't know, even after almost three years together. And now it didn't matter.

We'd gone back to her place from the awards ceremony. She'd insisted that I shouldn't be alone, and I didn't want to tell her I

15

would have preferred to go back to my own flat by myself. She sensed it, though. She was getting good at that.

We sat on Maria's couch and she asked if I'd like to talk about my mother, and assured me she completely understood if I didn't want to. All in good time, she said, and we could go straight to bed if I wanted to, and we could make love, or she would just hold me. Or not. Whatever worked for me.

'Thanks,' I said, and gazed at the floor.

She waited a moment, then stood up and left the room. Five minutes later she reappeared with a bottle of wine, poured two glasses, and sat down beside me again.

'Did you expect it?'

'No,' I said. 'I hadn't seen her for a while. We spoke on the phone about four months ago, but she didn't say anything.'

'Only seventy. That's so young. And she didn't tell you she was ill?'

'She never told me anything. Nothing important, anyway.'

Maria took my hand. 'I'm so sorry, darling.'

'My mother liked to surprise people.'

She glanced at me with a frown, but relaxed when she saw I was smiling. I knew she found it hard to read my mood sometimes. That wasn't her fault, especially at a moment like this, when I wasn't sure of it myself. I wasn't really feeling anything at all, to tell the truth, except a vague sense that something was over, like the end of a film or a concert. 'It's all right,' I said, patting her knee, 'don't worry. We weren't close.'

'As you've mentioned before,' Maria said, and refilled our glasses.

We went to bed not long afterwards, mostly because I couldn't think of anything else to do. In the morning we had coffee together, then I left.

Four days later, I was sitting up in her bed, watching the patterns cast on the wall by the morning sunlight as the slender trees outside her window, dusted with green, swayed in a light breeze. I'd started to tell her about the inheritance, but now I was gazing at the play of shadows dappling the plasterwork.

Maria nudged me. 'Go on.'

'Sorry, I was miles away. Yes, it's a huge house, apparently. Totally derelict.'

'How much is it worth?'

'It's not clear. Like everything else about this whole fucking legacy. For one thing, it depends on whether anyone would want to buy it in its current condition. If not, is it worth restoring? I haven't even seen pictures of it yet. Another thing that's not entirely clear is whether or not I actually own the place.'

'What do you mean? She left it to you! That what the lawyers said, isn't it?'

'Yes, but there are complications. Deeds, documents, god knows what. Stipulations and conditions. All kinds of paperwork that has to be verified. If it can even be found.'

'What a pain.'

'Tell me about it. But if I can get all that stuff straightened out, maybe someone will want to buy it from me. I mean, certain people might find it an attractive proposition, don't you think? Romantic, even. A huge mansion on a remote Scottish island with a small population. All very quiet, and out of the way. There's even a lake next to the house. It all sounds like *Brigadoon*, or something.'

'Like what?'

'That film. *Brigadoon*. The musical. About a magical place that comes out of the mist every hundred years.'

'Oh, I remember! We saw it one night when we were stoned.'

'That's right. It was funny.'

Maria was silent for a moment, then she said, 'Maybe you should go there.'

'Really? You think so?'

We were both naked, and I gazed at her, running my eyes appreciatively over her body. She smiled and rolled over to nestle against me. I put my arm around her, glad I didn't now have to face her. She'd said precisely what I'd wanted her to say.

She began to stroke my chest. 'You could use a break, couldn't you?'

'Could I?'

'I think so. That last film took it out of you. And the one before.'

'I wasn't undercover for the care home thing. Just a lot of editing.'

'Right. Sitting and watching that horrible footage over and over again. That's probably even worse. A month of your life, every day, seeing those poor, helpless people being abused and tormented. Don't tell me that doesn't affect you.'

'It did, I suppose.'

I thought about the footage she was referring to. It was certainly distressing to watch, and occasionally during the editing process I got a weird urge to wash my hands, despite having no physical contact with material which, by this stage, existed only as digital code. But had I been traumatised? I didn't think so. I remembered a medic I'd met in Afghanistan, an older guy who'd worked in a children's hospice for a few years. He told me he was able to get through his shift – which often included comforting dying kids, and dealing with their families – and remain composed. Then he'd go home, watch an episode of *ER*, and cry his eyes out. I found that interesting.

He said it didn't have to be *ER*, it could be any medical show – *Casualty*, *House*, or even *Scrubs* – just so long as it involved doctors, doing their work. I understood what that was all about. But nothing like it had happened with me.

'Believe me,' Maria continued, 'it affected you. And then you went straight into the trafficking film, with all the tension, and getting hit, and then the award, and now this news about your mother. I think you're burned out, Adam.'

'Yeah? I don't feel burned out.'

'You'd be the last to know.'

I gazed at the shadows on the wall again, letting her see I was thinking about it.

'Go and take a look at the place,' Maria said, 'as part of a way to sort it out. And at the same time, use it as an excuse to get away from everything. Have a complete break.'

'Maybe I will,' I murmured. 'You're right. I need to get away.'

'We could go together.'

I didn't reply, but I knew she felt the little spasm of tension that twitched through my arm.

She rolled off me and propped herself up on her elbow. 'What?'

'Nothing.'

'You don't want me to come?'

'I didn't realise that's what you meant.'

'What did you think I meant?'

'That I should...you know, just get away. Have some time on my own.'

'Is that what you want?'

'I don't know. But when you just suggested it a minute ago I suddenly thought, yes, maybe that's what I should do. It struck a chord. And it made me think of just being somewhere else, with a chance to recharge my batteries.'

'And you can't do that with me?'

'I'm not saying that.'

She gave me a long, deadpan look.

'What?' I said.

'I'm going to get some coffee.'

She was gone a long time. When she came back she'd showered and put on her thick bathrobe and wound a towel around her hair. She stood in the doorway. I raised the sheet so she could get back into bed, but she didn't move. I let it fall and met her gaze.

She looked away after a moment, and went to sit at her dressing table where she began to towel her hair, her eyes flashing at me in the mirror every so often.

I wondered how long this would take. 'Are you all right?' I said.

'Fine. I was just thinking.'

'Thinking what?'

'Maybe I'll take a holiday by myself, if I can't come with you. I could go on a romantic cruise for singles.'

'I didn't say you couldn't come with me.'

'You didn't have to.'

'Look,' I said, 'I'm sorry. Please come with me.'

She slung the towel around her shoulders, grasping the ends like a prize fighter, and took a deep breath and swivelled around to face me. Here it came.

'You planned this,' she said, 'didn't you?'

'Planned what?'

'So it would be my idea, as if it never crossed your mind that we could go together, and now it makes me look like I'm being pushy and needy if I say I want to come too.'

'Where do you get all that from?'

'This is the way it works, isn't it? You're the one who's

always leaving, and I wait here doing nothing, then you come back for as long as you want, but never long enough to commit to anything; god forbid, oh no, that would be too restricting, too much of a burden on your wild, noble, free spirit, wouldn't it?'

'You don't do nothing,' I said. 'You've got your work.'

'Oh, fuck off. In fact, really fuck off.' She stood up. 'Go on, go away and don't come back. Go and find someone else to rescue, before you get bored with me again. I'll be in the kitchen until you've gone. Leave your keys on the hall table.'

She draped the towel over her head like a hood, and walked out.

***

I looked down at the sea again and got a face full of spray for my trouble. As I raised my head and wiped my face I saw a low, dark mass on the horizon, dead ahead. I looked up and tried to catch Archie's eye, but the old man's gaze was focused on our destination, both hands on the wheel in front of him.

I took three unsteady steps away from the side and lurched for the handrail of the metal stairway up to the wheelhouse. The boat was no more than forty feet long, and the entire rear deck was occupied by a battered old Land Rover that was held in place by a couple of frayed ropes – not very securely, in my estimation.

As I entered the wheelhouse Archie glanced over his shoulder and nodded to me, then returned his attention to the horizon. He jerked his chin at the island that was now clearly visible ahead of us. 'Your first time over there, you said?'

'That's right.' I shuffled forward and stood beside him. I watched the way his hands seemed to move on the wheel intuitively, appearing to both steer and respond to the vessel at the same time.

Archie noticed me looking at his hands. He took them both off the wheel, which spun crazily. He raised a shaggy eyebrow at me. 'Steers herself, you see,' he said.

'I'll take your word for it.'

He grunted and took the wheel again.

He was almost too good to be true. If you asked a casting agency to provide you with someone to play the part of a grizzled old Scottish sea-dog you would have rejected Archie as being too obviously a stereotype. It was all there: the weather-beaten face, the wild red hair escaping from beneath a battered oilskin hat, the bushy beard in various shades of orange, grey and white. The man even had a pipe jammed between his teeth.

'So,' he said, 'you're the lad who's coming to take over the place by the loch.'

'I don't know about taking it over. My mother died, and–'

'Sorry for your loss,' he interjected. 'Her troubles are over. It comes to us all.'

I glanced at him. He was old-school, all right. Old Testament, even. 'Anyway,' I continued, 'it was only when she died that I discovered she seemed to have owned this place, this house, Stone Heart Deep.'

'Stone Heart Deep?'

'Isn't that what it's called?'

Archie gave me a flinty glance from beneath knitted brows. 'That's what the loch is called,' he said. 'But folks around there have another name for it.'

'What do they call it?'

He squinted into the distance again. 'I wouldn't know,' he muttered, 'I'm not from around there.'

I stared at the old man's craggy profile. I saw a fractional twitch at the side of his mouth, and heard an odd, rhythmic groaning sound leaking out from beside his pipe. I realised he was chuckling. The old bastard was fucking with me. I laughed. 'You had me there for a moment.'

Archie glanced at me again. 'Lighten up, man. Chill.'

'Right. It's just that I don't know what to expect. On the island there.'

Ahead of us, our destination was beginning to define itself as a formidable mass of rock, utterly isolated in a vast expanse of sea and sky.

'Well, don't expect any fishing,' he said. 'Too much peat in the water. That loch where your house lies is like a bog.'

'It may not actually be my house. My mother left her affairs in some disorder.'

'Aye, that doesn't surprise me.'

I felt abruptly wrong-footed. I turned sharply to him. 'Why not?'

'I met her once or twice.'

'Really? She said she was only on the island for a short time. Before I was born.'

'Did she, now? Yes, I dare say that's right. I didn't know her at all well.'

'I don't think anyone did,' I said, and immediately regretted it. Too much information. I cleared my throat. 'The thing is, she used to talk about a strange old house on a remote island, but I always assumed it was just one of her stories. I didn't even know if the island was real, to tell you the truth.'

'Oh, it's real enough,' Archie said, 'as you can see. But I wouldn't want to live there myself, all the same.'

'Why not?'

'That whole place is too damn quiet. You sneeze, and it's

news for a month. I like a bit of salt in my porridge.' He winked. 'I'm not dead yet, man.'

I liked Archie. I smiled, and when I turned to look at the island again I was startled because it suddenly seemed much closer. I could see a little harbour nestled among a cluster of cottages, and make out a man with a dog, waiting on the quayside.

TWO

I stood with my bag bedside me at the top of a concrete jetty that sloped down to the water, watching as Archie reversed the Land Rover up to the quay. The man with the dog walked slowly backwards up the slope, guiding Archie with hand-signals, which the old man ignored. As the vehicle drew level with me, Archie leaned out of the window and said, 'You're staying at the pub up in town, I understand.'

'That's right.'

'I'd give you a ride, but you're expected to take the taxi.'

'Expected?'

'Correct. Otherwise the taxi fellow might be offended.' He cocked an eyebrow at the man with the dog, who was now standing beside me. 'Isn't that right, Ogden?'

'Oh yes, Archie, we must not deprive the poor wee man of

his trade.'

Archie laughed. He raised a hand in farewell to me, and swung the Land Rover around in a tight circle. He gunned the engine, and the vehicle rattled away along the cobbles, exhaust belching.

The man beside me stepped forward and extended his hand. He was big and fleshy and he looked about fifty, but he had a boyish air, accentuated by a peaked cap perched jauntily on a mass of curls. The cap had a brass plate on the front that declared him to be the Harbour Master. His dog – a border collie, which looked as though it came from a disreputable branch of the family, more likely to rustle sheep than to herd them – lay at his feet, eyeing me warily.

'I'm Ogden,' the man said. 'Good day, and how do you do?'

I took the proffered hand. 'I'm Adam.'

'I know that,' Ogden said, pumping my hand vigorously and smiling at me. I smiled back. Ogden released my hand. He continued to smile, showing no sign of intending to do anything else for the foreseeable future.

'So,' I said finally, 'is the man with the taxi around?'

'Indeed he is. He will be with you momentarily.'

He removed his cap, and whistled. The dog at his feet sprang up and raced towards a row of cottages on the far side of the cobbled road lining the quayside, heading for an open door at end of the row. He threw his cap towards the dog, spinning it like a Frisbee. Without looking around, the dog leaped up, twisting in the air to catch the cap in its teeth, and disappeared into the cottage with it.

I glanced at Ogden, whose placid smile was inscrutable. After a few seconds the dog emerged from the cottage with a different cap between its teeth, ran up to Ogden, and sat on its haunches in front of him.

'Good lad,' Ogden said, and took the cap. He placed it carefully on his head and turned to me. 'Here he is.'

He raised a finger to the peak of the new cap in a salute, turned on his heel, and waddled briskly to a garage next to his cottage. He flung open the doors with a flourish to reveal an elderly but immaculate black London taxi.

I twisted around in the back seat of the taxi and looked down at the little harbour as the car began to climb a steep hill. The ferry bobbing at the end of the jetty seemed like a child's toy, washed up by the wide, endless sea beyond it. I could just make out Ogden's dog, prowling around in front of the cottages, on patrol.

'How long will the ferry stay there?' I said.

He glanced over his shoulder at me. 'Archie takes her back tomorrow. Twice a week he comes over and delivers supplies to folk. Weather permitting, of course.'

'Is it sometimes too rough?'

'Oh, indeed. And for bigger ships than Archie's, believe me. On occasion we have to wait several days before anything can reach us, especially in winter.'

'How do you manage?'

'How we've always managed. We tighten our belts when we need to.' He turned the wheel sharply and took a hairpin bend. The road was getting steeper.

'Do you like being so cut off?' I said.

He chuckled. 'Depends what you mean. We're not cut off from each other.'

'Right. But from the mainland?'

'We do well enough. We always have, and I expect we always will.' He swung the wheel again as he took another sharp bend. He wasn't slowing down for the turns, and this time the back of the car fishtailed slightly before he corrected it. When we'd set off, I noticed that Ogden seemed unconcerned about which side of the road he occupied, and as it got steeper and narrower the question became increasingly irrelevant. There was barely room for a single vehicle, let alone any oncoming traffic.

'Aye, we've always managed somehow,' he continued, turning around for a moment to grin at me, which didn't improve his driving.

'But it must get lonely sometimes,' I said, 'being so remote.'

'We're not bothered by it.' He squinted at me in the rear-view mirror. 'How much do you know about the history of this place?'

'Not much. I looked online, but I can't claim to have done much research.'

Ogden chuckled again. 'Oh yes, research. You're a newsman, after all.'

'How did you know that?'

'Archie told me. And people have been researching this place for thousands of years, it's just that in the old days they arrived in longboats and did their research with swords and spears and suchlike.'

I tried to remember whether I'd told Archie I was a journalist, but I was distracted by Ogden twisting around again to speak to me. I found myself tensing my leg, pressing an imaginary brake pedal.

'Now, that was Tallog Bay we've just left,' he said, assuming the tone of a tour guide, and nodding at the road behind us, 'and it used to be the main settlement, many hundreds of years ago.' He turned back to face the road ahead. 'But as you could surely see,' he continued, 'it is very exposed, and not just to the elements. However, it was a somewhat bigger place before folk moved up to the higher ground inland. This part of the island was more populated back then. Look over on your right-hand side there.'

I glimpsed a cluster of ruined crofts on a barren slope we were passing. Most of them were little more than piles of stones, overgrown with tough looking bracken.

'Why did people move inland?' I said.

'Pirates, Vikings, ruffians of every kidney. At first, the natives only used to go inland to hide up there, and they'd come back down when all the hooligans had gone home. But each time they ran inland they made their hidey-holes a wee bit more comfortable and cosy until eventually some lazy buggers couldn't be arsed to come back down again at all, and so Creedish up there became a town of itself.'

'That's civilisation for you,' I said.

'Oh, it's reasonably civilised, but it's not much of a town, to tell the truth, it's more of an oversized village. But it's where you'll find who you have come to see.'

After a pause I said, 'And who have I come to see?'

'The lawyer, Mrs Baird. To sort out all the bother with your house.'

I frowned at the back of Ogden's head, imagining that my displeasure could penetrate it like a kind of radiation, and make his brain itch. Attempting a tone of chilly courtesy I said, 'Does everyone here know my business?'

'Oh yes,' he replied cheerfully. Abruptly he leaned away from the wheel and peered up out of the passenger-side window. 'Ah, now this is interesting,' he said. 'You see those stones up there?'

He pointed to a windswept hill with a jagged ring of standing-stones encircling the top, looming against the slate-grey sky. The effect was bleak and unwelcoming. Perhaps that was the intention, I thought.

'Now, here's a mystery for you,' he said, accelerating into an oncoming bend and glancing around to look at me, an excited gleam in his eye. 'That hill is an Iron Age fort dating from a *later* period than the stones, which means they must have bee–'

He saw my expression change and whirled around to face the road. Too late.

An old woman on a bicycle had appeared from around the blind curve. Ogden slammed on the brakes in the same instant that the front of the car hit the bike. The woman's body flew into the air and struck the windscreen with a sickening thud before bouncing off to one side as the bicycle smashed onto the roof and cartwheeled away.

The taxi went into a skid and Ogden lost control. I braced my feet against the partition in front of me as the car lurched into a shallow ditch at the side of the road then ploughed into a steep bank. Ogden was jerked forward violently and struck his head against the wheel. He gave a surprised grunt and was still.

I tried to breathe evenly. The car was tilted over and the door next to me was jammed against the bank. I slithered across the rear seat until I could use the handle on the other door to haul myself into a position where I could open it. I pushed it upwards and outwards, taking care that it didn't fall back onto me as I scrambled out and lowered myself to the ground. I pulled Ogden's door open. Ogden groaned and raised his head. He had a small gash on his forehead but otherwise he seemed relatively unharmed.

I ran over to the woman who was lying in the road a few feet away. My heart sank as I knelt down beside her. One of her legs was bent beneath her at an unnatural angle and her foot was twisted almost entirely the wrong way around. Her legs were very thin.

Her bicycle was lying in a hedge beside the road, and the steady ticking of its spinning front wheel was the only sound I could hear. I leaned down to check the woman's breathing. Nothing. Her face was grey. Carefully I felt for a pulse in her neck. A flutter? Maybe.

A movement caught my eye. I looked up and saw two tiny, distant figures at the top of a field that sloped up from the bank where the taxi was embedded. They had abandoned a tractor and were running down the field towards us. As I turned my attention back to the old woman, I heard Ogden's voice, so close it made me jump:

'Bless my soul. That's old Mary Lennox. I haven't seen her around for months.'

I turned to find Ogden hunched behind me, almost breathing down my neck. His face was pale and he'd lost his cap; his curls flopped down over the cut on his forehead, which glistened wetly behind them, but didn't appear to be bleeding any more.

'She doesn't look good in very good shape,' I said.

'Aye, she hasn't been well for a long while,' Ogden said. 'She suffers from some class of trouble with her glands, I believe.'

'Have you got a phone?'

'A mobile phone? I have indeed. It's a Japanese make.'

'Who can you call for help?'

'Let me see,' Ogden said. 'How about the doctor?'

'Good, the doctor. Yes.'

Ogden fished a phone from his pocket and showed it to me. 'It's even got a camera inside it, you see? Do we need a photograph?'

'No, but please try the doctor.'

'Right you are. I'll see if I can get a signal. Sometimes we lose the connection for days at a time. It all depends on the weather. I'll just move it around a wee bit, and see what I can pick up.' Ogden held the phone aloft, and as he began to revolve slowly he caught sight of the two figures running down the field towards us. 'Oh look,' he said, waving at them, 'here come Barty and Sim.'

'Please,' I said, 'phone the doctor.'

'Of course, of course.' Ogden raised the phone again and began to take slow, ponderous steps away from me. 'Ah,' he said, 'I believe we're in luck. We're getting…a bit of a signal… over here.'

From the corner of my eye I saw the old woman's head move. A hiss of breath escaped her, and a spasm of pain crossed her face. As gently as I could, I slid my hand under her neck. 'It's all right, Mary,' I said. 'Just hang on. We're getting help for you.'

I called over my shoulder: 'We can't risk moving her. We're going to need a stretcher. Ogden?'

I glanced behind me to see that Ogden was now examining the twisted bicycle in the hedge. He put out his hand the stop the wheel spinning. 'Damn shame,' he murmured, 'this is a fine old machine.'

'Ogden! Did you reach the doctor?'

He looked up. 'What's that? Oh, yes! The doctor. I did speak to him. And as it happens he's not far away. He's in his car. He'll be here very soon.' He returned his attention to the bike. He grasped it gently with both hands and began to ease it from the hedge with great tenderness.

The old woman groaned. I leaned down close to her. 'Can you hear me, Mary?'

Her eyes snapped open. They were piercing blue. 'I know you,' she whispered.

'It's all right, Mary. The doctor is on his way.'

Mary's body convulsed. She struggled for breath. 'Mother,' she gasped. 'Mother?'

'Your mother's not here, Mary. I'm sorry. The doctor is coming soon.'

'Not...her,' she said. Her eyes widened. 'I know...you.'

I didn't want to keep contradicting her. 'Don't worry,' I said.

The woman suddenly grabbed my shoulder in a claw-like grip, pulled herself up with surprising strength, and hissed into my ear. 'She was right.' She sank back. Her eyes closed and her breath began to rattle in her throat.

I looked around. The two men from the field had reached the hedge. They scrambled over it, breathing heavily, and trotted up to Ogden, who was attempting to straighten the back wheel of the bike.

'You can't fix that,' panted the younger of the two men. He was large, and even though his overalls fitted him loosely it was evident that he was powerfully built.

The older, smaller man nudged him out of the way. 'What you mean is that *you* can't fix it,' he said scornfully. 'You haven't the skill, son. I can do it in the forge.'

'It's not yours to fix,' Ogden said, straightening up and placing himself in front of the bike protectively.

'You'll need my tractor to move your car,' the older farmer said. 'I'll do it in exchange for the bike.'

The three men became aware I was staring at them. They fell silent. Ogden smiled at me, casually placing a proprietorial hand on the bike's upturned front wheel. The older man placed his hand next to Ogden's.

'How is she?' Ogden said.

Before I could reply I heard a car engine, and almost at the same moment an old Bristol, dark plum red, in beautiful

33

condition, nosed around the blind curve. It came to a halt a few yards from me.

The driver who stepped out was a tall, keen-eyed man in his seventies, with a full head of silver hair swept back from a broad forehead. A black bag was in his hand. He ignored the men beside the bicycle, and nodded to me as he crouched down beside the woman on the ground. After a brief but close scrutiny he looked up at me.

'All I can do is ease her pain,' he said quietly.

He snapped open his bag and extracted a syringe, which he filled deftly from a glass vial. He found a vein in Mary's arm and injected her. Almost immediately her breathing became easier. The doctor took both of her hands in his and spoke to her in a low, soft voice:

'All is well, Mary. All is well.'

Mary seemed to sink into herself. Her face became tranquil. She shuddered, expelled a deep, rattling breath, and was still.

The doctor stood up swiftly. I got to my feet too, and noted that the old man was as tall as me. For the first time, he looked over at the men standing around the bike. Ogden removed his cap. The doctor addressed the older of the two farmers:

'Barty, will you please fetch your van and bring Mary up to the clinic for me?'

Barty jerked his head towards his companion. 'Sim will do it, Doctor. I had better stay here and help Ogden with his car.'

'Don't trouble yourself,' Ogden said.

Ogden and Barty each still had a hand on the bike wheel. The doctor took in their standoff. 'Whoever drives the van,' he said, 'I'd be obliged if you would bring that bike with you. The sergeant may wish to take a look at it.'

Ogden shifted uncomfortably. 'Why would he want to do that?'

'Perhaps the brakes were faulty,' the doctor said, 'or a wheel was loose. Something of that nature, do you see?'

I watched Ogden's expression change as the advantages of doing what he was told dawned on him. He nodded judiciously. 'Very true, Doctor. It will be best to check.'

'Precisely. You can stow it in the van along with the body, and I'll inform him.'

The doctor turned his gaze on me. 'You'd better come with me.'

I stiffened at his tone of command. 'Why?'

The doctor smiled. 'So I can give you a lift to Creedish. Unless you'd prefer to wait, and ride with the body. Or walk three miles uphill, and two more down to town.'

I felt foolish. 'Of course,' I said. 'Thank you. I'll get my bag from Ogden's taxi.'

'I'm Caleb Druce,' the man sitting next to me said as he reversed the old Bristol around the corner, executed a well-judged three-point turn, and accelerated back up the winding road. 'Doctor, obviously. People call me Cal.'

'I'm Adam Budd. But I expect you already know that. Everyone else seems to.'

'It comes with the territory, I'm afraid. Literally. It's a small place.'

'Small, but full of surprises.'

Druce shot me a glance. 'Yes, you've had a hell of a welcome. Are you all right?'

'I'm fine, thanks.'

There was a silence. I wondered whether to say what was on my mind.

He sensed my hesitation. 'Fine...but?'

'Since you ask,' I said, 'I have to admit I thought Ogden and

35

those men were behaving rather unusually.'

'In what way?'

'About the woman who died – Mary.'

'I think Ogden was in shock,' Druce said. 'Pretty deep shock, I'd say.'

'But those other two more or less ignored her. They seemed to be more interested in the bicycle, frankly.'

'They were probably embarrassed.'

'Embarrassed?'

'They didn't know how to behave in front of a stranger. They're farmers.'

'OK, but it was still a bit weird. I mean, you saw how they were.'

'Let me tell you something,' he said. 'Barty, the older man, knew Mary all his life, and saw her nearly every day. The young man, Sim, is his son. Mary was his godmother. They were both affected by her death, I can assure you.'

I stared at the road ahead. After a few seconds I said, 'I'm sorry. You're right, I don't know these people. This community. I'm behaving like a typical outsider, aren't I? Bringing my assumptions with me.'

'Don't be too hard on yourself. You just watched a woman die, after all.'

'Yes, I did.' I nodded thoughtfully.

After a pause Druce said, 'Is there something else you want to ask me?'

I turned to look at him. He kept his eyes on the road ahead, turning the wheel smoothly into the next bend. His aquiline nose and strong chin gave him a handsome profile. He was probably closer to eighty than seventy, but the flesh of his neck and throat had little of the looseness that age usually brings. 'All right,' I said, 'since you mention it, I'd like to ask you about that injection you gave Mary.'

'The morphine for the pain?'

'For the pain, yes. And for anything else?'

'Did I help her on her way? No, I did not. And if I did, do you think I'd be likely to admit it to a journalist, and one I've only just met, at that?'

I laughed. 'I guess not.'

'Correct. Now, let me ask *you* something. How old do you think Mary was?'

'I don't know. Eighty?'

'She was ninety-three. She was frail. I suspect there was dementia. She should never have been out on that bicycle.'

Again I hesitated. But what the hell – I would probably never see any of these people again after this visit. 'Yes,' I said, 'the bicycle that may be found to have had faulty brakes, or perhaps a loose wheel. Which would be convenient, I suppose.'

The car crested a hill and the road levelled out. Druce slowed down and parked on the flat verge.

I took in a spectacular view. The road ahead wound down in a series of gentle curves to a small town, nestled in a hollow. On the other side of the town a range of wild hills spread out, and beyond them was an endless expanse of sea. Low, scudding clouds allowed irregular patches of weak sunlight to play across the landscape, making it seem to shift and change all the time, almost as if it were breathing. It was lovely.

Druce turned in his seat and regarded me unhurriedly. His grey eyes were clear and bright. 'Very well. Let's cut to the chase, as they say. Is it your opinion that Ogden caused that woman's death?'

'I'm not sure if I can answer that.'

'Well, think about it. The local policeman will ask you that question. Reluctantly, I might add, but nonetheless, Sergeant

Glynn will do his duty.'

I nodded curtly. 'Good for him.'

He leaned back and studied me. 'How long do you plan to stay here?'

'A few days. A week, perhaps.'

'And what is your intention, if I may ask?'

'Sort out the legal situation with the house my mother left me, and sell it, if anyone will buy it. You may know more about that than me. What do you think?'

Before he could reply, we heard the sound of a vehicle approaching. Druce peered into the rear-view mirror. 'Talk of the devil,' he murmured.

I turned to see a minibus coming up the hill behind us, moving fast. As it sped past I glimpsed about a dozen people inside wearing bright yellow protective vests and hard hats. The driver honked the horn and Druce raised a hand in greeting as the minibus roared away and took the descent towards the town at high speed. A company logo on the sides and the rear of the vehicle depicted a circle that looked like a drilling platform seen from above, with the word SKANDIFLOW in the centre.

'Yes,' Druce said, 'those lads could be your customers.'

'Skandiflow. Who's that?'

'A big multinational, based in Norway. They have offshore drilling rights and an operation out to sea, just down the coast there.' He pointed to the horizon, where the hills rose and formed a bulky headland. 'You can't quite see it from here but it's only a couple of miles out. They've been expanding. They could be interested in your property.'

'What would they want it for?'

His mouth twisted momentarily into a thin smile. 'A conference centre, perhaps. Or a fancy training facility they could use as a corporate showcase. Something of that nature.'

I considered this for a moment. I was surprised by the idea, and I couldn't quite tell what Druce's attitude was. 'And would that be a good thing?' I said. 'Me selling a place that seems to be a local landmark to a big multinational corporation?'

He tapped his fingers gently on the steering wheel. 'It depends what you mean by a good thing, Adam.'

'Well, I don't particularly want to make myself unpopular.'

He turned to me. 'I'll tell you what will make you unpopular, if you really want to know. Getting Ogden prosecuted for manslaughter. That will do it, believe me.'

'What can I say? I saw what I saw.'

'Do you always report what you see?'

I returned his gaze levelly. 'That happens to be my job.'

Druce nodded slowly, not taking his eyes from mine. Finally he gave the steering wheel a brisk slap, and glanced at his watch. 'We'd best be on our way. I don't want you to be late for your appointment with Harriet Baird.'

'Christ!' I said, and shook my head. 'Is there anything you don't know about me? Do you want to tell me how my bowels are doing?'

He gave me a quick glance up and down. 'Fine, by the look of you.'

I burst out laughing.

'I'll drop you at her office,' Druce said, and put the car into gear.

THREE

The drive down into Creedish took ten minutes. The place turned out to be bigger than it had looked from the top of the hill, but I had to agree with Ogden's opinion that it was more of an oversized village than a town.

We drove the length of the narrow High Street, which seemed sleepy and almost quaint. A woman pushing an old-fashioned pram came out of a hardware store, and we passed a young man on a bicycle with what looked like a huge bunch of leeks poking out of the basket on the front. All very pleasant.

Druce pulled up outside a large house at the far end of the High Street. As we got out of the car, the front door of the house opened and man in a police uniform emerged, putting on his cap. When he saw us he walked over, raising a hand in greeting to Druce.

'Good day to you, Cal.'

'Hello, David.'

The sergeant stood in front of me and extended his hand. 'Mr Budd, I'm David Glynn. I regret you had to face such a terrible tragedy on your first day with us.'

I shook his hand. Glynn's grip was firm, but he didn't seem to be trying to prove anything. He was a compact man, a little shorter than me, and a few years older, I thought. Perhaps in his early forties. He had closely cropped dark hair and a neatly trimmed moustache.

'These things happen,' I said.

'Not very frequently, thank God. I hope you're not too shaken?'

'I'm fine, thank you.'

'Good, good. I may need to ask you a couple of questions, Mr Budd, if you can spare a few moments for me tomorrow?'

'I can give you a statement now, if you like. While events are still fresh in my mind. Wouldn't that be better?'

Glynn hesitated and his eyes flicked towards the doctor. I glanced at Druce but his expression gave nothing away. Some kind of message had passed between the two men, but I couldn't tell what it was.

'Thank you, Mr Budd,' Glynn said, 'but tomorrow will be more convenient. Perhaps I can talk to you while you're having your lunch at the pub.'

'I'm not sure I'll be having lunch there.'

'Oh, I recommend it, sir. Very highly. Finn and Penny provide excellent food.'

I regarded Glynn in silence. The sergeant smiled at me, eyebrows raised expectantly. I understood that he was simply waiting for me to agree. No other outcome was anticipated – or would be accepted, I sensed.

'That's fine,' I said. 'I'll see you there.'

'Good man.'

Druce stepped between us and handed me my bag. 'Harriet will take you to the pub after you've concluded your business. Goodbye Adam, I'll see you later.'

'Thanks. And thank you for the lift, Doctor.'

'Cal, please,' Druce said. He looked at his watch and turned to the sergeant. 'Shall I take you to the clinic, David? They should have got there by now.'

'That will be grand. Let the dog see the rabbit.'

As Druce walked to his car I heard him say to Glynn, 'Is everything all right in there?'

Glynn opened the car door. 'She knows, anyway,' he said, and got in.

I watched the car drive away. I walked up the steps to the front door of the house and found that the sergeant had left it open when he came out. I looked for a doorbell but didn't find one. I knocked on the door.

'Come in,' a woman's voice called out.

I sat facing Harriet Baird across her desk in a spacious Georgian drawing room that had been converted into an office. She examined the documents I'd just given her, taking her time. She was in her thirties and had chestnut hair. I'd been attracted to her from the moment we'd shaken hands, and I was conscious of trying to conceal the fact. Her manner towards me had been friendly and entirely professional.

She looked up at me and smiled. Her mouth was wide and her smile seemed to dissolve her formality. 'Thanks,' she said, sliding the documents across the desk, 'you can have these back. I just had to confirm your identity.'

'And am I who I think I am?'

'The real thing, apparently.'

'That's a relief.'

She smiled again. 'Are you sure I can't offer you some coffee? Or anything else?'

'I'm fine, thanks.'

'In that case, we'll get straight to the records of the property.' She reached into a file in front of her and pulled out a thick sheaf of papers. She flicked through them for a few moments, referring occasionally to a handwritten list on a notepad beside her.

'So,' she said, 'let me just summarise all this. Your mother inherited the property from her maternal grandfather, who was born on the island but didn't live here. Is that your understanding?'

'I think I remember her telling me that, yes.'

'But it seems her ownership was contested and she had to go through some legal difficulties to verify her claim?'

'She was very vague about it. She used to say it was all a frightful bore, which was pretty much her attitude to everything in her life that she preferred not to deal with.'

Harriet nodded, and studied the documents again. 'It appears she didn't spend long here, and as far as I can tell she never actually lived in the house. Is that right?'

'I don't know much about it, to tell you the truth. We were in London. I mean, that's where I was born, after she left here.'

'With your father?'

'No. He died just before I was born.'

'I'm sorry.'

'I never knew him. So it's no loss.'

Harriet glanced at me with an expression I couldn't quite interpret. Sympathetic, perhaps, but also puzzled. She seemed about to say something, but instead she looked down at the documents again.

'OK,' she murmured, 'apparently your mother inherits the house, clears one or two initial legal hurdles, and then, for some reason, she simply closes the place up and leaves, without registering the deeds.'

'And thereby handing me a legal mess.'

'Not for much longer, if you've got those deeds. May I see them?'

'Of course. That's what I've come here for.' I removed an envelope from my inside jacket pocket and passed it over the desk to her.

She slid out the documents it contained and unfolded them. 'Where did you find these in the end, if you don't mind me asking?'

'In an old hat box.'

She smiled to herself, and began to check through the deeds.

I watched the way her face registered her thoughts. A tiny frown appeared as she concentrated on each passage, and cleared as she mastered it. Occasionally she gave an almost imperceptible nod, as if to confirm her comprehension.

Abruptly a door at the far end of the room was flung open and a boy of about five stormed in. He was clutching paper and crayons.

Harriet looked up in alarm. 'What are you doing, Logan?'

'I want to draw in here!'

'Not now, darling. Remember the rule.'

The child scowled at his mother. She seemed flustered, and I thought she might be blushing. 'This is my son Logan,' she said to me.

'Hello Logan,' I said.

The boy pursed his mouth and narrowed his eyes at me in a pantomime of judicious appraisal.

'Logan,' his mother said, 'please say hello to Mr Budd.'

'Hello,' he muttered.

'Thank you,' Harriet said, 'and now please go back to your room. I'll come and fetch you very soon.'

'But I want to draw in here!'

'I'm afraid you can't, darling. I'm busy with work in here.'

Logan cast a sly glance at me, then spoke in a tone of injured innocence. 'But you told me this used to be the drawing room, so why can't I draw in here?'

'I've explained to you before,' Harriet said, 'that it was called a drawing room because that was short for "withdrawing room" in the olden days.'

'But it's not the olden days any more, so now it's the drawing room for drawing!'

'Logan, please stop showing off.'

'I'm not! I want to stay here!'

'I don't want you to annoy Mr Budd.'

'I won't annoy him! I won't!'

Without thinking I said, 'I don't mind if Logan stays here.'

Harriet glanced at me with a trace of annoyance. Immediately I wished I hadn't spoken. I smiled sheepishly at her. 'Sorry, I didn't mean to–'

'You see?' Logan crowed. 'He said I can stay!'

Harriet stared at her son impassively.

'Please?' he said.

'All right,' she said, 'but you sit quietly, all right? I don't want any fuss.'

The boy grinned. He sat down cross-legged on the floor and immediately became absorbed in drawing, no longer concerned with his performance.

Harriet glanced at me again. She raised an eyebrow in what I hoped was mock disapproval, then continued checking the documents in front of her.

I watched Logan as he drew. The boy wielded his crayons confidently, pausing occasionally to narrow his eyes and visualise something before pressing on. He was small and thin, and full of nervous energy. He became aware of my scrutiny and looked up at me with a mischievous, complicit smile, which I returned. I glanced at Harriet and saw she was watching us.

'The deeds seem to be in order,' she said.

'That's good.'

She leaned back in her chair. 'You could have just posted these things, you know. You didn't need to come all the way out here to this uncivilised place.'

'Civilisation is overrated.'

Harriet laughed. 'So I hear.'

'To tell the truth,' I said, 'one of the reasons I wanted to do all this in person was to be absolutely sure the whole thing is properly tied up. Finished. No more nasty surprises from my mother.'

'Oh dear. Did you not get on with her?'

'I didn't see much of her, to be honest. Even when I was a kid, she was...erratic, let's say. Very much present at certain times, then not around. Looking back, I think she was quite volatile, emotionally. People used to say she was full of life, and vivacious, and that kind of thing. Which may have been great fun at a party, but not so much fun when you were trying to find a clean pair of socks to wear to school and she was... busy. With whatever. Sorry. I don't really know why I'm telling you this.'

'Don't apologise,' Harriet said. 'You'd be surprised what people say in here. It can be very personal, dealing with an inheritance. Especially as it came as rather a surprise to you.

The house, I mean. You didn't know about it, did you?'

'Not really, no. I'm curious to see it.'

'Really? You want to see the house?'

'Why, is that a problem?'

'Not at all,' she said brightly. 'I just need to get hold of the keys, and so on. I'll make arrangements for you to see it in the next couple of days, if that's all right. If you're staying that long. Are you?'

'Sure, I'm planning to be around for a few days.'

'Good. Well, there's nothing more we need to do here,' she said, standing up and slipping some files into a battered satchel, 'so I'll take you over to the pub.'

I stood up. 'There's no need for you to do that.'

'It's no trouble,' she said. 'We're going there anyway, aren't we, Logan?'

Logan looked up from his drawing. 'Going where?'

'To Finn and Penny's. And you can go and play in Gully's room.'

'Cool.' Logan jumped to his feet. He walked up to me and held out the drawing he'd been working on. 'Can you see if this picture is right? It's the lady who was killed.'

'Logan,' Harriet said sharply, 'that's not–'

'It's all right,' I said, taking the drawing from Logan. 'Let me have a look.'

The picture showed a stick-figure in a triangular dress flying through the air with her limbs twisted and broken, and fragments of a bicycle whirling around her. The whole thing was decorated with big splotches of red that spurted out of the woman's head and body. I nodded thoughtfully as I inspected it.

'Excellent,' I said. 'It's just right. Maybe a bit less blood would be good.'

'I can't change it now,' Logan said. 'It's in crayon.'

'Actually, now I come to think of it, there was quite a lot.'

He gave me a satisfied smile. 'You can keep it if you like.'

'Thank you, Logan, that's very kind of you. I'll put it in my bag so I don't have to fold it up.'

'I don't mind if you fold it.'

'All right darling,' Harriet said, 'go and get your things.'

Logan trotted happily from the room.

'Sorry about that,' she said. 'He's got a lively imagination, and sometimes I find it hard to know where to draw the line, bringing him up on my own.'

I let that sink in. There had been no need for her to give me that information. 'Don't worry,' I said, 'kids can be like that. They love a bit of horror.' I widened my eyes briefly, play-acting, and smiled at her, letting the warmth show.

She smiled back. 'Have you got children?'

'No, but I hang out with a lot of journalists.'

She laughed. I met her gaze and held it.

'If you like,' she said, 'I'll drive you up to see the house tomorrow.'

'That would be nice. Thank you very much, Ms Baird.'

'Please call me Harriet.'

FOUR

Harriet drove back along the high street. After a few hundred yards, she turned left and swung the car onto a narrower road.

'It's about a mile to the pub,' she said. 'There used to be another one, back there in town, but it only lasted a while, and it's been closed for a few years now. The one we're going to is the old pub, that's been there for ever.'

'What happened to the other one?' I said.

'It was never very popular. I don't know why.'

'It was the man,' Logan piped up from the back seat.

I craned around to look at him. 'What man?'

'The man who owned it. He was a dickhead.'

Harriet stifled a shocked laugh. 'Logan! You mustn't say things like that! Where did you learn that word, anyway?'

'I don't know. Someone at school. They said nobody ever

liked Mr Pottinger, and he was a—'

'That's enough!'

'All right,' Logan muttered.

Harriet frowned and focused on the road. It was taking us steadily uphill in a series of climbs, dips and hollows. The banks on either side were steep, and I couldn't see much of the landscape. After a moment she cleared her throat.

'So,' she said, 'there's only one pub now. It's been up there, in one form or another, since people first started coming inland whenever the harbour was in danger.'

'Ah yes,' I said, 'I was getting the history lesson from Ogden, just before it was brought to an abrupt halt.'

She shot me a glance. 'Are you all right?'

'I'm fine, thanks.'

'OK. Well, naturally the folks fleeing from the harbour headed for the highest ground, to get as far out of the way as they could. Then, as things got safer, they began to trickle down the hill, and build themselves houses in Creedish. But the pub – or the inn, or whatever it was originally – stayed up on the top, even though it can get pretty bleak up there in winter. And despite various attempts to provide an alternative down in town, they've never had much success. People just seem to prefer it...up...*here.*'

With that, we crested a rise and emerged onto a grassy plateau with a panoramic view over the island and the open sea beyond it. A few buildings were dotted around its perimeter on three sides. It was as if a town square or outsized village green had migrated from its proper place and wandered to the top of a windswept hill, and settled down there.

The pub sat off to one side, on its own. Harriet parked next to a low stone wall which enclosed a garden in front of the pub, where a few wooden trestle tables were scattered. The building itself was long and low, with whitewashed walls and a slate roof. It looked old and sturdy. I could imagine it took a lot of punishment up there on the flat, exposed land when the weather turned bad.

As I got out of the car I saw a Land Rover I recognised in an open yard adjoining the pub. A man and a woman were unloading boxes and carrying them into the building by a side door while Archie stood watching them, drinking from a pint glass.

The woman put down the box she was carrying and walked towards us as we came through the gate into the garden. She was about forty, with a plump face and a sunny smile. Logan ran up to meet her and she gave him a hug, pressing him to her side until she reached us. She stood in front of me and extended her hand, which I took.

'I'm Penny,' she said, 'and you must be Adam.' She kept hold of my hand and began to pat it, gazing at me with maternal concern. 'You poor man, what a terrible thing to happen. Dreadful, dreadful. And you've had no lunch. Will you take some food?'

'No thanks, but I'd like a drink.'

'Of course, of course. What will you have?'

'I'd like a glass of red wine, please,' I said, and turned to Harriet. 'How about you and Logan? What can I get you?'

'I'll just have a coffee, thanks, and I expect Logan would like a coke.'

Penny finally released my hand. 'I'll go and get those right away. Will you come inside, or is it warm enough for you out here?'

'We'll be fine out here,' Harriet said, and led the way to one of the trestle tables in the garden. I sat opposite her, and Logan sat beside me, swinging his legs.

As Penny bustled away towards the pub, the man who'd been helping to unload the Land Rover approached us from the direction of the yard. When he reached our table he nodded to me, and winked at Logan. He looked about the same age as Penny, but where she was matronly and fleshy he was thin and angular. He had an odd, twitchy vibe, and his longish hair and beard gave him a touch of the hippie.

'Hi, I'm Finn,' he said. 'Is Penny sorting out your drinks for you?'

'She is, thanks,' I said.

'Right you are. I'll take your kit up to your room, shall I?'

Without waiting for a reply he picked up my bag and walked away with it. I watched him as he went into the pub, and tried to rationalise the prickle of dislike I felt for him. It was his attitude to Harriet, I realised. He'd ignored her. I wondered why I'd been offended by that, more than if – say – he'd been over-friendly towards her. And as I wondered that, I also wondered what the hell I was doing. I'd known Harriet for an hour, and now I was weighing up the possibility of being jealous. Which was totally ridiculous. I was here on business, and I was emerging from a relationship that had ended badly after nearly three years. Although that meant, of course, that I was on the rebound, which can be a dangerous time. Interesting, though. Whoa, I told myself. Get a grip.

My thoughts were interrupted by Archie's voice: 'Are you all right there?'

He had driven the Land Rover up to Harriet's car, on the other side of the low stone wall. He was leaning out of the window, looking at me.

'I heard what happened,' he said. 'I'm sorry you had to go through that.'

'I'm sorry for Mary,' I said.

He nodded and smiled at Logan, who had wandered over to the wall. 'Hello, young man,' Archie said, 'are you taking good care of that mother of yours?'

'Yes,' Logan said gravely, 'I'm doing my best, Archie.'

Archie chuckled. 'Good lad. Now, remind her to send me that bill.'

'Oh Archie,' Harriet called to him, 'there's really no need. It can wait.'

'No, no, I'm a man who settles my bills promptly. What if I suddenly decide to run off to South America without paying you?'

'I wouldn't put it past you! I'll have the bill for you next time you come.'

He waved, and gunned the Land Rover away.

'He's a sweetheart,' Harriet said to me. 'Every year he insists on paying me just to witness his signature on the licence for his boat.'

Penny arrived with a tray of drinks. 'Here we are,' she said.

Logan grabbed his glass of coke. 'Mum,' he said, 'can I take this up to Gully's room and play? Can I, Penny?'

'Of course you can, my pet,' said Penny. 'You run along.'

Logan trotted away to the pub, holding his drink out in front of him in an effort not to spill it. Penny watched him and shook her head. 'Sometimes he looks just like Gully.'

Harriet turned to me. 'Gully – Gulliver – was Finn and Penny's son.'

'We lost him,' Penny said, 'nearly a year ago now.'

I waited, expecting her to tell me more, but she just nodded slowly, gazing at me.

'I'm sorry to hear that,' I said. I raised my eyebrows. 'Was it...?'

'Yes,' she said, 'it was very sudden. But we've left his room

53

just how it used to be, and Logan likes to go up there and play with his old toys and things. He talks to him in there, doesn't he, Harriet?'

Harriet took a sip of her coffee and put the cup back on its saucer with careful deliberation. 'He's talking to himself, really.'

Penny shrugged. 'Children are funny little things.' She wiped her hands on her apron and smiled at me. 'Will there be anything else for now?'

'Can you give me a Wi-Fi password?'

She frowned. 'Wi-Fi?'

'Yes. Is there a password you can give me?'

'It's a bit...difficult,' she said vaguely. 'We haven't really got a...you know, a connection. It comes and goes.' She raised her eyes and gazed around, as if trying to catch sight of the elusive connection drifting through the atmosphere.

'Don't worry,' I said. 'It's not a problem.'

'Oh, good,' she said, and resumed her cheerful demeanour. 'Now, whenever you'd like to eat, just give us twenty minutes' notice. And if it gets too busy for you downstairs in the bar, I'll gladly bring your food to your room.'

'Thanks. I'm sure I'll be OK in the bar.'

'Will you have lunch? It's still not too late.'

'No, I'll wait and have something later, thanks.'

'Fair enough, I'll tell Finn. He's the cook around here!'

I glanced at Harriet. 'Would you like to join me?' I said. 'Can I buy you dinner?'

I saw Harriet and Penny exchange a quick glance. Harriet shifted around to look at me squarely. 'I appreciate the courtesy,' she said, 'but there's no need.'

'It's not a courtesy,' I said. 'I'd like to invite you to dinner.'

'I'd have to see if I can sort something out for Logan.'

'Hush woman!' Penny said. 'You know you can leave him here. He can stay and sleep in Gully's room. He'll be very welcome, and I won't hear another word about it.'

'In that case,' Harriet said to me, 'thank you. I'll see you inside at seven.'

***

I sat alone at the table, looking out of the window. It was dark outside.

We'd finished our food, and Harriet had gone upstairs to read Logan a story. I was waiting for her to come back. And what else? I tried to suppress a familiar feeling of anticipation. Calm down. Nothing was going to happen. I poured myself some red wine from the bottle on the table – still more than half full – and looked around the long, low room. There were about a dozen customers. Finn was behind the bar, serving Sim, the big farm boy who was at the accident. His father, Barty, was sitting at a table with Ogden and a sturdy-looking woman in her fifties with a strong, handsome face.

Barty caught my eye and gave me a wary nod. Ogden followed his gaze and locked eyes with me, staring at me impassively. I gave him a polite smile. Ogden didn't react. I turned away and looked out into the night. After a while, I slipped my phone from my pocket. It was force of habit – what I do when I'm waiting – and I didn't think about it until I was looking at the screen, and found there was no phone signal or any indication of an internet connection to be found. I recalled Penny's vagueness when I'd asked about the Wi-Fi. Since then, I'd discovered there wasn't even a TV upstairs in my room.

I experienced a sudden panic, as if my entire nervous system jittered with billions of hungry synapses, craving stimulation.

Even though I knew it was ridiculous, I felt bereft and fearful. How was I going to survive without those connections? Then, just as abruptly, the feeling was gone, replaced by what I can only describe as calm excitement. There was nothing I could do. I simply had to embrace the fact that I was a castaway, stranded on an unfamiliar shore, and see what happened next.

Harriet sat down opposite me. 'Sorry I was so long,' she said.

I poured her a glass of wine. 'How is he?'

'Fast asleep in Gully's bed. I'll leave him there for the night now.' She picked up her glass and drank appreciatively. 'Ah, that's good. I don't tend to relax completely until he's settled.' She drank again.

'You'll still have to drive, though.'

She gave me an amused look over the top of her glass. 'Trust me, I'm a lawyer. There's only one cop on this island, and I don't think David Glynn is going to bust me for drink-driving.'

'Why not?'

'Well, he's a friend, for one thing.'

'Just a friend?'

'Why do you want to know?'

'Sorry. Professional curiosity, I guess. It comes with being a journalist.'

'In other words, a nosy bastard.'

'Only if I'm any good.'

We both laughed. Our laughter faded and we gazed at each other. Harriet put her glass down and leaned towards me. 'Why not just ask if I'm single?'

'All right. Are you single?'

Harriet looked down for moment. She took a breath and was about to speak when a commotion erupted at the door.

Four large men tumbled into the pub. They were wearing jackets bearing the Skandiflow logo. They all looked pretty drunk, but one of them seemed ahead of the pack, and the other three were making good-natured efforts to keep him under control. He was a big, meaty young guy with blond hair under a knitted cap, and he was trying to bellow a repeated phrase in what I guessed was Norwegian while the others tried to shut him up. They steered him to a table in the corner, where he slumped down and appeared to fall asleep. The other men looked around, and exchanged eye-rolling shrugs and smiles with the bar's other occupants, who appeared to take it all in their stride. There seemed to be plenty of goodwill on both sides.

One of the Norwegians went to the bar and leaned over to whisper to Finn. He gestured to his slumbering companion, and pointed to his own wedding ring, shaking his head and making a grim face. Finn nodded sympathetically.

I returned my attention to Harriet. 'You were about to say something.'

'Was I?'

The drunk guy was suddenly on his feet. 'Fuck all the women!' he shouted. His friends gathered around him, trying to make him sit down. He lurched past them and grabbed a beer bottle from the next table and raised it to his lips. When he found it was empty he banged it down hard and yelled, 'They are all bitches!'

He pulled a crumpled sheet of paper from his pocket and waved it around. 'She is the biggest fucking bitch! Yah? Fuck her!'

The locals glanced at each other but didn't seem particularly concerned.

With surprising nimbleness the guy swerved past his friends and lurched to the bar, where he collided with Sim, who was walking away with a drink in each hand. One of the drinks spilled all over him. Sim stood stolidly in the Norwegian's path, staring at him calmly. Slowly he placed the glasses he was holding on the bar. The guy screamed at him, 'All the women! Your woman, she is a bitch!'

Sim didn't react. The guy grabbed a glass from the bar and smashed it. The other Norwegians edged towards him, preparing to jump him, but attentive to the jagged glass in his hand, which was now dripping blood.

The young guy screamed into Sim's face, 'Fight me, you fucker! Fight me!'

Very swiftly Sim clamped his hands around the drunk's wrists, stepping back slightly when he tried to knee him in the groin, but not loosening his grip.

Now the man's face was puce with rage and frustration. He spat at Sim.

Sim didn't blink.

The Norwegians swarmed their companion. The biggest one encircled him in a bear hug from behind while the other two secured an arm each. They nodded to Sim, who slowly released his grip. Carefully he forced the broken glass from the guy's hand and placed it on the bar.

The Norwegians hauled their friend away. One of them called out to the room in general, 'We are so sorry. It shouldn't happen. We will pay for anything, of course. Sorry for the disturbance.'

'It's all right, son,' said the sturdy woman sitting with Barty and Ogden. 'Woman trouble. We've all been there.'

Everyone laughed.

The Norwegians continued to manoeuvre their drunk friend towards the door. I saw him give us an ugly look as they dragged him past us, and the sight of Harriet seemed to stoke his rage again. He strained forward like a tethered bull, dragging his captors with him. 'Fucking bitch!' he screamed at her.

I sprang up, shielding Harriet. 'Control yourself,' I said. The guy lunged at me, and the men restraining him were taken by surprise, and almost lost their grip on him as he tried to head-butt me. I twisted away quickly, and assumed a fighting stance – sideways to assailant, left arm out at right angles, defining my boundary, right fist drawn back, cocked, ready to uncoil – as I ran through a checklist: is this necessary, is it appropriate, is it proportionate, is it likely to be effective? And as well as those questions, I was also asking myself why I was letting these people see me like this, and if it was justified. And the answer was yes. It was nothing to do with the way I felt about Harriet. There was a threat, the situation was unpredictable, and I needed to protect myself and my companion. Everyone froze, including the drunk.

'Go home,' I said. 'Sleep it off.'

For a long moment he stared at me. I watched the calculations moving slowly through his mind as he assessed me, and the situation. He seemed to slump. The fight was out of him, and he allowed his friends to bundle him out of the door without another word. I glanced around. Some of the locals were looking at me, but they seemed unperturbed. Barty gave me a brief nod, then resumed his conversation with the others at his table. Sim was occupied with replacing the drink that had been spilled, and laughed quietly at something Finn said when he passed it over the bar.

I sat down. Harriet was looking at me with a certain amount of surprise, not unmixed with what looked like amusement. I smiled at her, and nodded towards Sim, on the other side of the room. 'That big lad,' I said, 'seems to be a pretty cool customer.'

'He's not the only one,' Harriet said, 'is he?'

I tried to detect any mockery in her voice. 'If you're talking about me,' I said, 'I've had plenty of practice.'

'In the army?'

'What makes you think that?'

'Just a guess. But now I can see I'm right, aren't I?' There was a hint of mischief in her smile. She raised an eyebrow. 'Well?'

I smiled. 'I keep forgetting you're a lawyer.'

'What's that got to do with anything?'

'For a start, you're trying to change the subject.'

'Am I?'

'Yes. You're asking me questions, but you still haven't answered the one I asked you. Remember? Just before all that aggravation kicked off. Or more accurately, the question you asked me to ask you. Which is, are you single?'

Harriet threw back her head and laughed. The sound was rich and husky. I watched her throat and wanted to touch it. Just as she lowered her head and opened her mouth to reply she glanced abruptly to one side, startled.

Caleb Druce had materialised beside her. He raised the glass in his hand. 'Hello there, the pair of you. Can I get you anything?'

Harriet picked up the wine bottle and held it to the light. 'I think we're all right for now, thanks Cal.'

'Am I interrupting anything?'

'Not really,' Harriet said, without looking at me.

'Mind if I join you?'

'Please do.'

Druce sat down beside her. He ran a professional eye over my face. 'Any damage inflicted by that overexcited Viking?'

'I'm fine, thanks. How long have you been here?'

'Me? I came in just behind the pack of merry Norseman.

I had a suspicion the big one would try to mend his broken heart by breaking someone else's nose. It wouldn't be the first time.'

'Really? Do they cause a lot of fights?'

'No,' he said, 'that's not what I'm saying. You're putting words into my mouth, like the journalist you are. In fact, relations between the locals and the company employees are remarkably peaceable. Much more so than in many other places.'

'What other places?' I said.

'My God,' Harriet broke in, 'you're right, Caleb. He can't stop asking questions!'

'I'm sorry,' I said.

She patted my hand. 'I'm only teasing you. I apologise. And I'm sure Caleb will be only too happy to tell you about his travels. He's been all over the world.'

Druce shrugged. 'I've knocked around a bit.'

'Tell Adam about working in Africa,' Harriet said.

I stood beside the car, my hand resting on the top of the open door, breathing in the crisp air. The sky was ablaze with stars.

'You can have breakfast with Logan,' Harriet said from the driver's seat. 'I think he likes you.'

'Good, I think I like him too.'

'And what about Caleb Druce? Do you like him?'

I considered the question for a moment. 'I like the fact he likes animals,' I said.

'Animals?'

'Didn't you notice? He said he was going to tell us a story about being a doctor in Botswana, but he barely started it. We ended up talking mostly about wildlife.'

'I suppose we did. By the way, I hope you didn't mind me

asking him to join us.'

'No, he seems to be an interesting man.'

'I sometimes wonder if he's lonely. That's why I asked him.'

'Has he got no family?'

'Not any more,' she said. 'It's a long story. I'll tell you another time.'

'Another time. That will be nice. I look forward to it.'

Harriet looked down and rummaged through the bag on her lap. She found the car key and put it in the ignition. 'I'll come by and pick Logan up at around ten tomorrow morning,' she said, 'so I'll see you then. We can go and inspect your property.'

'Fine, as long as I'm back here for lunch. I've got to give a statement to your friend Sergeant Glynn.'

'What are you going to tell him?'

'I thought I might tell him the truth.'

'So, you'll tell him what you think happened?'

'I'll tell him what I saw.'

'What you think you saw.'

I laughed. 'God save us from lawyers!'

Harriet started the engine. 'I'm sure you'll be a truthful witness.'

I began to close her door for her. I paused. 'Talking of sergeant Glynn...'

'What about him?'

'I'm still waiting for an answer. As to whether you're single.'

She peered around theatrically. 'There's nobody else here, is there? Just me.'

'And me.'

'Oh yes. But not for long, right?' She put the car in gear.

'See you tomorrow,' I said, and gently closed her door.

FIVE

I was woken by rain drumming against my window. It was nearly eight, and I'd slept for longer than I'd intended. Perhaps it was to be expected. I'd been up at five the previous day, and I'd travelled for three hours to get to the ferry, which had taken another hour to reach the island. Then there was the shock of the accident, followed by the meeting with Harriet, and my dinner with her.

I gazed up at the low, whitewashed ceiling, and pictured her face. I could still feel the touch of her hand on mine when she'd told me she was teasing me.

I was hungry. I thought about breakfast, and got out of bed.

I paused at the top of the stairs. A door on my left was partly open, and from the room behind it I heard Logan's voice, talking quietly but intently.

I walked softly to the doorway and looked in. Logan was sitting on the floor in the bedroom of a typical six-year-old boy. His back was to me, and in front of him were two large groups of toy soldiers, lined up to face each other in battle formation.

'Yes,' Logan said, 'but then my army men start shooting with their special guns that can even get through your tanks and everything.'

Logan paused, as if he were listening to a reply. He shook his head. 'No, no, your guys don't have time, so loads of them get killed, pow, powee!' He leaned over and flicked some of the enemy soldiers over with his fingers. He listened again, cocking his head, then said, 'But it *is* fair, because the guns are special and they fire, like, bullets that are like bombs and they explode!' He reached over and knocked down a few more opposition soldiers, with appropriate sound effects. Abruptly he stopped, his hand poised in mid-air, on the point of visiting more destruction on the enemy.

'No, wait,' he said. 'I don't *totally* win, actually.' He sat back on his haunches and spread his hands, as if he were trying to placate his unseen opponent. 'Because,' he continued, groping for a persuasive argument, 'because…you've got a special plane, see?' He grabbed a model aircraft from a shelf beside him. 'And it comes and bombs all my guys, kaboom, kaboom!' He swooped the plane over his own soldiers, knocking some of them down. 'Then,' he said, 'my men shoot it down, after it's killed, like, loads of them.' He put the plane into a slow spiral and landed it carefully. He paused.

'No way!' Logan said. 'It doesn't kill my whole army!' He put on a dopey, strangulated voice, obviously imitating someone, and squeaked, 'Get real, dude!' He began to laugh. 'No *you* get real!' He laughed louder. 'No, *you*!'

Logan's laughter overcame him. He fell to the floor and rolled around, kicking over the rest of his own soldiers. Abruptly he sat up, breathing heavily. 'Look what you made me do!' he said angrily. 'You suck!' He reached over and swept away all the remaining opposition soldiers, then sat back, his face set in a sulky scowl.

Slowly his expression softened. He muttered, 'Neither did I,' and a crafty smile twitched his lips as he added, 'Dude.' He raised his eyebrows. 'No, *you're* a dude!' He started chuckling. 'No, *you're* a dude, Dude!'

He laughed himself to the floor again, and as he rolled over he caught sight of me, watching him from the doorway. He sat up quickly, blushing.

'Hello,' I said, and indicated the soldiers lying on the floor. 'Looks like a big battle you've just had.'

'Yes,' he said, 'it was pretty serious.'

'I expect you could use some breakfast.' I glanced out of the window. 'It's stopped raining, so maybe would could have it outside. Are you up for that?'

'I'm up for it.'

Logan and I sat in the pub garden beneath a pale blue sky. Two large, empty plates were on the wooden table in front of us.

I finished my mug of coffee. 'That was a good breakfast,' I said.

'Yes,' Logan said. 'Very delicious sausages.' He reached into his pocket and took out two of the toy soldiers he'd been playing with, and put them on the table facing each other. Slowly he moved each one forward in turn until they were almost touching, then he hunched down and glared at them, as if daring them to attack each other.

I said, 'Did you often play soldiers with Gully?'

'Yes,' he said quietly, still intent on the soldiers.

'You two must have been good friends.'

He nodded, but didn't raise his head.

'What about other friends?'

Logan looked up. 'They've gone,' he said. 'Some of them.'

'Really?' I said. 'Where have they gone?'

he shrugged and turned to gaze out at the sea. 'I don't know. It was after the game. Last time.'

'What game is that?'

'In Summer School. Everyone has to do it. You have to do it when you're six.'

'Everyone?'

'Not, like, everyone in the world! Just us islanders have to do it.'

'So all the kids on the island play this game when they're six, is that right?'

'Gully played it last time, and William and Nicola, because they were all a bit older than me, so it was their turn. Last year.' Logan was still looking out to sea. Absently, he curled a hand around each of the soldiers on the table and grasped them tightly in his fists. He dropped his voice to a whisper. 'I've got to play it next time. It's soon. Summer School is at the end of the summer.' He scanned the horizon slowly, as if searching for something. He seemed to be miles away.

I saw that Logan's knuckles were white. I reached over and gently unclenched the boy's fingers from the plastic soldiers. He glanced at me, startled, then looked down at the red marks on his palms. 'Sorry,' he said.

'Don't worry,' I said, trying to soften my tone, and to sound less like an interrogator. 'But tell me what happens in Summer School, and the game you're talking about. What kind of game is it?'

'I don't know,' Logan said. 'They don't tell you.'

'And what about your friends, William and Nicola? You said they've gone. I expect you were a bit upset about that. It's always sad when your friends go away. Did they move somewhere else with their mummies and daddies?'

Logan caught sight of something over my shoulder and his eyes widened with excitement. 'Look,' he cried, 'it's the chopper!'

As Logan spoke I heard the familiar sound of distant rotor blades. I turned to see a large transport helicopter swinging in around the headland from the direction of the drilling platform that Druce had told me was located offshore.

Logan jumped up from the bench and ran to the dry-stone wall and scrambled up to stand on it. I got up and followed him. The aircraft was approaching fast, and seemed to be making directly for us. I realised it would land in the wide expanse of flat grass that stretched away from the pub. I began to feel the downdraft on my face and hair, and I saw that Logan was having difficulty keeping his balance on the top of the wall.

'Logan, get down from there!' I shouted.

He showed no sign of having heard me, so I moved into position behind him and held him firmly around the waist. He glanced over his shoulder briefly, grinning at me. He looked wild with excitement.

The helicopter landed gently about sixty yards away. As the blades slowed to a stop a door opened at the front of the aircraft, on the co-pilot's side, and a tall blond man wearing a dark suit jumped down. He was clutching a large bouquet of flowers, and he held them close to his body to protect them as he hunched over and scuttled clear of the blades. Behind him, a cargo-door opened in the side of the helicopter. Half a dozen men emerged. They removed their lifejackets, which bore the Skandiflow livery, and slung them back into the helicopter.

The tall man in the suit approached me and Logan with a smile. He waved to someone behind us, and I saw Finn coming out of the pub.

Logan jumped down off the wall and ran to meet the man in the suit as he reached the garden. 'Hi Lars,' Logan said, 'when can I go on the chopper?'

'Hello Logan,' the man said. 'How are you?'

'I'm OK, thanks, but when can I go on the chopper?'

I heard Finn's voice behind me: 'Whoa there, Logie, let's not forget our manners. Don't you think we should introduce Adam to Lars?'

He stood behind Logan and placed a restraining hand on his shoulder. 'Adam,' he said, 'this is Lars Hansen, the boss out at the drilling rig. Lars, this is Adam Budd, the new owner of Stone Heart House.'

We shook hands. 'Adam,' Hansen said, 'it's good to meet you.' He dropped his voice and bent his head closer to mine, his rimless spectacles glinting in the sun for an instant. 'I was very sorry to learn your mother had passed away. It's such a painful loss when one loses a parent.'

'Thank you.'

Hansen straightened up and smiled. 'And now you have to think about that old place by the lake. What will you do with it?'

'I don't know yet. Maybe sell it.'

He glanced at Finn, then said to me, 'If you decide to sell it, please contact me. I'd be interested. In fact, if you'll forgive me for coming straight to the point like this, I'll make you an offer right now.'

'I haven't even seen the place yet.'

'Nonetheless,' he said, 'I will make you an offer.' He turned to Finn and held out the bouquet of flowers. 'Finn, will you take these please?'

As Finn took the bouquet Hansen extracted a small leather-bound notebook and a gold pen from his inside pocket. He scribbled something down, tore off the page, folded it, and passed it to me. 'I think you'll find that's generous,' he said.

I tucked the note into my pocket without unfolding it. 'I'll certainly consider your offer,' I said, and smiled blandly at him.

He nodded thoughtfully. 'Please do,' he said, 'but don't take too long. Without wishing to hurry you, I must tell you the offer will stand for only a limited time.'

I continued to smile. I could see Hansen was a bully beneath the Scandinavian courtesy and the mild manner, and I suspected he wanted me to see it. I knew all about these corporate types on power trips. Fuck him, and the helicopter he rode in on.

Logan darted forward and tugged at Hansen's sleeve again. 'Lars, when?'

Hansen hitched the knees of his trousers and squatted down to bring his face level with Logan's. 'I understand your impatience, Logan, but I can only say what I've said before. We cannot take children.'

Logan glared fiercely at the helicopter. I followed his gaze and saw that the men who'd emerged were dispersing. Three of them were making their way to the pub, and they crossed paths with four people who were heading for the chopper. As the two parties exchanged greetings I recognised one of the outbound group as the sturdy woman who'd been sitting with Ogden and Barty the previous evening.

Hansen leaned close to Logan and pointed at the workers. 'When you are as big and strong as they are,' he said, 'then you can come! Are you strong yet?' Playfully he tried to squeeze Logan's biceps, but the boy pulled himself from Hansen's grip and turned his back, and scuffed his way over to the wall.

Hansen got to his feet and shrugged ruefully at me and Finn. 'What can I do? The health and safety people would go crazy – and I would go out of my job!'

Finn laughed, and I joined in. I was being polite, but unlike Hansen I wasn't interested in making a point of it, or of anything. Not at that moment, anyway.

Hansen checked his watch. 'Talking of which, I should get back. They'll be ready to go in a minute.' He looked at the helicopter. The four people who'd emerged from the pub had reached the aircraft and were pulling the discarded lifejackets out of the hold, and putting them on. Two more figures were approaching from a car that had just parked at the end of the road leading up from the town.

Finn held the flowers out to Hansen. 'Are you taking these?'

'No, no. They are for you! Or more specifically they are for Penny. To apologise for the trouble last night. In addition to any financial recompense we must make you, of course. I thought I would hitch a ride in with the shuttle and deliver them in person, but now I don't have time to see Penny myself. A pity. But in compensation I have met Mr Budd, and I hope that our meeting will prove to be fruitful.' He held out his hand again.

As I shook it I said, 'Where do you find flowers on a drilling rig, if you don't mind me asking?'

'Not at all. The company flies them in every week. It has been established they are good for morale, and for mood enhancement in the work environment.'

'What kind of work are you doing out there?'

'Oh, the usual type of thing,' Hansen said. 'Minerals, and

so on. You know. Very dull, really. Now, if you'll excuse me, I must go. I hope we can discuss that little matter soon, my friend.' He took a step back, bobbed his head, and strode away. He avoided the gate and instead he trotted straight to the wall and vaulted over it. As he jogged away he raised a hand in farewell without looking back.

I watched him climb back into the aircraft. 'So,' I said to Finn, 'the locals work out there on the rig as well as the Norwegians?'

'That's right,' Finn said, 'the Norwegians are just the... specialists.'

'Specialists in drinking, some of them, judging by last night.'

Finn stared at me blankly. 'What do you mean?'

'It was a joke.'

'Oh, I see. Right. Very good.' He exposed his teeth briefly, in what I guessed was intended to be a smile. 'I'd better get inside,' he said, 'and give these flowers to Penny.'

'I expect she'll be pleased.'

'Not really.'

'Why not?'

'She'll say it's a waste of money.'

'You think so?'

He shrugged. 'Well, it is, really, isn't it?'

I watched him walk back to the pub, the bouquet dangling from his hand like a dead animal. I caught a movement from the corner of my eye and saw Logan throwing a stone at his toy soldiers, which he'd placed on the top of the wall. He missed, and threw another stone, which also missed. Logan saw me and glared at me. He scanned the ground at his feet for more ammunition, but couldn't find any. He ran to the wall and began trying to pull a large stone out of it.

I strode over to him and put a hand on his shoulder. 'Wait,

Logan, that's not cool.'

He shook me off. 'It's not fair!' he shouted above the noise of the helicopter, which was lifting off. He raised his voice and shouted again, 'It's not fair!' He stopped trying to pull the stone from the wall, and swept the soldiers from the top of it, and stomped them into the soft grass at his feet. His face was red and tears were brimming.

The sound of the aircraft faded. 'You're right,' I said. 'It's not fair.'

'Then why can't I go on it? Why?'

I bent down and retrieved the soldiers from the grass. 'I can see you're pretty angry,' I said to him.

Logan didn't reply. He watched as I slowly cleaned the mud off the soldiers. When I was finished I held them up and inspected them. 'But when you get those feelings,' I continued, 'like being angry or upset, think about soldiers. Like these ones.'

'Why?' Logan muttered.

'If you were in charge of them, like if they were in a battle, and you were in command, they'd have to do what you said. They'd have to obey orders, wouldn't they?'

'Yes,' Logan said sternly. 'Otherwise it's mutiny.'

'That's right. And what if they suddenly didn't feel like obeying orders?'

'They'd get shot for mutiny!'

'But maybe they're feeling angry or upset,' I suggested, 'and so they decide they don't want to fight the enemy. They're feeling too pissed off. They'd rather just go home and have a nice cup of tea and a biscuit. How about that?'

'In the middle of a battle?'

'Yup. Right at the most important moment.'

He smiled despite himself. 'That would be crazy!'

'You said it, mate. You wouldn't allow that, and you're in charge – am I right?'

He nodded firmly.

'Same with getting angry. You're in charge of that, too.'

'Like being in charge of the soldiers?'

'Same thing,' I said. 'You don't take any nonsense from yourself. You're in charge of your feelings. You give the orders. Quick march! Left, right, left, right.' I began to march on the spot. I pointed at Logan. 'You there! Fall in, soldier! Left, right, left, right!'

He stood beside me, imitating me.

'Quick march!' I said, and set off along the grass. Logan kept pace with me, swinging his arms. 'Left, right, left, right,' I called out. He joined in.

'And…right turn!' I called, swerving sharply. Logan began to turn, and I barked out, 'And halt!' and stopped so abruptly that he crashed into me.

Logan laughed. 'No, you've got to keep going! Left, right, left, right!'

I began marching like a malfunctioning robot, goofing around, and he laughed even more.

I heard Harriet's voice: 'Give that man a medal.'

I saw she was leaning over the wall, watching us. Her car was parked in the road behind her.

'I'm in charge!' Logan shouted to his mother.

'Yes, sir!' Harriet said. 'Can you go and get your stuff now, please sir?'

'No, we're being soldiers!'

'Adam has to be back in time for lunch.'

'That's true,' I said. 'Go on, Logan, quick march!'

He marched towards the pub, turning to call over his shoulder, 'I've just got to put my stuff in my backpack, but I won't be long!'

'While he's doing that,' Harriet said to me, 'I may just go in and grab a quick coffee, if that's all right with you?'

'Sure.'

As we walked to the door, I saw Finn's face at the window beside it. He moved away quickly, and by the time we got inside the pub he was waiting for us and holding out a mug of coffee to Harriet.

She laughed as she took it from him. 'You know me too well, Finn.'

He smiled and raised his eyebrows at me. 'Another one for you, Adam?'

'No thanks.'

He nodded and walked away to the kitchen. Harriet drank her coffee, gulping it quickly. 'Ah,' she said as she put the mug on the bar, 'I needed that.'

Logan clattered down the stairs, swinging his backpack. 'Ready, sir!' he said, and marched to the door, flinging it open and striding out.

Harriet and I followed him, only to find him standing motionless halfway along the path to the gate. He glanced back at us with a questioning look.

Two men were standing beside Harriet's car, and I recognised them as two of the workers who'd disembarked from the helicopter earlier. They stared at me impassively. Harriet hesitated, then she smiled and waved at them. They ignored her and walked away from the car, along the road to the town.

I glanced at Harriet. 'What's their problem?' I said.

Harriet shook her head, frowning as she watched the men walk away.

SIX

We drove through a wooded valley with steep sides. I was struck by how abruptly the landscape had changed. It was only ten minutes since we'd set off from the pub, on a broad upland plateau, and now we were in a dense, dark green forest. Harriet said the island was deeply scored by a dozen of these gorges, running its entire length.

'They were probably formed in the last ice age,' she said, 'but they're unusually deep. There's some speculation that a few of them may have been excavated artificially, to make them even deeper, but nobody seems to know quite when that happened, or who might have done it. It's all a bit vague. A lot of what happened around here in the distant past is shrouded in mystery.'

She slowed down. 'There are some tight bends coming up.'

She steered carefully through a series of curves as the road emerged from the woods and climbed the side of the hill. A drop on the driver's side began to fall away steeply.

'Shit,' Harriet said.

I saw she was frowning at the dashboard. Before I could ask her what was wrong, the car slowed, then jerked forward abruptly. The engine began to misfire and cough.

'That's weird,' she said, 'I'm sure I had nearly half a tank yesterday, and now it's showing empty. Uh oh.'

The engine spluttered, then the car bucked once and came to a halt.

Logan leaned forward between us. 'What's happening, Mummy?'

'We've run out of petrol, darling.'

'There's a can in the boot!'

'That's right, Logie.' She glanced at me. 'Everyone here carries extra fuel, because there are only two garages on the whole island.' She began to open her door. 'I'll get it.'

'Wait,' I said. 'If you're sure you had plenty in the tank, there must be a reason why it's gone. Let me check, and see if I can find a leak.'

The lever to open the bonnet was in the footwell on my side. I popped it, and got out of the car. There was a strong smell of petrol.

I opened the bonnet and peered inside. Like most of the vehicles on the island, the car was several years old, which was an advantage. Modern engines seem designed to thwart people like me, whose expertise with cars is twenty years out of date, and it's easier to see what's going on in older cars. It took me less than a minute to discover that the clip securing the fuel line to the carburettor was so loose it had nearly fallen off. It was conceivable that the line had worked itself free – after all,

I told myself, the roads on the island were very bumpy – but I was pretty sure someone had tampered with it. I reconnected the fuel line and tightened the screw on the clip with a coin from my pocket.

I slammed the bonnet, and smiled at Harriet and Logan. 'Fuel line was loose,' I said, leaning in through the open passenger door, 'but I've tightened it up. And since I'm out here, I may as well get that petrol can from the boot.'

I walked to the back of the car and opened the boot. It took me a moment to register what I was seeing, then I recoiled. Two dead birds were lying in there. They were black and glossy. Crows. Shockingly large at such close quarters. They were completely intact, and clearly hadn't been dead for long. The eye of one bird was half-open, just beginning to cloud over with an opaque film. The corpses had been placed there with evident care, and were arranged breast-to-breast, their beaks overlapping, and their legs tied together with thin wire.

'Are they dead?' Logan said from beside me.

I lowered the lid of the boot swiftly. 'Get back in the car.'

'Why are they there?'

'Please, Logan, get back in the car.'

He hesitated. I gazed at him impassively. He backed away and got back into the car, and through the rear window I saw him talking to his mother. She turned to look at me anxiously, and seemed undecided about getting out. I held up a hand, and mouthed, 'It's all right.' She nodded.

I opened the boot again and picked up the two birds by the wire that was wrapped around their legs, which were surprisingly thin and delicate in contrast to the sudden weight of their bodies. I took a step back, whirled around, and hurled them away, sending the twinned corpses spinning out over the tree canopy, thirty feet below the edge of the road, and saw them drop down into the dense, dark green mass of trees.

I became aware of the stillness and silence. The only sound was a faint hissing, like background static, as the treetops swayed in the breeze.

I lifted out the jerrycan of petrol that was jammed between the wheel-arch and a large toolbox, cushioned by a pile of old coats. I took it to the side of the car, and opened the petrol cap.

We drove in silence for a few minutes. Harriet glanced anxiously in the rear-view mirror at Logan, and when I turned to look at him, he seemed lost in thought.

I smiled at him, and he did his best to smile back. Eventually he spoke: 'But Mummy, who put them there?'

'I don't know, Logie. But please don't worry about it.'

'But why did they do it?'

'It was probably just a joke. Probably someone we know, who decided to play a silly prank; that's all.'

Logan thought for a moment, then he said, 'Was it the two crows from the story?'

I saw Harriet's hands tighten on the steering wheel. 'No, darling. Nothing like that.'

'But can I tell Adam the story?'

Harriet frowned. 'I don't think he'll want to hear it, Logie. It's just an old folk tale.'

'But I want to tell him!'

I was about to say I'd like to hear the story, when I remembered the look of annoyance Harriet had shot me the last time I intervened in a battle of wills between her and Logan, back in her office, the first time I met them. I bit my tongue.

'Perhaps another time,' she said.

'I want to tell him now!'

I glanced at Harriet. Her lips were clamped shut, and she was breathing through her nose. I waited for what I expected from Logan – escalation, and a tantrum as his weapon of last resort – but it didn't come. He sat back, and in a low, patient voice he said, 'Please, Mummy, it won't take long, and I'm sure Adam would like to hear it.'

Logan's tone was so comically adult and reasonable that Harriet and I couldn't help smiling. She shook her head with a sigh. 'Go on, then.'

'Well,' he said, leaning forward again, 'it's a very old story and it's about these two crows, and they were the first people to live here. Animals, I mean, but animals who were like people, who could talk and everything. Creatures. Some type of creatures. They told us the word for it at school. What's that word, Mummy?'

'Mythical?'

'That's right. Mythical creatures. Anyway, they were here when the first human people arrived, and they'd always been here. And one crow was good, and one crow was bad. And if you were thinking of doing something bad, like, I don't know, like maybe robbing someone, or killing them, or something like that, then the good crow would come and talk to you, and remind you to be good, and try to make you change your mind. But the bad crow might come as well, and try to make you do the bad thing. Or, if you were going to do a good thing, like, I don't know, give some medicine to someone, the bad crow would come and be like, "Don't do it, because the medicine is expensive, and you should keep it for yourself." Things like that. Oh, and I forgot, the crows had names, which was how you knew which one was which, and the good one was called Arak and the bad one was called Krak. And if you wanted them, you could call them, like, "Arak!" and "Krak!"

and they'd come.'

'Hey,' Harriet said, 'not quite so loud, Logie. That was right in our ears!'

'Sorry. Anyway, after a long time – maybe a hundred years – people began to get the two crows mixed up. Actually, it was probably longer than that. Hundreds and hundreds of years. Maybe a thousand years. But anyway, people couldn't tell which one was which, and it was no good calling their names, because if you say both of their names, one after the other, it just sounds like one name, and it's the noise a crow makes, like, "Arakrakarakarak!" so it all gets mixed up. And then people started forgetting how to talk to the crows, and how to listen to them, and so they kept doing bad things, and fighting and stuff. And after a long time, the chief of the human people got fed up, and killed both of the crows, so at least people wouldn't be so mixed up. That was the idea, anyway. So he killed the crows.'

Harriet nodded. 'Thank you, Logie,' she said, 'you told the story very well.'

'Wait, it's not finished!'

'We're nearly at the loch, darling. Perhaps the rest can wait.'

'No, it won't take a minute,' Logan said, and before Harriet could object, he continued, 'The thing is, the crows weren't really dead, you see, or they were dead, but they were kind of like ghosts, and that's why the crows here are always so angry, because we killed the old crows, the first ones, and so now all the crows are trying to...you know, get their own back, and get...what's the word?'

'Revenge?' I suggested.

'Yes, revenge. That's right. They want revenge, and they go around in pairs, two of them at a time, and if you see two black crows, and they get really close, it's a sign you're going to...'

Logan trailed off, as if he'd suddenly realised the implications of what he was saying. I heard him swallow.

'It's a sign,' he said in a much quieter voice, 'that you're going to die. But it's only an old story. So it doesn't mean anything. Does it, Mummy?'

Harriet gave me a worried glance. 'No,' she said, 'of course not.'

'Well,' I said, 'I liked the story. I thought it was great. Nice and spooky.'

Logan brightened up. 'Really?'

'Sure. All the best old stories are about spooky warnings, and ghosts, and that kind of thing. That's what makes them good.'

That seemed to satisfy him, and we drove on in silence. The road began to wind its way downhill, and we were level with the forest again.

'Excuse me, Adam,' Logan said, 'but what happens when you die?'

'Darling,' Harriet said, 'I've told you before. Nobody really knows.'

'I bet they do,' he said, 'but they're just not telling.'

I turned in my seat to face Logan. 'What do *you* think happens?'

'I don't know,' he said. After a moment he added, 'You go away.'

'Perhaps you're right,' I said. 'We're all living on an island, and when you die you sail away.'

'Where to?'

'Another life.'

'We're here,' Harriet said.

I turned back to face the road, and saw the trees had thinned out and we were descending into an open valley. Harriet slowed down to take a corner, and the car rolled to a halt. We were at the edge of a huge lake surrounded by wild, steep hills.

'Here it is,' she said. 'Stone Heart Deep.'

A veil of mist lingered over the still, grey water, rising like wisps of smoke in the morning sun to reveal glimpses of a dark mansion squatting on the far shore, about a mile across the lake. 'And there's your house,' she said.

We sat in silence, watching.

I said, 'It almost looks as if the house is growing out of the rock.'

'It is, in a way,' Harriet said. 'The back of the house is built directly into the mountain.'

'Pretty impressive.'

'Wait until you see the inside.' Harriet steered the car onto a rough, narrow track that hugged the shoreline, and began to drive around the lake, towards the house.

I stood between Harriet and Logan, taking it all in. The massive entrance hall was like the interior of an abandoned cathedral. Blades of sunlight stabbed through broken shutters and grimy skylights to fill the huge space with a cubist patchwork of light and shadow. At the far end of the hall, across a vast expanse of marbled floor, a wide stone stairway curved up into the dusty gloom.

Even before we'd gone inside, it became clear that the house was more ramshackle than it had seemed from a distance. And bigger. Viewed from across the lake, it looked substantial but conventional: square and unfussy, like a straightforward stately home of perhaps Georgian design. But as we drove around the lake and our perspective shifted, the shape of the house seemed to change, revealing a building that was more complex and less symmetrical than it had appeared. An entire wing on one side seemed to emerge as a distinct structure only when you approached the house from a certain angle, as if it had been designed deliberately to trick you. Of the main building, there were four storeys above the ground floor, and although all their windows were tall, and gave an appearance of uniformity at first glance, in fact very few of them were exactly alike, and those that did conform to a single pattern weren't necessarily adjacent to each other. It was as if they'd been constructed at different times, or that entire sections of wall had been removed at some point and swapped around. At the top of the house, dormer windows of various shapes and sizes jutted haphazardly from a complicated roof. But what was disturbing, rather than merely eccentric, was that as we got closer to the building, and its proportions became increasingly bewildering, it also seemed to grow larger.

By the time we parked in front of the huge front doors, the house loomed over us darkly, and seemed to enfold us within a façade that thrust forward at either end in a pair of hulking, mismatched extensions. Everything about the place seemed irregular and irrational.

We began to explore the ground floor, where some of the rooms and passageways still contained a few scattered items of heavy furniture, dark paintings that hung askew, and faded tapestries dangling in tatters. We investigated nooks and alcoves. After a few minutes, we drifted apart, and went off on separate expeditions.

It was easy to get lost in Stone Heart House, partly because of an architectural oddity that I only began to notice when I tried to count the rooms.

There were too many corridors. You'd walk into a room, and out of it by a door opposite you, and find yourself in a corridor lined with doorways into other rooms, some of which gave access to further corridors, or possibly different sections of corridors you'd already encountered – it was hard to tell, especially as some of the passages ran at odd angles, and intersected confusingly. You never quite knew where you were, and whether you'd doubled back on yourself. It didn't help that the sparse furniture remaining in the house had a generic appearance, and many of the rooms were entirely empty. After a while, wherever you went, you had the feeling you'd been there before.

As we wandered around, we called out to each other, and with the help of this navigational aid – a kind of echolocation – we converged eventually at the back of the ground floor in a single huge room that spanned most of the house. It was a sprawling kitchen area, dark and dank, and as far as I could tell, it abutted the solid rock of the hillside behind it. We poked around for a few minutes, examining ancient cooking utensils and grim contraptions that suggested the preparation of meat in stultifying quantities, including a pair of rusting animal traps that dangled from the ceiling on hooks.

I found a passageway at the far end of the room, and it appeared to lead deeper into the hillside, but after a few steps I found it was closed off by a door that proved to be locked when I tried to open it.

I turned and called to Harriet, 'Have you got a key for this?'

'No, I haven't got any keys for the inside doors. Just the front.'

I realised I couldn't see Logan anywhere, and just as I was wondering where he'd got to, we heard his distant voice: 'Hey! Come up and look at this!'

We found him on the first floor in an echoing ballroom lined with mottled, flaking mirrors. Light filtered in through decaying curtains.

Harriet walked to the middle of the room and pirouetted slowly. She faced me and curtsied. I smiled and performed a sweeping, elegant bow. She held out her hand. I took it and we began to waltz, slowly and gracefully at first, then faster and faster. Logan joined in, capering around us in his own mad dance. We all whirled around wildly, raising swirls of dust, until finally we had to stop, gasping and laughing. I bowed again, and Harriet fluttered her lashes behind an imaginary fan.

Harriet and I gazed out at the lake from a tall front window on the second floor. We were standing close to each other.

'Are you excited?' Harriet asked.

'About the house?'

'What else would you be excited about?'

I glanced at her. We seemed to be even closer to each other now. Harriet searched my eyes. Then she turned to gaze out at the lake again.

'Nothing can live in that water,' she murmured. 'Too much peat, apparently. But it preserves things. Anything dead, which is creepy.'

'What can you tell me about Summer School?' I said.

If I'd hoped to catch Harriet off guard, I failed. She betrayed no surprise at my question coming out of the blue, and continued to stare at the placid water. 'It's just an old island tradition,' she said.

'Were you born here?'

'I was.'

'Then you must have played it. When you were six, right?'

'All I can remember is this little ceremony, about being a true islander. That kind of thing. All very quaint, I seem to recall.'

'Really? Logan seems worried about it.'

Harriet nodded slowly. 'I know.'

'And?'

'The thing you need to know about Logan...' she paused, and seemed to come out of a trance. She looked around. 'Actually, where is Logan?'

'He was around a minute ago. Playing by the stairs, I think.'

'I hope he hasn't–' Harriet broke off and ran to the top of the stairs.

'Logan? Where are you? Logie!'

I joined her. We listened to the silence.

'I'm here.' We both jumped at the sound of Logan's voice, unexpectedly close. He was above us, on the stairs up to the next floor. He was holding a big, dusty book.

'God, Logie,' Harriet said, 'you gave us a fright. What have you got there?'

'There's loads of them upstairs. It's got pictures in it. Old photographs.' He handed the photo album to his mother. I looked over her shoulder as she flipped through it. The pictures were faded; some of the older ones were clearly sepia to begin with, and others that began as monochrome prints were now washed out to nearly the same tone. The pictures featured men almost exclusively, individually and in groups, many of them with guns and dogs. Hunting parties.

'Amazing,' Harriet said, peering at a cluster of laughing men standing in front of a small wooden building in a rocky landscape. 'So many people smoking.'

'What's that place?' I asked. 'It's like a little Swiss chalet.'

'It's the old hunting lodge, just along the loch. They still use it.' She flipped some more pages. 'Maybe there's a picture of your father.'

I felt a jolt of shock. 'My father was never here,' I said.

Harriet looked at me with a puzzled smile, which vanished abruptly. 'Oh my god,' she whispered, 'I'm so sorry.'

'That's OK.'

'No, I'm an idiot. Forgive me. It was your grandfather – no, your mother's grandfather – who owned this place, wasn't it?'

'That's right, although he never actually lived here, apparently.'

'Yes, I remember now. I don't usually get mixed up like that over deeds and records and documents. I'm sorry if I upset you.'

'Don't worry,' I said. 'It's fine really. And even if I saw a photo of my father, I wouldn't recognise him. I think I mentioned that he died just before I was born?'

'Yes, you did. But didn't your mother ever show you any photos of him?'

'I don't think she kept any.'

'Same here,' Logan said. He swung himself around the bannisters and nestled himself against his mother's hip. 'We haven't got any of my dad, either.'

Harriet checked her watch. 'Oh my god, we need to get you back, Adam, or you'll be late for David Glynn.'

I summoned up a smile. 'We mustn't keep the sergeant waiting.'

***

Harriet pulled up outside the pub.

I got out and rested a hand on top of the car, leaning back down to talk to her through the window. 'Thanks for doing that. I appreciate it.'

'It was my pleasure. What do you think of the place?'

'It's extraordinary.'

'Has the visit changed your plans at all?'

'I don't know. It's certainly given me a few things to think about.'

'Let me know what you decide.'

'I will. And by the way, remember what I said about that fuel line. Let me check it again in a couple of days.'

'Thanks, I may take you up on that.'

Logan crawled over into the front passenger seat and looked up at me. 'Let's go there again, can we?'

'OK,' I said. 'Maybe we should.'

'Logie,' Harriet said, 'put your seatbelt on if you're going to sit in the front.' She began to release the handbrake, then paused. She leaned forward and looked past her son at me. She seemed to be hesitating over something. I waited.

She said, 'Would you like to come to dinner tonight?'

'I'd love to.'

'It will be nothing special.'

'Nothing special is my favourite meal.'

Logan frowned, then laughed as he got the joke.

Harriet nodded to me. 'Come at seven-thirty.'

SEVEN

I watched the car until it was out of sight. Was it likely that she would she invite me to dinner just to be polite? Part of me – my instinct – knew the answer, but I decided to ignore it. I didn't want to permit myself that gratification. Not yet. But I was pretty sure I knew where I stood with Harriet, and what would happen if we allowed it to.

'Right on time!' a voice behind me called. It was David Glynn, emerging from the pub. He was carrying a tray. I went through the gate and into the garden.

Glynn stopped at a table and put the tray down on it. As I approached, he unloaded its contents: two plates of food, cutlery, and two pint glasses.

'I've taken the liberty,' he said as he sat down, 'of ordering for both of us, Mr Budd. It's lamb stew, and I anticipate that you'll enjoy it. The same goes for the cider.'

'What if I'm a vegetarian?'

He glanced at me. 'Then you wouldn't have eaten three sausages for breakfast, would you?'

I gave him a quick smile and sat down. By now I should have got used to the idea that everyone here knew everything I did, and that Glynn, especially, would have put in the detective work to discover not only what I'd eaten for breakfast, but precisely how many fucking sausages I'd consumed.

Glynn began to eat, and waved his fork at my plate. 'Go ahead; try it.'

I did as I was told.

'I thought,' he said, speaking through a mouthful of food, 'that we could have a little chat while we were eating. Less formal, don't you think?'

'Sure.'

'How do you find the stew?'

'It's delicious,' I said, truthfully.

'Good, good. Now, Adam – do you mind if I call you Adam?'

'Please do. And you're David, right?'

'Correct. Let's not stand on ceremony for god's sake. And what do you make of that cider? Not too dry for you?'

I took a drink. 'It's very good.'

'It is, isn't it? Pressed locally, you know. From imported apples, obviously.' Glynn took another mouthful of food. 'So,' he said, 'Did Ogden kill her?'

I gazed at him impassively. I wasn't going to let him see he'd taken me by surprise.

'Old Mary Lennox,' he prompted. 'The accident. Was it Ogden's fault?' He paused with a forkful of food halfway to his mouth, scrutinising me.

'I don't think Ogden was responsible for her death,' I said.

90

'You don't think so? Are you not sure?'

I put down my knife and fork. 'No, I'm not sure. But I don't think it was Ogden's fault that she died.'

Glynn chewed his food, keeping his eyes on me. When he'd finished he took a swig of cider, still looking at me, and banged the glass down.

'Then that's settled,' he said.

'Don't you want to ask me anything else?'

'No,' he said. 'Not about that.'

'About something else?'

'Indeed. If you'll forgive my curiosity, Adam, I wondered if perhaps you've changed your plans?'

'Which plans?'

'About how long you're thinking of staying with us. I recall you saying you planned to be here for just a few days. And I wondered if you'd changed your mind, that's all.' He leaned back and assumed an amiably quizzical expression.

'I may stay a little longer than that,' I said.

'A while longer, eh? Well, it's a fine place, and if you have no pressing business elsewhere to call you away, I dare say you'd have your reasons for wanting to stay.'

I leaned back, matching Glynn's posture. 'You're right – it's a fine place.'

'It is. And how do you find the people, Adam? What do you make of us?'

I shrugged. 'I hardly know anyone yet.'

'Not yet, no. But tell me, what about Harriet Baird? What do you think of her?'

'Why do you ask?'

Glynn leaned forward. 'I'll be honest with you, Adam,' he said quietly. 'I'm fond of Harriet Baird.'

'And is she fond of you?'

He looked down at the table. He fiddled with his knife and fork, arranging them symmetrically. He looked up abruptly and his eyes glittered. 'I wouldn't like to see her hurt,' he murmured.

'I wouldn't hurt her,' I said.

He nodded thoughtfully. 'That's good to know, Adam.' He sat back again. 'Any plans for the rest of the day?'

I gestured towards the distant cliffs. 'I thought I might go for a walk.'

'Ah yes, it's a lovely walk along there. And a good day for it. I hope the weather stays mild for you.'

'Me too. But I'll take a coat, just in case.'

'Very wise. And later on? Do you have plans for the evening?'

'I'm having dinner with a friend.'

'Be careful,' Glynn said.

I kept my eyes on him and said nothing.

'On the cliffs, I mean,' Glynn continued. 'The path up there can be more treacherous than it looks. Don't go too near the edge; that's my advice.'

'I never go too near the edge of anything.'

'Is that so? I find that hard to believe, Adam. A military man like you.'

'I'm a journalist, David.'

'But a military background, yes? I can tell. I have a nose for these things.'

I suppressed an urge to tell Glynn what he could do with his nose. He was smiling at me expectantly, and there seemed something childlike in his desire – his need – to have his suspicions confirmed. He was clearly a man who liked to be proved right.

'As it happens,' I said, 'I spent some time in the Army Air Corps.'

Glynn slapped the table. 'I knew it!'

I spread my hands. 'You can read me like a book.'

'Oh, I wouldn't go that far,' he said. 'But the Air Corps, eh? Well, that military training is difficult to hide. And I expect it means you can take care of yourself, Adam.'

'If I have to.'

'Let's hope you don't have to,' he said. He stood up abruptly and held out his hand. 'Thank you, Adam, you've been most helpful.'

I shook his hand, feeling at a disadvantage because I was still seated. 'Thank you for the lunch,' I said.

'It was my pleasure.' He was still gripping my hand, and now he leaned down towards me, exerting more pressure. 'There's just one more thing I'd like to mention, if you'll permit me.'

'What's that?'

'Don't get too friendly with my son.'

I stared at him blankly.

He squeezed my hand even harder. 'Didn't she tell you? Logan is my boy.'

This time I couldn't conceal my surprise, and Glynn noted it with satisfaction. He released my hand. 'Now,' he said, 'I hope you'll enjoy the rest of your day.' He put on his cap and straightened the peak. 'And your evening,' he said, and walked away.

I was glad I'd brought a coat. There was no rain, but the gusts of wind whipping along the cliff had a keen bite.

The path was narrow, and in stretches where it hugged the cliffside I was only a few inches from the edge, looking directly down to the sea-lashed rocks.

I rounded a corner and stopped. A few miles out to sea was the drilling platform. It was the only feature visible for as far as the eye could see in an otherwise empty seascape, and it looked innocuously small from this distance. Beyond it, the horizon was a flat, unbroken line.

I heard distant, human sounds borne to me on the wind. I looked down and saw some people about a quarter of a mile away on the shore, back in the direction from which I'd come. The cliffs were lower and less steep back there, and instead of presenting a precipitous drop onto jagged rocks like those directly below me, the land sloped more gently down to a stretch of flat, stony beach. A family was having a picnic there, and a small child with bare legs was at the sea's edge, toddling into the water and squealing as the shallow waves splashed her ankles and chased her back to safety, where she turned and repeated the process. The girl's mother called to her, and she ran back to her family as the woman began handing out food from a large basket. They looked happy, huddled together against the wind in the pale sunshine.

I turned away and began to walk on – and stopped again. Two men were on the path ahead of me, and as they approached I saw it was Ogden and Barty. There was barely room for them to walk side by side along the narrow path. I glanced over my shoulder and saw the hulking figure of Sim, blocking the path twenty yards behind me. I adjusted my breathing, and directed energy down through my body, into my legs and feet. I wanted to be planted firmly on the ground, but also ready to move. I kept my eyes on the two men ahead of me, but I was aware of Sim behind me, and I knew exactly where he was.

Ogden walked up to me and stood close. 'I'm much obliged to you,' he said.

'What for?'

'For what you told the sergeant.' He thrust out his hand. 'Thanks.'

I took his hand, and felt Ogden's grip tighten. 'And now,' he said, 'you'll be leaving us.'

'What makes you think that?'

'I've heard you're selling the house.'

'I haven't decided yet.'

With his free hand Ogden grasped my upper arm. 'You should,' he said, stepping forward and shoving me back. 'You really should.'

My heels were on the edge of the path. There was a sheer drop behind me. From the corner of my eye I saw Barty and Sim moving closer. My hand was still gripped by Ogden's. I jerked it back, pulling Ogden towards me, bringing him off balance, and at the same time I spun around and pulled Ogden's arm up behind his back.

Now it was Ogden who was teetering on the cliff edge, and the only thing preventing him from falling was the armlock I had on him. Barty and Sim froze.

I put my lips close to Ogden's ear. 'Don't threaten me.'

'I don't make threats,' Ogden said. He was gazing down at the rocks far below him, and seemed completely calm. 'How about you, Adam?'

My face was close enough to see the pulse in the side of Ogden's neck. It was slow and steady. Not raised at all, as far as I could tell. I stepped back and pulled him with me, and slowly I released him from the armlock. He turned and gazed at me levelly for a moment, then walked away towards Sim. I stood still. Barty shuffled past me with his head down, and the three men set off down the path the way I'd come. None of them looked back at me.

EIGHT

As I came down the stairs from my room a flash of colour caught my eye. The flowers Lars Hansen had brought with him in the chopper were now stuffed in a metal waste bin between the wall and the doorway into the bar. I wondered why they hadn't been thrown out altogether. It was almost if they'd been left there to be noticed. To make a point.

It was seven in the evening, and I'd just made a final attempt to get online before giving up on the whole idea. The bar was deserted and the lights were low, but as I crossed the room to the front door I caught the sound of voices. I paused. They were coming from the kitchen. The door wasn't fully closed, and light spilled out into the area behind the bar, glinting on the bottles. The voices stopped abruptly. After a moment the door swung wide and Penny strode out. She stopped and faced me. Her smile was as placid as usual but it didn't reach her eyes.

'Can I help you, Adam?'

Her husband emerged from the kitchen behind her, speaking quietly to sergeant Glynn. They both halted abruptly when they saw me, causing someone right behind them to stumble, then retreat hastily back into the kitchen and close the door, but not before I had time to see it was Ogden. I was pretty sure someone else was still in the kitchen.

Finn nodded briefly at me and shuffled behind the bar counter. Glynn didn't move. Penny cleared her throat. 'Can I get you something?'

'No thanks. I'm just on my way out.'

'Oh yes,' Penny said, 'of course. And would you like to borrow a torch? It will be dark when you come back.'

'That's OK,' I said, 'I expect I'll find my way.'

'We'll leave the side door open for you, and a light outside.'

'Thanks.' I glanced back as I stepped out of the door. No one had moved.

I was about half a mile along the road into town when I heard a car behind me. As I scrambled up onto the narrow grass verge to let it pass I recognised the purr of Caleb Druce's old Bristol. It pulled up beside me and the doctor leaned over and shoved open the passenger door.

'Can I give you a lift?'

'Thanks,' I said, 'but I'm going to be early if I get a ride with you.'

'Then perhaps we can take the opportunity to have a talk.'

'Sure,' I said, 'why not.' I got in the car. As it pulled away smoothly I said, 'I don't suppose I need to ask whether you know where I'm going, do I?'

'I assume you're going to see Harriet.'

I sighed and shook my head in mock despair. I caught the glint of the low moon through gaps in the tall hedgerow bordering the road. I glanced at Druce. 'Doesn't it drive you a bit crazy, living here?'

'Why would it?' he said, then laughed. 'I'm not denying that I'm a bit crazy, of course. Certainly no less crazy than anyone else.'

'You know what I mean. Don't you find it weird, or at least oppressive, or intrusive, that everyone knows what everyone else is doing all the time?'

Druce considered for a moment. 'I'd say that's rather ironic.'

'What's ironic?'

'That you accuse us of knowing everyone's business. Think about it. We're not the ones spending our lives obsessively checking our phones and computers, hooked into an internet that's constantly collecting information about us. Sometimes, out here, we can't get online at all, even when we want to. There's no cable broadband here, the phone signal is terrible, and whatever we get via satellite is very erratic. Looking at it from my perspective, you're the one who's living in a surveillance society where everyone knows what you're doing – not me. Perhaps you're so used to living in a global village that you've forgotten what a real one is like. I'm not necessarily saying this place is a village, exactly, but it's an isolated, close-knit community, so there's a similar mindset.'

'Maybe.'

A minute passed in silence. Druce said, 'What are you thinking about?'

'Villages. I get what you're saying, but I'm thinking about some of the places I've been to, when I was abroad. And it's not quite the same.'

'Are you talking about when you were in the military?'

'Specifically, I'm talking about Afghanistan. Even in really remote places you'd see people with phones, satellite dishes, whatever. Maybe those places used to be different, but they're not now. They're just as connected as the rest of us.'

'Take it from me, they used to be different.'

'You've been to Afghanistan?'

'A couple of times, briefly. Nearly fifty years ago now.'

'What were you doing there?'

'What I've always done,' he said. 'I was being a doctor. Medicine is a bit like tennis: if you're reasonably good at it you can find a game of some sort almost anywhere in the world. I enjoyed travelling, and by practising medicine I was able to see interesting places, and to keep learning. That's important, Adam. Never stop learning.'

'Are you saying you were doing research?'

Druce gave a dismissive grunt. 'Research makes it sound too grand. I was just a restless man satisfying his curiosity. I find the world endlessly fascinating, to say nothing of the strange creatures that live in it, of whom the strangest, of course, are us.'

'And yet you've ended up here on this tiny island.'

'I was born here. Did you know that?'

'I didn't. But that still doesn't tell me why you've come back, especially after seeing so much of the world. What drew you back here?'

Druce slowed down and took a turning. I saw we were nearly in the town, approaching the main street that led up to Harriet's house. Before we reached it, he pulled in and parked. He switched off the ignition and rolled down his window.

We listened to the silence.

'I'd seen enough,' he said. 'I worked with aid agencies. I did relief work in war zones with refugees. Victims of torture, famine, genocide, mutilation. Every kind of misery and horror that humans are capable of inflicting upon one another. It's astounding, the variety of ways people devise to hurt each other.'

'Yes, I've seen some ingenuity in that respect myself.'

Druce glanced at me and grimaced sympathetically. 'So much rage and violence in the world, isn't there? And I grew to hate it. All that madness. I think that's why I'm back here, if you really want to know.'

I looked out of the car window. The moon was higher now. It seemed to have climbed very quickly. 'All right,' I said, 'I get everything you're saying, but all the same, I can't shake the feeling there's something creepy about this place.'

'Beware,' Druce intoned in a spooky voice, 'the island of zombies!'

I laughed. 'I'm not suggesting that, exactly.'

'Look,' he said, 'isolated communities tend to develop their own distinctive culture; you must know that.'

'Sure, but human nature is the same everywhere, isn't it?'

'When people talk about human nature they usually mean their own nature. We assume everyone is the same as us, but I prefer to think of ingredients, or a repertoire, from which we construct ourselves, in different proportions. Does that make sense?'

'OK, but regardless of the mixture, the basic ingredients you're talking about are common in every culture. People experience the same feelings, the same passions.'

'But what do you do with them, Adam? That's the question. How do you control them? Don't you agree that much of what we were talking about – the horror and violence we've witnessed – is a consequence of unchecked emotion?'

'Sometimes, yes. Of course. It happens all the time. People get swept away by emotions they can't control.'

'Like that boy in there?' Druce nodded in the direction of Harriet's house.

'Who, Logan?'

'Yes. A troubled child, don't you think?'

'I don't know about that. I think he's lonely.'

'And that's something you know about, is it?'

'What?'

'Being a lonely little boy.'

I gave Druce a long, deadpan stare. 'Did I say that?'

'Sorry, I can see I've hit a tender nerve there.'

Before I could object, Druce smiled brightly and said, 'Well, Logan seems to like you, at any rate. And so does his mother.'

'Really? I'm glad to hear you think so. It's a relief to know she probably won't try to poison my dinner.'

He chuckled. 'She's an interesting woman, but I don't think she'd go that far.'

'What do you mean when you say she's interesting?'

He said nothing for a moment, then he turned to me. 'You're right, Adam. There was a bit of ambiguity in the way I used that word, wasn't there? And I didn't notice until you challenged me. It's astute of you to pick up on these things. Let's see, why do I say Harriet Baird is "interesting" in that way? I suppose it's because there's a part of her I find a little unpredictable. I think that's it. She can be impetuous, you know. Irrational, perhaps. At times I wonder if she lacks impulse control.'

'Are you suggesting she's...what, unstable?'

'No, no. I wouldn't go that far. Certainly not. But as we've agreed, everyone displays a different mixture of the same ingredients, and in some people the mixture is more volatile, let's say. But that's the great thing about a community like ours. We can tolerate all the differences, and find a place for everyone. We look after each other. We're aware of each other's strengths and weaknesses, and we make allowances. For example, if Harriet wants to drive herself home after having a drink or two, fair enough. People can take that into account, and allow a bit of leeway.'

'Are you talking about people like Sergeant Glynn?'

Druce regarded me evenly, but behind his eyes I sensed he was trying to gauge how much I knew. I wasn't about to tell him.

He smiled. 'I'm talking about everyone, Adam. Please don't think I'm picking on Harriet specifically. Lord knows, we all have our idiosyncrasies, myself included. For example, sometimes I can get a little abstracted – forgetful, on occasion. And people are aware of that, and make allowances for me. Do you understand?'

I cocked my head and looked at him. Somehow I didn't buy the idea of Druce being an absent-minded professor type.

He saw my scepticism. 'Oh, it's true enough,' he said. 'But look, I don't think I'm explaining myself very well. Let me tell you a story, if I may.'

'Go ahead.'

'Many years ago, I spent a few months in a small village, a very remote place in southern Italy. There was a man there – a youngish man – who lived with his mother, and he used to steal people's clothes from their washing lines. In those days we'd probably have called him a simpleton, or even a village idiot. Now we'd probably say he had a learning disability. Stealing people's washing was the only problem he caused. Nothing else. But he couldn't stop doing it, no matter what anyone said or did. Every week the priest took his confession, along with everyone else's, and told him to stop, and he said he would, but he didn't. Technically, he was committing a crime, because it was theft, but it was a very minor crime, and a very minor sin. And although some of the clothes he stole were underwear, that didn't seem to be the point. He took all kinds of clothes. He didn't do anything with them, he just took them home. And he was happy to give them back, too. He just liked taking them. And everyone in the village knew that if you found your washing had been taken from the line, you simply went to Stefano's house and asked for it back. And he'd give it back. Do you see what I'm driving at, Adam?'

'Sure. The community was able to absorb it and deal with it.'

'Exactly. And would it have been better if people had tried to cure Stefano? If he'd been institutionalised, or medicated?'

'No,' I said, glancing at my watch. 'Of course not.'

'You're still in good time.'

'Thanks. But tell me, doctor, what if Stefano were to do something more serious?'

'Then you deal with it on a case-by-case basis. That's precisely what I'm saying, or part of it: that you have to take a lot of factors into account, in each individual situation.'

'But in general, you believe communities can solve their own problems better than outside agencies? And that sometimes enforcing the laws that operate in wider society isn't the appropriate response?'

'Sometimes, yes. Do you disagree with that?'

I didn't respond. Druce looked at me expectantly.

'I wasn't going to tell you this,' I said finally, 'but maybe I should. Something happened when I was walking along the cliffs today. The three men who were at the accident, when you first saw me, they were up on the path there. Ogden and the two farmers, Barty and Sim. I'm pretty sure they'd followed me, or were waiting for me.'

He frowned. 'What did they do?'

'They threatened me. At least, it was pretty clear to me that they were trying to scare me off. Persuade me to sell the house and leave.'

'Were they violent in any way?'

'Not quite. It was there, though. Under the surface.'

'But did they seem angry, or upset?'

I cast my mind back, seeing the men's faces. 'No. That's the weird thing. It was all very calm. Even when I put Ogden in an armlock. He didn't turn a hair, even though I could have dropped him off the cliff edge.'

'Hold on,' Druce said, 'it sounds to me as if *you* were the one getting violent.'

'No, it wasn't like that. I felt threatened – physically threatened – and I had to respond by neutralising the threat.'

He nodded slowly. 'You're probably right. I wouldn't be surprised to find they don't want you here.'

'Why not?'

'Why don't they want you here, or why wouldn't I be surprised?'

'Both.'

'There could be any number of reasons why they don't want you here. They don't like change, for one thing. They're naturally suspicious of newcomers, and people who appear to be different to them. Does that seem terribly primitive to you?'

'That's a trick question,' I said. 'We both know that in evolutionary terms a suspicion of outsiders can be a survival strategy. But don't forget the other side of the coin, which is that diversifying the gene pool is also an evolutionary advantage. Which requires at least some members of the tribe to interbreed with strangers, even if they're only the outliers.'

Druce regarded me with what seemed like amusement.

104

'Statistically,' he said, 'they *have* to be outliers. Mutations on the margins. Is that what you are, Adam? A mutation who's come here to diversify our gene pool?'

'That's not really the right thing to say to a man on his way to have dinner with a single woman. You're not exactly an incurable romantic, are you, doctor?'

'I'm an old man. Forgive me.'

I waved that away. Neither of us was being serious, and although I was enjoying that, I wasn't going to be distracted by it. 'What other reasons,' I said, 'would those men have for not wanting me here?'

Druce shrugged. 'It could be simply that they want to protect Ogden. They want to hear you say, unequivocally, that he wasn't at fault in the accident. And if you won't, then they want you gone.'

'Nothing to do with Harriet?'

'I doubt that very much.' He smiled. 'She may be unattached, but they're sensible men. They'd be realistic about their chances with her.'

'That wouldn't stop them being jealous.'

'I think it would, if they're rational about it. And as I said, they're sensible men.'

'It sounds as though you're taking their side.'

'No, Adam, not at all. I'm simply telling you what kind of men they are. And I'm also answering the second part of your question, which was why it wouldn't surprise me to find they don't want you here. It's because I know them. It's not in their interests, as they see it, to have you around, and they will do whatever is in their best interest.'

I felt a flash of anger, and didn't restrain it. 'Oh, so you think they were justified in threatening me up there on the cliff?'

'Did I say that? No. I said they were acting rationally. That's why I asked you if they seemed angry or upset. But no, you said they weren't. So, whatever they did, it was as a result of a calculation they made.'

'And that makes it OK, does it?'

'You're putting words into my mouth again, Adam. We've been talking about controlling one's emotions, and I consider that to be a good thing in general because in my experience, in the long run, it increases the overall likelihood of a good outcome in most situations. But I'm not claiming it's a virtue in itself. We still have to make our choices, and we have free will. But perhaps we can see those choices a little more clearly when we have our emotions under control. Does that seem so unreasonable?'

'No, doctor. It seems eminently reasonable.'

Druce chuckled. 'You see? Two civilised men, with a measure of goodwill between them, can usually find a way to agree. And I'm all in favour of that, especially if it's me they're agreeing with. Now, much as I enjoy your conversation, I don't want to keep you from your appointment. Shall I drive you to the door, or will you walk from here?'

'I'll walk.' As I reached to open my door I paused and said, 'What happened to Logan's father? Why did he leave Harriet?'

Druce didn't miss a beat. 'Don't try to catch me off-guard, Adam. It's not friendly.'

'Sorry. But it's a genuine question.'

'I'm sure it is. But I think you'd better ask Harriet. She'll tell you if she wants you to know. I'm already starting to think I may have breached professional confidentiality by talking about her at all, in view of her being my patient.'

'Wait, are you saying you *are* treating her for something?'

Druce patted my knee. 'No,' he said gently, 'I'm saying I'm her doctor. I'm everyone's doctor. I'm the only doctor on the island, do you see?'

'Yes, I see.' I opened the door. 'Thanks for the lift.'

'It was my pleasure. I enjoy your company, Adam. I hope we can continue our philosophical ruminations soon.'

'Me too.' I stepped out of the car and closed the door.

NINE

'Your timing is perfect,' Harriet said as she led me into an open-plan area that combined the kitchen with a dining room. 'I've just got Logan off to sleep.'

I saw that the table had been laid for two, with silver cutlery, snowy linen, candles, and an open bottle of wine. 'You've gone to a lot of trouble,' I said.

Harriet poured two glasses of wine. 'It's nice to have someone to take trouble for,' she said. As she handed me a glass our fingers brushed. She didn't move, and we remained facing each other, standing close. We raised our glasses and drank.

'How long have you been on your own?' I said.

'About four years. Since Logan was nearly two.'

'What happened to his father?'

Harriet hesitated fractionally. 'He left me.'

'Really? He must be crazy.'

Harriet laughed. 'What a nice thing to say.'

I noticed she had a slight overbite. We both drank again. When we lowered our glasses we held each other's gaze.

'What have you made for dinner?' I said.

Harriet set her glass down on the table. 'Nothing that can't wait.'

I put my glass down. I cradled her face and kissed her. She put a hand behind my neck and pulled me close, responding urgently. With our mouths still locked together she grabbed my belt and steered us out of the room, pulling my shirt loose as we reached the stairs. We stumbled up the steps, Harriet walking backwards, pressing my face against her breasts, my hands beneath her skirt, half-lifting her. At the top of the stairs she pulled me into a bedroom. 'We need to be quiet,' she gasped, 'because of Logan.'

I freed myself from the tangled sheets and lay on my back. We'd been greedy with each other, and the need to keep the noise down had imposed a restraint that proved erotic, bringing an intense focus to everything we did, and inspiring us to careful ferocity. Several times we'd had to pause, in a stifled ecstasy of tension, straining to listen for any sign we might have woken Logan up.

Now Harriet lay sprawled across me. I stroked her hair and said, 'Have we ruined the food?'

'No,' she murmured into my chest, 'it was on a timer. It's cooked, but we may have to heat it up. Don't worry. We don't have to race downstairs. We can stay here. Unless you want to run off, now you've had your way with me.'

'No chance.'

'Good.'

We were silent. Harriet's breathing was deep and I wondered if she'd gone to sleep, but when I shifted slightly she moved her head accommodatingly.

'Did you know,' I said, 'that I've had an offer for the house?'

'From who?'

'Lars Hansen. The boss out at the drilling rig. For a lot of money.'

'Will you take it?'

'Do you think I should?'

'What's the alternative?'

'I don't know. Keep the place, I guess. Maybe stay here. If that was…the right thing to do.'

Harriet laughed and propped herself up on her elbow. 'You're a very moral person, aren't you, Adam? I wonder where that comes from.'

'Am I? I don't know. Maybe it's my mother's influence.'

She pushed herself further upright and scrutinised me. 'Really? From what you were saying she doesn't sound very… well, very much like a moral influence.'

'That's the point. I think I reacted against her kind of life. There were always different men around. I never knew what was happening. It was very chaotic.'

Harriet laid her head on my chest again. 'Is that why you joined the army?'

'Probably. Although it seems I needed a bit more chaos before I was ready for that.'

'What kind of chaos?'

'I left home as soon as I finished school. I'd been living in the middle of nowhere with my mother. Well, Berkshire, which amounts to the same thing.'

'What did your mother think about you leaving home?'

'I'm not sure she really noticed, to be honest. Anyway, I went to London, and I spent a couple of years getting into various kinds of trouble, until I woke up one day in an alley with no money and a broken arm, and a very clear message from the people who'd broken it that I should make myself scarce. Two months later I was doing army basic training. Eventually I got into the Army Air Corps, and one thing led to another, and by the time I was twenty-one I was flying helicopters in Afghanistan.'

'And did it work?'

'What do you mean?'

'The military life. Did it give you the structure you'd been looking for, or the discipline, or whatever?'

'Not really. It turns out I don't like people telling me what to do.'

Harriet laughed and rolled off me. 'You sound like Logan!'

'That's probably true of all kids, isn't it?'

'Wait, are you upset because I compared you to a kid?'

'No! Well, maybe a bit.'

'Sorry. Anyway, don't change anything. Logan likes you.'

'I like him too. He's...he's a good kid.'

'I hope so,' Harriet said.

'Why do you say that? Are you worried about him?'

She sighed. 'I don't know. Perhaps I am. But probably no more than any other mother in my position.'

'Which is what, exactly?'

Harriet glanced at me. She shifted in the bed and sat up, propping herself against the pillows. I did the same. I waited for her to speak, but she didn't.

Eventually I nudged her shoulder and said, 'What's up?'

She shrugged. 'I don't know. You keep asking me different versions of the same question, and I'm not quite sure what you want me to say. And at the same time I get the feeling you're the one who's not telling me everything. I don't know. Maybe I'm imagining it, but whenever we talk about Logan, you seem to get tense, and it's like you're holding something back, and then you change the subject and start asking me about my... my situation.'

I looked away. I wondered what it would be like if I stayed here, with this woman, and how I would feel if I changed my life. I was aware that Harriet was looking at me intently. Slowly she moved her head forward and around, widening her eyes cartoonishly, making a joke of the fact she was inspecting me, waiting for me to speak.

I laughed. 'Sorry.'

'In your own time.'

I took her hand. 'I need to tell you something.'

'Uh oh. That sounds ominous. Will I need to see a doctor?'

'No, but I might. Depending on how you react to being... misled, let's say. It's just that when you asked if I'd had any kids, I didn't exactly tell you the whole truth.'

Harriet leaned back. 'Oh, right. Here it comes. What are we talking about? A wife and family? More than one wife and family? Give it to me straight. I can take it.'

'No, that's not it.'

She realised I was being serious, and sat up again. She squeezed my hand. 'Sorry, I'm making assumptions and being flippant. What is it? Tell me.'

'When I came home from the army I was angry,' I said. 'I'd been given an honourable discharge, but they'd wanted to throw me out, or even lock me up, and the only reason they didn't was that I had evidence of things that could have been awkward for them if I'd gone public. It was about something that had happened – an atrocity, or something close to it –

that was being covered up. Whitewashed. I found out about it almost by accident, because I'd worked on some intelligence missions, as well as the flying, and I got to know a few good people. Only a few, though. Mostly, I hated what we were doing.

'Don't get me wrong, I've got no romantic illusions about the people we were fighting, and they were capable of doing truly dreadful things – and they did them, frequently. But I suppose I did have one illusion, which was thinking that somehow we shouldn't have been as bad as them. But we were, a lot of the time, and the only real difference was that we tended to be more discreet in our barbarism, and more cynical about it. Where they might relish the opportunity to present you with the severed head of one of your colleagues, and do it in person, perhaps wrapped in his entrails for good measure, we preferred to betray our enemies to their rivals, and let them do our dirty work for us, out of our sight.

'But the one thing both sides shared was the compulsion to talk about how fucking honourable we all were, and I got so sick of that bullshit I would have left anyway. As it was, I left in a kind of fog of moral compromise that made me feel like I needed to take a cold shower for the rest of my life. I needed to find some clarity. Or purpose, or peace, or something. Whatever it was, the very last thing I needed was what actually happened.' I stopped, and looked away again. I needed to maintain a distance from the events I was about to describe.

'I'm going to take a wild guess here,' Harriet said, 'but did it by any chance involve a woman?'

I exhaled. 'It did. Three weeks after I got back to England I fell in love. I was twenty-four, and she was a few years older. Nearly thirty. She was called Lucy.'

'And you had a kid?'

'No. She already had a daughter. A seven-year-old called Florence. She was a lovely kid, and we got on really well. Her father had left her mother when Florence was three. Her mother and I decided we wanted to have a child of our own, but it wasn't happening: Lucy had two miscarriages, and I didn't want her to keep trying after that. I was happy to be with her and Florence. More than happy. I was madly in love with Lucy, and I loved being a stepdad to Florence, and it was wonderful. Not perfect, because nothing is, but it was as good as it gets, I think. More than good enough for me.

'I got some work as a freelance journalist, and a few times I went away, reporting on conflicts. I wouldn't call myself a war correspondent, because most of the conflicts I reported on weren't really wars, they were just – well, conflicts. But I did go back to Afghanistan twice, and I can't pretend it didn't feel like I had unfinished business. Like I was scratching an itch. It was mainly to do with some Afghan guys who'd worked for our side as translators, and were being put in danger by the army's refusal to honour its obligations to them. There it is again, that word honour. It never got fully resolved, but I like to think I helped, and I was able to protect some of the people I knew. But the second time, after I got back – and this was after Lucy and I had been together for about five years – things started to change. With Florence.

'She was always quite mature for her age, and by the time she was twelve she was obsessed with her appearance, and I'm not just talking about the usual teenage girl stuff – the things that get exaggerated and manipulated by all the shit they see online now. This was something else. Sometimes she would just stand in front of the mirror for hours and cry. And there was a lot of anger – and I mean serious anger, not just tantrums. It seemed out of control. She smashed a lot of things up, and she was harming herself – cutting herself – which completely freaked us out, me and Lucy. We exhausted ourselves trying to deal with it, and it took us months to realise that not only was she clinically depressed, she was anorexic. Like, severely anorexic. And I didn't know how to talk to her. Every time I tried, I got the whole "You're not my real father" thing, which was ridiculous, because I'd never tried to fulfil that role; never even went there, never got close to it. How could I, even if I'd wanted to? I was only fifteen years older than her, and I was more like a big brother. Or I had been, until it all went wrong.

'She was thirteen when she left the house one evening without telling us and stayed out all night. We were frantic. The next day she said she'd been to a party – a friend of a friend – and she'd missed the last bus home. Then she did it a few more times, and each time we thought we'd sorted it out, and got her to agree not to do it again. Then one morning she came home at about seven when I was in the kitchen and I saw she was on heroin. I could tell immediately. Even before I went to Afghanistan I'd spent enough time around opioids to see it straight away. I didn't confront her there and then, and I didn't want to tell her mother. I took her aside the next day and tried to ask about it, and she raged at me, and denied it, and tried to hit me. Then it got worse.

'Thirteen years old. It broke our hearts. She was hanging out with a gang of older kids, and some people who were more than kids – men in their twenties – and she was being used to move drugs, and to sell them, and she was using drugs herself. And when she became properly addicted, which doesn't take long, the older ones, the men, started pimping her. It was a classic grooming process, and I was watching it happen in front of my eyes, and I was desperate to try and stop it. We'd tried everything we could think of in terms of doctors, and medicine, and counselling, and cures, and we'd tried taking Florence away, but it was a nightmare, and as soon as we got back she just started again. The only thing left was to get the police involved, and Lucy ruled it out. Florence kept disappearing and coming back, getting clean and relapsing – which is a depressingly predictable cycle – until finally she didn't come back at all. We waited and waited. She phoned once, to say she was alive, and then nothing. Then, of course, we told the police, but they didn't find her, and Lucy blamed herself for leaving it too late. I couldn't bear seeing her in such pain, and the thought of what was happening to Florence was driving me crazy. So I took action.

'I went undercover. I drew on my own experience of that world, from the days when my life was falling apart before I joined the army, and I called up the skills I'd learned when I was doing intelligence work. Character, back-story, trust, misdirection, double bluff; the whole bag of tricks. I didn't try to find Florence directly. It was more like circling, and circling, and getting closer to her that way. A few times I had to do serious drugs – heroin, crack – in front of people I wanted to deceive, and that pushed me close to losing my grip, but I kept it together. Finally I found myself alone in a room with her, in a house that was too squalid to be called a brothel. It was a shithole where humans were nothing more than a series of primal functions and transactions.

'She was so shocked. It was one thing to do what she was doing while keeping it in a separate world from the one her mother and I lived in, but the sudden reality of me being there – that other world breaking in on her in that place, and the horrible pain it brought with it – that was too much for her. She fell apart completely. I had to damage a couple of people to get her out of there, but it was nothing they didn't deserve. If I'd done what they deserved, they wouldn't be alive. And I know it was a brutal thing I did to her, confronting her like that, but leaving her there would have been worse.

'I got her home, and I devoted myself to her recovery. Lucy gave her all the love in the world, but it takes more than love to help someone in Florence's condition. Looking after her became my full time job, twenty-four hours a day, and slowly, very slowly, she seemed to be getting better. After about three months we saw Florence coming back to life – not just to how she'd been before she disappeared, but back to what I thought of as her real life, the one she should have been living. She seemed genuinely healthy and happy. For about six months it was like a miracle. We were in a kind of heaven, I think.

'Then one day she disappeared again. We waited. Three days later we were told her body had been found on some cliffs near Dover. She'd taken heroin, then died of hypothermia, they said. At first I didn't believe them. I went crazy. I was convinced the people who'd groomed her and abused her had found her, and abducted her, and spiked her, and I actually got ready to set off and hunt them down; I even got hold of a gun. But I didn't do it. It was stupid. I was trying to project all my rage and grief onto some kind of lurid melodrama.

'I had to face the fact that it was simply the ordinary, banal death of a relapsed addict. One day she'd just wanted to get high again. Maybe she really believed she was only going to do it one last time, or there was some other story she told herself. There's always a story, with addicts. Maybe her mother or I had said something thoughtless, or done something silly, and she built that into a justification for running away. Fuck knows, and it doesn't matter. But she hadn't done heroin for about nine months, and she probably scored what would have been her usual dose, from back when she'd been using constantly and had built up a tolerance, or maybe it was a strong batch, or whatever, but she took too much, then she nodded out, then she froze to death. Her life ended.

'And so did Lucy's. Her misery was fathomless and unending. A year after Florence died she still wouldn't go out, or do anything, or talk about anything. Nothing. She was numb, blank, absent. I couldn't bear it. It was happening all over again: I was watching someone I loved disintegrate and I couldn't do anything about it. I tried to get help for her, but she wouldn't see anyone. She told me to leave her, but I didn't, of course. Until she began to say it every day, month after month, and then she started this horrible ritual, of packing a suitcase of my clothes, and putting it next to the door, and saying she was going to bed and she didn't want to see me again. After a month of that I left. Eighteen months later she died of breast cancer. She was thirty-nine.'

I waited for Harriet to speak. Eventually I glanced at her and saw she was gazing into the distance, her eyes glistening.

'Sorry,' I said.

'For what?'

'Well,' I said after a moment, 'for one thing the dinner will be cold by now.'

Harriet looked startled for an instant, then she smiled. 'You've got a pretty dark sense of humour, haven't you, Mr Budd?'

I shrugged. 'Sometimes you've got to laugh, or it would all get too much, right?'

'What would?'

'Everything. Life. Not that I know very much about yours, of course, because all you've done is listen patiently while I lie here, unspooling my dismal history.'

'I like listening to you.'

'That's nice. But now I've told you my story, how about yours?'

'It's not terribly interesting. Not as...dramatic as yours. Is that the right word? I don't want to say "exciting" because it must have been terrible, whichever way you try to think about it now. And I get it: I get that making dark jokes is one way of dealing with these things. It's a defence mechanism, wouldn't you say?'

'You're playing for time.'

'Am I?'

'I asked you about yourself, and you're trying to deflect the conversation.'

'Yes, I suppose I am. I'm not very good at talking about myself.'

'OK, how about if I ask you some questions, would that help?'

'Like a quiz? Or more like an interview, seeing you're a journalist. We could pretend I'm some terrifically interesting celebrity.'

'Good. So, my first question is this. Why didn't you tell me that Logan's father is David Glynn?'

Harriet stiffened. She turned to look at me and folded her arms. 'You're a bit of a bastard, aren't you, Adam?'

'You say that like it's a bad thing.'

She laughed despite herself. 'Fuck off.'

'Sorry. I thought I'd just jump straight in there.'

'No, don't apologise. I can see it's an effective interview technique. Get the subject off-balance right from the start. Very impressive.'

'Thanks. And what's the answer?'

She uncrossed her arms and lay back. 'I suppose,' she murmured, 'I figured you'd find out soon enough. Was it David who told you?'

'It was, yes. And I must say, I was pretty surprised to find out you two had been a couple. You seem an unlikely match, if you don't mind me saying so.'

'No, I don't mind. It's true. We weren't really suited, right from the start.'

'And what was the start? Want to tell me about it?'

'I could, but it's part of a bigger story, and I'd have to tell you the whole thing.'

'That's the general idea.'

She laughed again. 'Damn, you're good.'

'It's a living. OK, I'm all ears.'

Harriet shuffled closer to me and pulled the sheets up to cover us. I put an arm around her, and she nestled against me. 'I suppose it all starts with my mother.'

'A lot of stories do,' I said.

'Sorry to be predictable.'

'Not at all. That's pretty much the way mine started, if you remember. So, what was she like?'

'Formidable. That's what a lot of people used to call her, and sometimes I thought of her that way too. But she was also very kind, and very loving to me. I think she spoiled me a bit, especially after my father died. I was only eleven. He drowned, in a fishing accident. Well, in a storm – if you can call that an accident. He was just doing his job, as he saw it.'

'He was a fisherman?'

'Not exactly. You might say he was a small businessman. He owned five boats, and employed people to crew them. One day, the weather changed suddenly while four of the boats were out, and only three made it back before the storm broke.

My dad went out in the spare boat, which was meant to be undergoing repairs, and tried to find the missing crew, but he never came back. Ironically, the boat he was trying to find limped home the next day, when the storm had passed.'

'That must have been rough on you. Losing your father at that age.'

'I suppose it was. But it's funny, isn't it? You remember things that happened to you, but do you actually remember the feelings you had? I don't think so. I remember missing him, and wishing he was still here, but thinking about it now, the closest I can get to an emotional response is a feeling of... disappointment. They say we forget pain, don't they? They always use the example of having babies, and say that if we remembered how painful it was, human reproduction would grind to a halt. Which brings me back to my mother. We definitely grew closer after my father died. She became quite protective of me, and spent as much time as she could with me, which meant I got to know quite a lot about her work, and that influenced me, of course, as well as everything else.'

'Her work? What work?'

Harriet raised her head and looked up at me with an expression of surprise. 'She was the lawyer here. Didn't I tell you?'

'No, I didn't know that. That's interesting.'

'I suppose it was a kind of tradition, because my grandmother was the lawyer too.'

'Wow. Like a matrilineal thing?'

'Not specifically, although it did come down through the family. My grandmother's father was the lawyer here – my great grandfather.'

'And before that?'

'It's hard to know, because about a hundred years ago

there was a big fire at the Town Hall and all the records were destroyed. But I'm pretty sure it was in the family for a long time.'

'That must have made it difficult for you.'

'Why?'

'All that tradition behind you. It must have made you feel you had no choice. Or didn't you think of it that way?'

Harriet was silent. Her hand was resting on my chest, and I felt her fingers kneading my flesh very gently. 'It crossed my mind,' she said finally, 'although I was pretty sure I wanted to do it. But there was a brief period when I tried hard to imagine what it would be like if I turned it down. I was testing myself, I think. I was about seventeen, and it was as if I was trying to summon up some kind of rebellious teenage attitude, and try it on for size. But it didn't fit, that's the truth. In the end I realised I was proud to carry on the tradition.'

'And your mother didn't pressure you?'

'No.' She paused. 'Well, it wasn't pressure, but I knew she'd be disappointed if I didn't study law, and take on the job. That was pretty obvious, I'd say.'

'That sounds like pressure to me.'

'What, you mean like a kind of emotional blackmail?'

'Well, now you mention it...'

'It's not that simple, Adam. We all take other people's feelings into account when we make our choices, don't we? Especially when you're part of a community. We weigh up the pros and cons, and take everything into consideration, and make a decision that might not be absolutely black-and-white, but it's generally the best for us, and for everyone else. Or perhaps that doesn't apply to big, tough, hard-boiled reporters who roam the world and treat everything as a story to be investigated?'

I laughed. 'I think you may be stereotyping me a bit.'

'Really? No shit.' She made a fist and tapped my chin playfully. 'And is it remotely possible that you've just being doing exactly that to me, do you think? Can't you accept that other people are just as complex and conflicted as you are?'

I was about to object, but I sensed an edge beneath her playfulness. And she had a point. I took her hand and kissed it. 'Fair enough,' I said. 'Please continue.'

'Well, I made my choices, and I went to Edinburgh, to do a law degree. I'd never left the island before, and it was pretty strange. And I'll admit, the longer I was away, the more I questioned some of the things I'd taken for granted. For the first three years, I came back every summer, for the long vacation, and one time I came back at Christmas, and of course my mother and I wrote to each other. We spoke on the phone as well, but the land line here is just as unreliable as the mobile signal, and half the time you spend the entire conversation asking the other person if they can hear you.

'Then, in my final year, things got hectic. I was working hard, and I'd met someone, and I thought I might be in love with him, although that was mostly because he kept telling me how much he loved *me*. He was involved in various human rights causes, and at the time I thought that was rather romantic and noble, although he never seemed to do anything about them, just talk. God, that man talked. Looking back, I can't believe I put up with him.'

'Ah,' I said, 'love's young dream.'

'Yeah. Well, I would have woken up eventually, but everything changed before I had a chance to. I found out my mother was very ill. I knew she was getting frail, and each time I came back for the holidays I could see she was ageing, but she never gave any sign that anything serious was wrong. During my final year on the mainland, she sometimes mentioned she'd been unwell, but in her letters and phone calls she always insisted she'd got over it, and she was fine. Then, about a month before I was due to come back for good, I got a message from Caleb Druce. He told me she had cancer, and didn't have long to live. It was a total shock, and I simply couldn't understand why she hadn't told me.'

'Maybe,' I said, 'she thought it was important for you to get your degree and complete your training, and she didn't want you to break that off.'

'Obviously,' Harriet retorted, 'that was part of it. Of course it was. But what you have to understand about my mother is that underneath it all she was fiercely loyal to this place. And I always knew that, but it was still difficult to accept that she'd been prepared to keep the truth from me – and about such a personal thing between us – just to make sure I would take her place. You know, this island may seem like a remote backwater to you, but there are still a lot of things that require legal work. All kinds of transactions and contracts – between people here, and between us and the mainland. It's a full-time job, and sometimes it can be quite difficult.' She paused, and sighed. 'Sorry.'

'What for?'

'I'm sounding defensive. I suppose I'm just as loyal to the island as she was; that's what it comes down to.'

'Nothing wrong with that,' I said, and gave her a squeeze with the arm that was around her shoulders.

She nestled into me more closely and said, 'I came back as soon as I could. It was terrible to see her. She was like a skeleton. Doctor Druce said it had been very swift.'

'What type of cancer was it?'

'A type of blood cancer. Quite rare, he said.'

'Was Druce the only one who was treating her? I mean, did

she see specialists, or anything like that?'

'No. He sent off various samples, but there was nothing much to be done, apparently. There was some talk of possible treatments, but it was pretty clear they didn't hold out much hope, and she didn't want to be moved anyway. She wouldn't hear of going to the mainland. I was able to spend the last couple of weeks of her life with her, and I'm grateful for that. It was like she'd been waiting for me, and as soon as I got here she kind of...let go.'

She fell silent, and I waited. I could feel her heartbeat against my chest, then her ribs moving as she took a deep breath. 'After my mother died,' she said, 'I felt totally lost, as though I couldn't remember my place in the world. I couldn't find anywhere to be. And I didn't know how I was supposed to feel, although that probably sounds a bit weird. But it's true: I didn't know how to grieve.'

'There aren't any rules,' I said. 'It's different for everyone.'

'Yes, I know that, but it didn't help. I felt completely cut adrift, like I was wandering aimlessly. And I don't mean just metaphorically. I drifted around without knowing where I was, or where I was going, and I went for long walks on the cliffs, and didn't think about turning back and going home. I was often out late. I walked and walked, all the time. And that's when I began to notice David.'

'Notice him? In what way?'

'He was just...there. I started to see him when I was out walking. Not in a creepy way, not like he was stalking me. It was more like he was watching out for me. He wasn't obvious or intrusive, but sometimes I'd meet him when I was out, and occasionally I'd become aware of him walking along beside me, and then we'd exchange a few words, and then he'd kind of... be on his way. And sometimes I'd see him when I was going home, and I began to realise he was there because he wanted to make sure I got back all right. He was a policeman, after all, so it felt natural that he might be keeping an eye on me. And I suppose I got used to him being around. It was reassuring to see him, because he was a steady presence, and he was quiet, and he didn't say much, but he seemed practical, and down-to-earth and capable. That's what made me think that Conrad, the guy I'd been seeing in Edinburgh, was a bit of a wanker.'

I chuckled. 'That was, in fact, the word that sprang to mind when you were describing him, although I didn't want to be the one to use it.'

'I'm being harsh, really. But at that particular time, the whole idea of someone like Conrad seemed unreal. I was in a different world – David's world, it turned out, although I didn't realise it at the time. It was like he surrounded me, and then, after a few months, he married me.'

'Really?' I said. 'That makes it sound like something he *did* to you. Didn't you have any choice in the matter?'

'Of course I did. I wanted to marry him. Or I thought I did. It was almost as if I couldn't think of anything else to do. I was back at home, I was taking over from my mother, I was an islander, it all seemed like...fate. My destiny. So, we got married.'

'It sounds like you were still traumatised from losing your mother.'

'I was, probably. I was certainly in a bit of trance. But a few weeks after the wedding, I woke up. Literally. I remember opening my eyes one morning, and seeing David beside me, and thinking, why the hell am I here with this man? I mean, we had nothing in common. Nothing. And I started to feel trapped, and stifled. And over the next few months it got worse, and then I found I was pregnant. I felt that I couldn't get away. He was always there, as a kind of dark, brooding presence. It was the other side of the coin that I'd found so reassuring – his solidity, his silence, his rootedness – it was all suddenly oppressive. And I began to understand that he was very controlling.'

'Was he violent?'

Harriet shot me a quizzical look. 'Why do you say it like that?'

'Like what?'

'As if you were hoping I'd say yes. That he hit me, or something.'

'Sorry, I didn't mean it to sound like that. But maybe you're right. It's true that I dislike him, and I suppose it would give me more of a reason to justify it.'

'He wasn't violent. Not physically. But sometimes he let me see his anger, although he never lost control of himself. I just knew it was there; that's all. He had ways of making me feel wary of him. He didn't like me doing anything without him, and he even resented me reading, so I used to pretend that anything I was reading was for my work. I felt more and more isolated, and eventually I decided I had to get away from him, and when Logan was about a year old I started making secret plans to take him to the mainland. But David found out about it somehow. Not that he did anything – he just became even more quiet and watchful, and sullen. I tried to talk to him about it, but he wouldn't engage with me. It was like I was in a limbo. I don't know what I would have done if it had gone on much longer. I was pretty desperate.'

'So what happened?'

'I went to Caleb Druce, and told him everything. He said he'd talk to David. I don't quite know what went on, but David finally began to discuss what was happening, and I told him

I wanted us to separate. He didn't like it, but we negotiated an agreement. Logan was to understand that David was his father, but that was all. David would have no access rights, except at my discretion. In return, I agreed not to take Logan away from the island. I wouldn't say it was amicable, but at least David moved out quietly. We'd been living here together, you see, which was one of the problems, I think. He had a small flat above the police station, and he went back to live there.'

'So you're still married to him?'

'No. About a year later, I got an uncontested divorce. I'm a lawyer, remember, so it wasn't too difficult. And now you know all about me.'

'Thanks for telling me. But can I ask you something else?'

'That depends. What's it about?'

'About growing up here.'

'Hmm. Can I ask you something first?'

'Sure,' I said. 'What?'

Harriet smiled. 'Are you hungry?'

'Why, are you?'

'I could be.' She pressed herself against me. 'But I'm just as happy to stay here in bed with you.' She stroked my chest, and moved her hand down until it was under the sheets, her fingers brushing my pubic hair as my cock rose up to meet them. 'On the basis of the evidence currently available,' she said, 'perhaps we should postpone dinner again.'

We began to kiss, then I pulled away and said, 'I still want to say sorry. I mean, I didn't intend to tell you my entire life story.'

Harriet gazed at me. 'Why are you so keen to apologise about everything?'

'Am I? I don't know. I'm probably not expressing myself very well. It's just that sometimes I don't know what to do with my feelings.'

'You don't necessarily have to do anything with feelings. You can just have them.'

'All right. I will.'

'Good. Let's have some feelings together.'

TEN

I got back to the pub at dawn, and slept for a couple of hours. When I woke up I went in search of coffee, feeling surprisingly energetic as I trotted down the stairs.

I walked into the sunlit bar and stopped dead.

Harriet was standing near the front door, holding Logan's hand. Sergeant Glynn was beside her, and Finn and Penny were facing them from across the room. I hadn't heard them talking, but I sensed they'd broken off a conversation when they heard me coming downstairs. There was an odd, tense atmosphere in the room.

'Adam. Good morning to you,' Glynn said. 'I was just leaving.' He looked around at the others and smiled genially. 'Thanks for the coffee, and the little chat.' He put his cap on. 'Good to see you, Harriet. And you too, Logan. Be a good boy, won't you?' He smiled down at Logan, who raised his eyes and nodded, then stared at his feet.

'Ah well, duty calls,' Glynn said. 'I trust you'll all have a fine day.' He walked out and closed the door behind him.

Penny looked around brightly without meeting my eye, then walked off into the kitchen. Finn went behind the bar, where he opened a trapdoor and clattered down some unseen steps. In the silence that followed, Harriet cleared her throat. 'Adam, I wonder if I could ask you a favour.'

I thought she looked pale. 'Of course,' I said. 'What can I do for you?'

'Some work has come up suddenly, and as we're in the middle of the school holidays at present it's left me in a slight predicament.'

I wondered why she was being so formal. I tried to detect some acknowledgement of what we'd been doing only a few hours earlier, but her manner was simply polite, and nothing else. I smiled at her encouragingly. 'Do you want me to look after Logan?'

'That would be very kind,' she said, as if I were a total stranger to her. 'You see, usually when these things come up, I'd leave him with Finn and Penny, but they have to change the barrels this morning, and I don't want Logan getting in their way.'

'No problem. What do you think, Logan?'

Logan nodded at me briefly. 'Cool.'

'You can borrow my van,' Finn said from behind the bar, emerging from the steps up from the beer cellar. 'Maybe take yourselves up to the loch again?'

'Thanks Finn, that would be great,' Harriet said. She looked down at her son, stroking his hair. 'Would you like that, Logie? To go up to the loch with Adam?'

'OK,' Logan said.

Harriet straightened up and gave me a bland, professional smile. 'Thank you, Adam. I really appreciate it. Now, I must run!' She bent down and kissed Logan on the cheek swiftly, then turned and left without looking at me again.

Finn picked up an adjustable wrench and began descending the cellar steps. 'The van keys are on a hook at the end of the bar,' he called to me. 'See you for lunch!'

***

I stood at the edge of the lake, gazing at the house on the distant opposite shore. I tried to identify the window from which Harriet and I had looked out across the water yesterday, standing close to each other, erotic tension sparking between us like static. For a moment, I had a feeling someone was watching me from over there. Perhaps it was me, and I'd slipped through a gap in time, and was back in the house, watching myself here a day later. Or perhaps it was the house itself that was watching me. I looked around. There was no mist, and I felt dwarfed by the surrounding hills in the vast morning stillness.

'It's no good,' Logan said, as the surface of the water settled and the ripples died away, 'I can't do it.'

'Don't give up,' I said. 'It just takes a bit of practice.' I dropped down onto my haunches and tried to look Logan in the eye, but the boy turned away and scuffed his feet.

'It's partly about getting the right stone,' I said. 'Let's look for a couple of really good flat ones.' I selected two large pebbles from the shingle at my feet and handed one to Logan. 'Here you are, have another go.'

'You go first,' he said, 'and I'll watch.'

'OK, good plan. Right, you need to get down low, like this,

so you can keep the stone nice and flat. Here we go.' I skimmed my stone across the glassy lake and it kissed the surface in a chain of low arcs until the water swallowed it. I stood up and patted Logan on the shoulder. The boy bent his knees and shuffled to the edge of the water, then flung his stone. It plopped beneath the surface a few yards away.

'That was shit!' he said. He turned away from the water miserably.

'Hold on,' I said, 'Let's keep going. Look, I've got two more good ones. Here's a really flat one for you. Shall I go first again, and you can watch how I do it?'

He nodded. I saw the beginnings of tears brimming in his eyes. 'You'll get there, Logan,' I said, 'I know you will. Now, watch how I keep my arm level with the water, OK? Here we go.'

I skimmed my stone again, and it seemed to skip for ever before it sank, almost out of sight. 'That was a lucky one,' I said. 'Now, come over here, close to me.'

Logan stood beside me. 'Let's practise a couple of times' I said, 'to get the angle of the swing right. Like this.' I took his arm and moved it gently, showing him the way. 'All right, now go for it. Keep it smooth.'

Logan threw the stone carefully. This time it skipped once before the water gulped it down. 'Shit!' he said.

'No, it was good!' I said. 'Better than the last one! I reached out to take his shoulder but he sprang forward and began kicking at the water furiously.

'Stupid water!' he shouted. 'It's all wrong!'

'Whoa, come on Logan,' I said, and reached out to him just as he slipped over and fell into the shallows, where he rolled around, thrashing savagely at the water with his arms and legs. I pulled him up swiftly, but he squirmed out of my grasp and flung himself face-down onto the pebbly ground.

'It's not fair!' he yelled, his voice muffled.

I stood over him, and was about to raise him up, but held back. I waited a few seconds, then said, 'Hey Logan, remember the soldiers.'

He rolled over and looked up at me sulkily. 'What about them?'

'You're giving the orders, right?'

He squeezed his eyes shut and balled his fists. 'But this is different!'

'Well,' I said, 'maybe you're right. I'll tell you about another way to do it.'

'Do what?'

'Take charge. Be the boss. OK?'

Logan sat up slowly. 'All right.'

'But first take your shoes and socks off. They need to dry out.' I waited while he pulled off his shoes and laid out his socks carefully on the pebbles. He looked up at me, wriggling his toes.

'What's your favourite story?' I said. 'Have you got one?'

He squinted into the distance for a long time before he said, 'I quite like all the *Thomas the Tank Engine* stories.'

'Excellent call,' I said. 'Those are good stories, for sure.'

'I've got all of them except two.'

'I'm impressed. Now, remind me about this: does anyone ever get angry or upset in those stories?'

'For sure,' Logan said. 'Gordon the Blue Engine. He's always angry.'

'What does he get angry about?'

He shrugged. 'I don't know. He's always angry about something or other.'

'I guess he's just that type, right? Some people will always find something to be angry about, if they want to be angry.'

He nodded gravely. 'Some people are definitely like that.' He thought for a moment. 'But I didn't decide to be angry with the water, or the stones. It just happened.'

'I know,' I said. 'That's what it feels like. But all the time it's happening, you can actually do something about it.'

'How?'

'By telling a story about it. But you tell the story as if it was happening to someone else, like you do with the stories about Gordon the Blue Engine.'

He frowned. 'I don't get it.'

'You turn what's happening into a story. You say, for instance, "Logan tried to skim a stone, but it didn't go right," or something like that. Try it.'

He looked dubious. He drew his knees up and rested his chin on them. 'Logan tried to skim the stone,' he muttered, 'but it didn't go right.'

'Carry on,' I said. 'As if it all happened to someone in a story.'

'Because the water was all wrong,' he continued, 'and the stone was all wrong as well, and it's not fair, and that's why I got–'

'Wait,' I said, and held up my hand. 'It's all about someone else, remember? So you don't say, "it isn't fair," and, "I got angry," you say, "it *wasn't* fair," and "*Logan* got angry." Like that, you see?'

'OK,' he said. He took a breath. 'The water was wrong, and the stone was wrong, although really it was just that I – no, that *Logan* couldn't do it, and he got angry, and they said don't get angry but he couldn't help it and he got more angry and that's what always happens, I mean *happened*. Used to happen. To Logan. He got angry.' He stopped abruptly, breathing heavily.

'Is it working?'

'I don't know.'

'Does Logan still feel angry in the story?'

He nodded.

'And what about you, now? Do you feel angry?'

He narrowed his eyes, considering. Slowly he smiled at me. 'Is that how you did it in the war?'

'Which war is that?'

'Mummy said you were in a war and then you wrote stories about it.'

I wondered what Logan was seeing when his large, clear eyes settled on me like that. 'She's right, kind of,' I said. 'I was a soldier for a little while, and after that I sometimes used to go to places where there was fighting, and write about it. For the news, you know?'

'Did you see dead bodies?'

'I saw a few, yes.'

'Cool.'

'Well, it's not really cool, though. Because it meant somebody killed those people, so they couldn't be alive any more, and enjoy themselves. And not only them: it meant other people got hurt and were really sad. Their friends, and their mummies and daddies, or their children, all those people got really hurt. Think how unhappy they were.'

'I see,' Logan said. 'But with the bodies, did heads come off, and stuff?'

'No,' I said after a pause. 'Heads stayed on. Mostly.'

'My friends are dead,' he said, 'but I don't know who killed them.'

I tried to keep my tone calm. 'I don't think anyone killed them, Logan. I know Gully died, which must have made you very sad, and he was your friend. But nobody killed him. And

136

your other friends, William and Nicola? They left the island and went to live somewhere else. You said that yourself.'

'But they're dead, really. I'm not meant to know, though.'

'Why do you think they're dead?'

'Simon told me.'

'Who's Simon?'

'He's Finn's nephew. You know, Finn, at the pub? And Simon's twelve, so he should know.'

'I think maybe Simon is just telling you stories, Logie. He's probably trying to scare you. Big boys sometimes do that. I'm pretty sure William and Nicola just moved away from the island, with their families. Their mums and dads just decided to go and live somewhere else, don't you think?'

'But their mums are still here! And their dads! Except Sarah. But she never had a dad, I don't think.'

'Wait, who's Sarah?'

'Simon's sister. She's dead too. They're all dead.'

Logan was breathing heavily. I knew I should stop interrogating the boy, but I was sure I was on the verge of something. 'How do you know they're dead, Logan?'

'I just do.'

'Can you tell me any more than that? What makes you sure they're dead?'

He shook his head slowly.

'Is it a secret?' I said. 'Is that why you can't tell me?'

The tears that had been brimming in his eyes spilled out.

'It's all right,' I said. 'It doesn't matter, Logan. Never mind. You don't have to tell me. Here, up you get.'

I reached out my hand and Logan took it. But instead of pulling himself up, he squeezed my hand as tightly as he could, and raised an anguished face to me.

'Am I going to get killed?' he whispered.

I dropped to my knees beside him and put my arms around him, and drew him to me gently. 'No, I promise you'll be all right.'

Logan pressed his face into my shoulder and wailed, 'How do you know?'

'I won't let anything happen to you. I promise you.'

ELEVEN

Logan and I handed our empty plates over the bar to Penny.

'Thanks,' I said, 'that was a lovely lunch. Wasn't it, Logan?'

'Yes. Very delicious pie. Thank you, Penny.'

Penny beamed at him. 'You're most welcome, my pet.'

Logan looked up at me. 'Can I go and play with Alice, please?'

'Who's Alice?'

'By the window,' Logan said.

I glanced around. A little girl of about Logan's age was sitting by herself on an upholstered bench beneath one of the windows, looking out at the garden. She turned to smile shyly at Logan, and I saw she was pretty, with dark curls.

From behind me Penny said, 'She's waiting for her dad. He'll be coming in from his shift on the rig fairly soon.'

Logan tugged at my sleeve. 'Can I be excused, please?'

'Of course, off you go.' I watched him trot over to the girl. After a whispered conference they went outside. I turned back to the bar. Penny beamed at me.

'Logan's a nice boy,' she said, 'don't you think?'

'He is, yes,' I said. After a pause I continued, 'It's a pity he doesn't have more friends his own age, though.'

'Ah, very true. He misses Gully terribly, of course. They were great pals.'

'Yes, that must have been hard on him. And he's lost a couple of other friends too, so I hear. Some kids called Nicola and William?'

Penny folded her arms and leaned on the counter. 'Sadly,' she said softly, keeping her eyes on mine, 'the little girl passed away. Nicola. It was the same thing that took Gully. Some kind of virus. They never found out what it was. And the boy, William, well now, he's away at boarding school, you see.'

'Doesn't he come back?' I asked. 'I mean, for holidays or whatever?'

Penny frowned. 'I'm not sure about the arrangements, Adam. I believe he stays there on the mainland, and the parents go over to visit him. I seem to remember they have a relative over there. Something like that, I think.'

'Logan seems to think they both died.'

Penny looked down and wiped the surface of the counter with her sleeve. 'Oh dear,' she said with a sigh, 'he's been talking to that boy Simon again. Finn's nephew, you know.' She looked up at me and chuckled. 'He's a menace, that one. Always putting dreadful notions into the younger ones' heads, the little devil. He tells them all kinds of morbid tales, and frightens the life out of them.'

'And he's got a sister as well, is that right? Sarah, is it?'

Penny studied me for a moment. 'If you really want to know,' she said, 'young Sarah lives with her father on the mainland. He split up with Finn's sister, and he took the girl with him. These things happen. Sometimes a marriage will break, and it can't be mended, and it's for the best if the folks leave each other alone. I'm sure you know that.'

'Oh, I see. Thanks, I didn't mean to pry. It's just that Logan seems to think–'

'Sorry Adam,' Penny said, 'but there are people waiting for their food. I'll have to attend to them, if you don't mind.' She walked away towards the kitchen.

'Be careful, Adam,' a quiet voice beside me said.

I spun around to find Caleb Druce standing next to me, leaning on the bar.

'You need to give these people a little space,' he continued. 'They don't much like being interrogated, you know.'

'How about you? Can I interrogate you, doctor?'

'You're a proper bulldog, Adam. It's an admirable quality in some circumstances, I grant you. But it's a pain in the backside in others, and I have to wonder if perhaps you lack the gift of telling the difference between the two.'

'Are you telling me to fuck off?'

'Not at all, dear fellow. Ask me whatever you want.'

'All right, I will. What's the infant mortality rate on this island?'

Druce straightened up. He said nothing, and appeared to be inspecting the array of bottles lined up on shelves behind the bar. Then I realised he was looking in the mirror behind the bottles. 'It's a fine day,' he said amiably, 'shall we go outside for a while?'

I turned to follow Druce outside and almost bumped into Ogden, who was right behind me. The handsome, middle-aged woman I'd seen a couple of times before was standing next to him. I skirted around them and made for the door.

Druce and I sat at a table in the part of the garden farthest from the pub. A few yards away, Logan and the little girl, Alice, were kicking a football against the low stone wall.

'I thought we'd be better off out here,' Druce said, 'given the level of interest you seem to be attracting.'

'I get it,' I said. 'I'm a stranger, and it's a small community. OK. But those two in there were pretty blatant about eavesdropping on us. Doesn't it bother you?'

'*Tout comprendre, c'est tout pardonner.*'

'I'll take your word for that. By the way, who's the woman who was with Ogden in there? She's quite striking.'

'That's Meg. A strong-minded person. It's worth keeping on the right side of her.'

'Or else what?'

He laughed. 'I don't mean to be melodramatic. Simply that she has a certain degree of influence around here. A good influence, I would say, by and large.'

'That's nice to know. So, are you in a position to give me an answer to my question now?' I looked around pointedly. 'We're alone. Nobody here but us chickens, as they say. Unless you think those two kids are fitted up with listening devices.'

Druce glanced at Logan and Alice, who were now deliberately colliding with each other as they slammed the ball against the wall, yelping and laughing.

He gave me a wry smile. 'I think we can speak freely. And I'll try to be plain about it. Statistically, the infant mortality rate is a little higher here than on the mainland. But that's not unusual in a remote place like this. It follows a discernible trend: the figures tend to rise as you get further away from

142

large, centralised medical resources, like hospitals and clusters of expertise. It stands to reason, when you think about it.'

'So the answer is yes, it's relatively high?'

Druce sighed. 'Yes, if you insist.'

'And you don't think there's a particular reason for that? Apart from the generalised trend you just mentioned?'

'A particular reason? Like what, Adam?'

'Like, perhaps, that drilling operation out there.'

'How would that be connected with infant mortality here on the island?'

'If, for example, the operation discharges toxic waste, and the tide brings it to the shore, and it gets into the food chain.'

'If something like that were happening, do you think I wouldn't know about it?'

'So, you're absolutely positive there's no connection between the activities of the drilling company and the number of child deaths on the island. Is that right?'

Druce leaned back and regarded me with sour amusement. 'That would be a good story, wouldn't it? "Is This Multinational Corporation Poisoning Kids and Paying Their Parents to Keep Quiet?" That would make a great headline, from your point of view.'

'And would it be true?'

'No.'

'What if I want to make sure? Just for my own peace of mind, you understand.'

Druce leaned forward again. He looked me in the eye, then slowly turned his head towards the pub. I followed his gaze and saw Ogden and the woman, Meg, standing at the window, watching. They moved away as I looked at them.

'Just remember,' Druce said quietly, 'that half the people on this island work for that company.'

I scrutinised the doctor's face. 'Does that include you?'

'I work for everyone. I'm a doctor.' He glanced at his watch. 'And as it happens, I have patients to see.' He stood up. 'Give yourself a break, Adam. If you want my professional opinion, I think you were more shaken up than you realise by witnessing that accident just after you arrived. You should take it easy, that's my advice.'

I thought about the old woman lying in the road, and the syringe Druce had produced so swiftly from his bag. 'By the way,' I said, 'when's the funeral?'

'It was yesterday.'

'Really? That was quick. And I didn't hear anything about it. I would have liked to pay my respects.'

Druce smiled. 'We don't make much of a fuss about that kind of thing here. It was a very small, peaceful affair. But a fitting farewell, I can assure you.' He checked his watch again. 'I'm not being rude, Adam, but I really must go. I'll see you later.'

Druce strode away. He waved at the two children as he passed them, now sitting on the grass and whispering with their heads together. They waved back, and glanced over at me before exchanging a smirk and collapsing into giggles.

I wondered what they found so funny. I found myself gazing out at the sea, lost in thought. A web of connections was trying to form itself in my mind, like a distant constellation in the night sky, glimmering faintly and fitfully through storm clouds.

'Adam!'

I saw Finn in the doorway of the pub, beckoning to me. I walked over and followed him as he led me through the pub, and into the kitchen.

'There's a call for you,' Finn said over his shoulder. 'It's Lars, out at the rig.' He pointed to one corner of the big kitchen space, where a cabinet stood open. I recognised the equipment on the shelf inside it.

'I didn't know you had satellite,' I said.

'We have to stay in touch with the rig. The mobile signal is hopeless. Can't rely on it at all. Here you go.' He handed me the headset. 'I'll be outside when you've finished.' He walked out, closing the kitchen door behind him carefully.

'Hello?' I said into the microphone.

'Hello Adam.' Lars's voice was surprisingly clear. 'How are you doing? Enjoying life on the island?'

'It's an interesting place.'

'And nice people, don't you think?'

'Very nice.'

'So, the purpose of my call. Have you considered my offer on the house?'

'Yes, I've considered it, but I haven't decided anything yet.'

'I will double the offer.'

'Really? That's a lot of money, Lars.'

'I know. And that's why there is a condition. The offer is open until tomorrow morning only. Hello? Are you still there, Adam? Did you hear what I said?'

'Yes, I heard. I was just thinking. Why the time limit?'

'That's the way I do business.'

'And exactly what business are you in, Lars?'

'The offer is open until tomorrow, Adam, and you can take it or leave it. That's all you need to know. Goodbye.'

There was a click and the connection ended. I put the headset back on the shelf next to the satellite tuner. As I stepped back from the cabinet I noticed an open laptop on a small desk beside it. The screen was dark. I tapped the space bar on the keypad. No response. I clicked on the track pad and the computer screen sprang to life. I searched for any indication of an internet connection.

'Everything all right with the call?'

I hadn't heard Finn coming back into the kitchen.

'Yes thanks,' I said. 'All good. I was just wondering: what kind of internet connection can you get from that satellite setup? Is it any good?'

'We can't really get online,' Finn said. He closed the doors of the cabinet.

'But it looks like you've got it set up on that laptop.'

'Sorry, yes, what I meant was that it's not very good. It doesn't work well at all.'

'Could I try it anyway? I've got my laptop with me. Do I need a password?'

Finn stared at me blankly. Slowly he shook his head.

Through the window behind him I saw Harriet's car approaching. 'Never mind,' I said, 'I'll try it later, if that's OK with you? Now I'd better go and hand Logan over to his mother.' I turned at the door to see him closing the lid of the laptop. 'Thanks for letting me use the satellite,' I said. 'See you later.'

I walked quickly back through the pub and into the garden. I jogged to the stone wall and vaulted over it just as Harriet was getting Logan into the car.

'Good jump,' said Alice, who was sitting on the wall, dangling her feet.

Harriet straightened up and glanced at me. 'I see you've acquired another fan,' she said, nodding towards Alice as she got into the driver's seat. 'I hope Logan wasn't too much trouble.'

'No, he was fine. We had a good time. How was your morning?

'Fine, thanks.'

'And the work that came up?'

Harriet shrugged without looking at me. 'It was nothing special,' she said.

I leaned down closer to her. 'I've just had an interesting conversation with Lars Hansen. I don't know what to make of it. Perhaps you can give me some advice.'

She looked down. 'I don't know if I can help you. Not just at the moment.'

'What's the matter? What have I done?'

'Nothing. I'm sorry.' Finally she looked up at me. 'I can't talk now, Adam,' she murmured, 'not while they're watching.'

'Who?'

'Anyone. Anyone from the pub.'

I shifted casually so that I was screening her from view. 'What's up?'

She leaned forward. 'Can you come later? To dinner?'

'As long as it's nothing special. Again.'

She smiled, despite clearly being tense. 'Nothing special. Again. Same time.'

'I'd love to. See you then.' I waved to Logan in the back seat, smiled at Harriet, and closed the car door gently.

I took an afternoon walk on the cliffs again, following the pathway I'd taken before. I went about half a mile beyond the point of my encounter the previous day, and stopped at the tip of a promontory where the cliffs jutted out to sea like a long, bony finger. I gazed at the drilling rig, trying to picture Lars Hansen out there, and wondering what he was doing. Was he sitting in an unostentatious office at the top of the superstructure, tapping his fingers on his desk as he waited for me to call him back? Or perhaps he was on the platform, wearing a hard hat, consulting his engineers, examining charts, checking supplies, moving confidently among the workers, emanating amiable efficiency. Neither image changed my opinion of him. I was sure he was hiding something.

I retraced my steps without seeing another soul until I reached the pub.

I'd only intended to take a short nap, but it was early evening when I woke up. I opened my laptop and found I could get online, although the signal wasn't strong. I spent half an hour trying to find out about Skandiflow, and all I unearthed was their own glossy website and a few links that took me to what looked suspiciously like paid promotions disguised as news items in trade publications.

I composed an email to an old friend called Gavin McLennan. I trusted Gavin completely. He was part of a loose network of ex-service personnel and reporters who'd become – more by chance than intention – a pressure group, dedicated to getting fair treatment for the interpreters who'd worked with allied forces in Afghanistan, and whose lives had now been put at risk because the British and American governments were failing to provide the protection they deserved. The fight to help these people and their families was still going on, and Gavin was a mainstay of the network. Unlike me, I thought. Not for the first time, I questioned my motives. Sure, I chipped in now and again with whatever help I thought I could give, but I was involved for my own reasons as well. The truth was that I was a journalist, and it was a story. OK, some of the others were reporters too, but I always had a sense they were more sincerely committed to the cause than me. I felt like I was a parasite. Maybe it was time to commit myself to the kind of work the others were doing. Alternatively, maybe it was time to stop beating myself up and get on with my job. I tried to brush these thoughts aside as I composed the email:

Gavin, please dig deep on multinational corp 'Skandiflow' offshore drill, maybe gas, minerals, oil? Poss toxic/ environmental/chemical damage + cover-up. Zero on web except PR. Special interest in LARS HANSEN, status within company, etc. Please treat all as confidential, usual protocols. Best, Adam.

I hit *send*, and at that moment the internet connection dropped. I tried to reconnect a couple of times, but it wasn't happening. I closed the laptop and left my room.

Nobody seemed to be around downstairs. I walked to the kitchen and opened the door. Finn was standing in the middle of the room, facing me. I was certain he'd been expecting me.

'Hi there, Finn. I just lost the internet connection.'

'Yes, it happens.'

Something had changed in the room since I'd last been in it, and after a moment I realised what it was: the laptop was gone from the small desk. 'How about you?' I said casually, 'have you got a connection on that laptop of yours?'

Finn shook his head.

I let my eyes wander to the desk. 'Oh, right,' I said, 'I see it's not here. But could you give it a try for me?'

'There's something wrong with it,' Finn said. 'It just stopped working, I've no idea why; I'm not very tech-savvy, I'm afraid. But a friend of mine who knows about all that stuff has taken it away to repair it. Or have a look at the damn thing, at any rate. Modern technology, eh? What can you do?' He gave me a rueful smile.

'But the internet signal comes from the satellite connection, right? Is it worth having a look at the equipment?'

Finn frowned. 'The dish is on the roof. Would you be wanting to climb up there? I wouldn't advise it. It's a wee bit treacherous on those tiles.'

'Not the dish, no,' I said. 'But maybe we could take a look in there.' I gestured towards the cabinet.

Finn stared at me. He began to pat his pockets. 'Where did I put the key?' he said. 'I may have taken it behind the bar. Or is it still in here?' He looked around the room with a vague, bemused expression. Abruptly he pointed at the cooking range. 'Hey, time to fire up for dinner. By the way, are you eating here this evening?'

'No thanks, I'll be going out.' I glanced at the window and saw it was beginning to get dark outside. 'In fact I'd better get going soon.'

'Fair enough, Adam. Have a nice walk.'

TWELVE

A full moon was rising above the top of the tall hedgerow that flanked me, casting a delicate filigree of shadows on the road. I estimated I'd covered about half the distance to Harriet's house. I'd taken this road twice before by car, and it was no more than a mile, even allowing for the fact that Harriet's house was at the far end of the high street, but I'd allowed myself twenty minutes to cover it on foot.

I was thinking about Caleb Druce. He was an interesting man, and I enjoyed his company, but I wasn't sure if I liked him, exactly. I wanted *him* to like *me*, of course, but who doesn't want to be liked, especially by someone you find impressive and charismatic? But there were things about Druce that bothered me, although I was finding it difficult to put my finger on them. And maybe that was the problem: it wasn't so much that there was something about him – some quality he possessed – that bugged me, it was that something was missing. When I was with him there seemed to be a spark, but no flame. The warmth never arrived.

The road curved, and I began to walk down into a dip where the banks on either side of me became higher and pressed in to form a narrow culvert. As I reached the bottom of the dip I heard a rumbling sound behind me. I turned to see a mass of dark, heaving shapes at the top of the hill. I realised they were cattle. A lot of them. The moon emerged from behind a cloud, and I saw that the animals were jostling out of an open gate, spilling into the road, and starting to flow down the hill towards me. As the stream of lowing beasts continued to grow, the silhouette of a large tractor crested the top of the hill behind them. The herd quickened its pace, filling the road, hemmed in by the narrow embankments. They were being driven towards me. I looked for a spot where I could climb up one of the steep banks that enclosed me and get out of their path, but I couldn't see one. The tractor revved its engine, nudging against the cattle at the back of the herd. All at once the animals at the front broke into a trot, and those behind them surged forward, transforming the herd into a dark, fast-flowing river, churning through a crevasse. The tractor continued to press closely behind them down the hill, and the panicked creatures rushed ahead blindly.

They were close enough now for me to hear them snorting and bellowing and I saw the moonlight glinting in their rolling, terrified eyes. I began to run up the slope ahead of me, glancing over my shoulder to see the dip filling with a dense, roiling mass. The tractor accelerated again, its engine whining and roaring, and the cattle burst up out of the hollow and began to pound up towards me, gaining on me.

The incline became steeper and I gasped as I forced my legs to pump faster, trying to stay ahead of the tumultuous wave of animal flesh swelling up the hill behind me, hooves thundering, throats open. There were no breaks in the high banks on either side of the narrow road, and even if I'd somehow been able to scramble up them, the tangled hedgerows on top of them were as impenetrable as prison walls.

I stumbled. The frenzied cattle were almost upon me. I could feel the heat from their bodies and their breath. I pushed myself up and leapt forward and ran for my life. I reached the top of the hill, and as the road levelled out the bank on my left dropped away, and I saw a gate. I lurched at it, and flung myself over the top of it with the hooves of the foremost cattle inches behind me.

I tumbled forward and landed on my back, knocking my breath out of me. I sat up and grabbed at the bars of the gate, sagging against them as the tide of animals flowed past, only a metre from my face. After more than a minute the last of the cattle thundered away and the tractor appeared, looming high above me.

The driver was just a dark shape up in the cab, and soon the noise of the engine faded, leaving me alone with the sound of my own ragged breathing.

'Does that hurt?' Harriet said.

I shook my head. I was sitting on the couch with my shirt off.

She dipped another pad of cotton wool into the bowl of warm water and wiped the cut on my shoulder where I'd scraped it as I tumbled over the gate.

I held her wrist gently. 'It's fine,' I said. 'It's not deep. And it's clean now, thanks.'

'Are you sure it was deliberate?' Harriet said. 'I mean, it must have been pretty dark out there. Perhaps he just didn't see you.'

'He saw me. The moon was bright enough. And if he didn't see me, why did he deliberately drive the cattle so hard?'

'But you said you didn't see him.'

'Just a quick silhouette. I was on the other side of the gate by then, and the tractor drove by pretty fast.'

Harriet put the bowl on the floor and leaned against me, stroking my chest. 'I suppose it could have been Ogden,' she said. 'If he thinks you're going to change your mind about the accident, or testify against him back on the mainland, or something like that. Or he might have got Barty or Sim to do it. They're pretty rough types.'

'Maybe. But I think there's more to it than that.'

'In what way?'

'I don't want to sound too melodramatic about this, but I think there's something going on here that people don't want me to find out about.'

Harriet kissed my cheek. 'Even if you're right, let's not think about it now.' She stood up and took my hand. 'Come on, let's get you into a bath.'

I stood. She put her arms around me and kissed me, caressing my back. She pulled away slowly and whispered, 'You know, we may have to skip dinner again.'

'Can I ask you something?'

She smiled. 'Are you going to invite me into the bath with you?'

'That's a good idea. But first I just want ask you about Skandiflow.'

'What about them?'

'What's their environmental record like?'

154

Harriet leaned back and looked at me searchingly. 'Pretty good, I think. They seem very responsible about recycling, and that type of thing. Why are you asking me?'

'Because this island seems to have an unnaturally high infant mortality rate.'

Harriet stepped back and stood with her arms at her sides. 'What's the matter, Adam? Are we too boring for you without some kind of dark secret to uncover? Can't you just take me as I am? Isn't it enough? Why can't we simply be together, as we are?'

'Sorry.' I shook his head. 'It's just that... I don't know–'

'Well, I do. I know I want you.' She lurched forward again and kissed me, pressing herself against me, running her hands down my back and slipping them under my waistband, grasping my buttocks as she pulled me against her. I began kissing her neck and throat hungrily and lifted her skirt.

She arched her head back and gasped, 'We may have to skip the bath as well.'

I stood at the bedroom window and watched the first glimmer of dawn creeping into the sky. Behind me on the bed Harriet was sleeping. I buttoned my shirt, picked up my shoes, and slipped out of the room.

As I padded towards the front door I passed Harriet's office, and through the open doorway I saw that a desk lamp had been left on overnight. I went to switch it off and my eye was caught by a document on the desk, just beyond the edge of the pool of light, with a familiar design at the top of it. I picked it up and began to read the text below the Skandiflow logo.

'I meant to tell you last night,' Harriet said from the doorway. Her face was pale and she clutched her bathrobe at her throat.

'You work for them?' I said.

'Sometimes, yes.'

'Why?'

'Why do you think? I've got a child to support. I get a lot of work from them.'

'OK, I understand that, but does that mean–'

'No, you don't understand, Adam. If you understood, you'd sell Stone Heart House and leave. Right away.'

'Is that what you want?'

She made a dismissive gesture. 'It doesn't matter what I want. Just sign the document that Lars has drawn up. He's doubled his offer, and what he's prepared to pay is way more than double what the house is worth. Just sign it.'

'Is that where you were yesterday? With Lars Hansen?'

'No. But I spoke with him. I've got a satellite phone. If you agree to sign, I can call him now, and get it over with. Just sell him the house and leave the island.'

'Why should I leave?'

'Because you're in danger.'

'Why didn't you tell me last night?'

She gazed at me for a moment. 'Because I wanted another night with you.'

I moved towards her and stood close. 'How can I trust anything you say? You work for them. All that bullshit about their environmental record. Jesus. Don't you care about your own child?'

Harriet slapped my face with all her strength. I didn't move. She stared at me, her face chalk-white, then buried her head in her hands. Her body heaved.

'You have no idea,' she sobbed.

'Then tell me! Tell me what the fuck is going on here.'

She looked up at me, wiping her eyes. 'Please just do it, Adam. Sign the contract and leave.'

'I'm not leaving. Not until I know why.'

'Just believe me. If you won't do it for yourself, then do it for me and Logan. Because if you don't, and you stay here, you're putting us in danger too.'

'What kind of danger?'

She took a breath. 'Look, I really appreciate what you've done for Logan, and what you've been teaching him, but it's not enough. Can't you see that?'

'What do you mean? What have I been teaching him?'

'You've helped him to control himself. To deal with his temper and not to be so impulsive, and all over the place.'

'What's that got to do with anything? Look, just answer my question: why are you and Logan in danger?' As I searched her eyes for an answer I saw them change, and react to something behind me. I turned to see Logan in the doorway. He was wearing a tartan dressing gown over his pyjamas.

'Mum,' Logan said, yawning, 'can I get my own cereals? I won't put too much sugar on them, I promise.'

'That's fine, darling,' Harriet said. She looked at me imploringly while Logan shuffled away. 'Oh god,' she whispered to me when he'd gone, 'just sign the contract and go. Please.' She seemed exhausted.

'Come with me,' I said.

Her eyes widened. She shook her head slowly. 'I can't,' she whispered.

'Why? Because of your work? Is it to do with Lars, and the company?'

'Not just them. It's everyone. All of them. They won't let us leave.'

'That's crazy. How can they stop you? I mean, what are they going to do?'

She clasped her hands together and twisted her fingers. 'I

can't explain.'

'Take a moment,' I said. I reached out and gently separated her hands and held them in my own. 'Just tell me, Harriet. I have to know.'

She pulled her hands away. 'I can't! I can't tell you!'

I saw she was trembling. 'All right,' I said, 'that's all right. You don't have to tell me now. Don't worry. Just let me take you and Logan away from here.'

She was still trembling, but I realised it wasn't fear that was affecting her. She was shaking with rage. I had a sudden memory of Druce's face when he'd spoken to me about her. I'd asked him if he was implying she was unstable in some way, and he'd denied it, but the message in his expression had been ambiguous. Now, as I stared at Harriet in confusion, she mastered herself quickly. Before I could say anything she flung herself at me and put her arms around my neck and pressed herself against me. 'I wish I could come with you,' she said, her voice muffled by my body.

I stroked her hair. 'You can. Really, you can do it. I'll help.'

She pulled her head back, and gazed at me. 'I don't know how to get away,' she whispered.

'What about the ferry? Couldn't we just get on it and leave? Archie – the skipper, is he one of…the people who'd try to stop you?'

'No, he's not an islander. And he likes me. He's a friend.'

I thought for a moment. 'OK, call Lars. Tell him I've signed. That'll buy some time. Then we'll contact Archie. Can you reach him?'

Harriet hesitated. Her gaze drifted past me, towards the kitchen. We were both silent for a moment, listening to the clatter of Logan's spoon against his cereal bowl. 'I won't let anything happen to him,' I said. 'I promise.'

'I don't know,' she said. 'I'm not sure if we can do it.'

'What about Caleb Druce?' I said. 'Would he help us?'

I felt Harriet stiffen in my arms. 'No.'

'Why not?'

'You don't want to know. Believe me.'

'But I thought you said he helped you. When you were trying to leave Glynn. You implied he was very understanding.'

She shook her head. 'There are things about him I can't tell you now, and about David. Not while I'm on this island.'

I released her from my arms and took a step back. 'What are you saying? What is it that you don't want me to know? This is crazy. I need you to tell me.'

She pressed her lips together. Her face began to twist with anguish, and I saw the depth of her misery. It was as if she were being torn apart, or collapsing inside. 'It's all right,' I said, and placed my hands on her shoulders. 'You don't have to tell me now, not if you can't. Look, I just want to help you do what's best, for you and Logan. And if that means you have to get away from here, I can help you do that. Will you trust me?'

Harriet nodded. She took a deep breath and turned away, and walked over to a tall mahogany writing bureau that was next to her desk. She opened the top. Inside was a satellite phone rig, like the one at the pub. She flicked a switch, and lights began to blink on the front of the transmitter as she pulled a keypad out from a recess at the bottom, and picked up the headset.

'Maybe call Archie first,' I said. 'Ask him to bring the ferry over here as soon as he can, and not to tell anyone about it. Then we can contact Hansen.'

Harriet reached for the keypad.

'Wait,' I said. 'What about Ogden? Will he be down at the harbour?'

'No, he's only at the harbour when he knows the ferry is arriving. The rest of the time he stays up here in town with his sister.'

'Fine. Just tell Archie to alert you when he's on his way, and we can all go down to the harbour and meet him there. You, me and Logan.'

Harriet shook her head. 'No. We can't go together. Logan and I can be together, but not the three of us. They'll see us, and know what's happening.'

'Who will see us?'

'Everyone. They're watching all the time.'

I studied her face. She was pale but she seemed composed, and it was clear she believed what she was saying. 'All right,' I said, 'we'll figure something out.'

'Good, I'll call Archie and get him to see what's happening with the tides.'

She began tapping at the keypad. I walked to the window and pulled aside the edge of the curtain. The street outside looked flat and dimensionless in the leaden light of dawn, and the fronts of the houses across the street were like blank, lifeless faces. Then I caught a movement. Where had it come from? I scanned the street in both directions as far as I could see. Another flicker of movement. I focused on an upstairs window in a house five doors down on the opposite side of the street. Had the curtain moved? As I stared at it, waiting, I heard Harriet's voice behind me:

'Hello Archie, did I wake you up?'

I strained my eyes, trying to decide if I could see someone in the room behind the window, or if it was just an effect of the dawn light on the glass. Behind me, Harriet continued: 'I need to ask you a favour...yes, a big one. I need you to bring the ferry over. I can't tell you why, but it's really important...

Yes, as soon as you can please, Archie, but don't tell anyone...
I'll explain when I see you... OK, please do that...'

Another hint of movement? Or just the light as the pale sun rose? No, I was increasingly certain there was someone there, in the window. I stepped back and turned to Harriet. She put her hand over the microphone. 'Archie is just checking the tides,' she said to me. She held up a finger and spoke into the headset again: 'Is that the earliest..? OK, that's fine... Three passengers. Thanks, Archie. I love you.'

She ended the call and looked at her watch. 'He can be there at ten. That's three hours. You need to leave now, and get down there later, by yourself. Will you be able to do that?'

'Sure, no problem. What about you?'

'I'll drive down there with Logan at the last moment. And just before I leave I'll call Lars Hansen and tell him you've signed the deal.'

I thought for a moment. 'Maybe better to tell him you're bringing me the contract at ten, and I'm going to sign it then. That buys a bit more time, and it gives you an excuse to be on the move, if you need one – pretend you're on your way to find me, right?'

'Good idea. You'd better go now.'

I crossed the room and took her in my arms. She pulled me close and kissed me hard on the mouth, then released me and walked to the kitchen without looking back. I went to the front door, opened it, and walked swiftly away from the house, wondering about eyes behind the upstairs window across the street, and all the other windows.

THIRTEEN

As the day grew lighter I felt increasingly exposed on the road back to the pub. But trekking across the fields would have made me even more conspicuous: at least the road was shielded on both sides by the steep banks topped by hedgerows. I prayed I didn't meet any vehicles, and I was relieved when I crested the top of the final hill without having encountered anyone. As I approached the pub I scrutinised it for any signs of life, but the squat, whitewashed building seemed as inert as a tombstone. I found the side door open and slipped upstairs to my room.

It was clear someone had been in there. My laptop had been opened – the hair I'd placed under the lid had been dislodged – and no effort had been made to return it to the position in which I'd left it. I locked my door, set my alarm, and slept for forty minutes.

At nine-fifteen I crept downstairs with a few things in a small backpack. The bar was empty. As I stepped behind the counter and plucked the keys to Finn's van from their hook, I heard the kitchen door open. Finn emerged. He was holding a large meat cleaver in his right hand.

'All right, Adam?' he said. 'Can I help you with anything?'

'I wondered if I could borrow your van.'

Finn walked into the middle of the room, placing himself between me and the front door. 'Not today, mate,' he said quietly.

I moved out from behind the counter. Finn was about three inches shorter than me, and his slight frame and wispy beard made him look unthreatening, but I wasn't about to underestimate him. It's the wiry little fuckers you have to watch out for. I noted the way he was holding the cleaver. He wasn't waving it around, or doing anything particular with it except letting it fill his grip, and feeling its heft, just so. His hand was steady and his eyes were calm. I took a step forward. He shifted slightly and I could see he was nicely balanced, weight just a little forward on the balls of his feet. I slipped into a fighting stance, and moved forward and feinted to his right. He didn't buy it, but I hadn't expected him to: I just wanted to see how quick his reactions were. They were quick. He had himself under control. OK, I thought; time to find out if I can still do this shit.

I took two quick steps forward and pivoted to my left in a full circle as he swung the cleaver. It missed my shoulder by a millimetre, and by the time he was raising it again my straight left arm had struck his throat. He staggered back slightly, and I spun around again, bringing my other arm up underneath his and twisting around, forcing Finn's hand up and back over his shoulder. With my left arm around his throat in a choke hold, I grasped his wrist as I got behind him, and pulled his arm further back until I was able wrench the cleaver out of his hand. He tried to bring his hip around to my groin, but it didn't work and I felt a very faint tremor shake his body. He wasn't giving up, but he knew it was over. From the corner of his eye he must have seen the cleaver going up as I raised it in my own hand, and he made a frantic effort to free himself. I spun the handle of the cleaver around and brought the blunt edge of the blade down on the side of his head. He made a noise like a dog trying to cough something up, and his body went limp.

I lowered him to the floor. There was some blood seeping from the wound on the side of his head, but it looked like it would clot soon. I checked his pulse and his breathing, then grabbed his ankles and dragged him behind the bar counter. I dropped his legs, and pulled up the trapdoor to the cellar. As I lifted his ankles again, I saw his eyelids fluttering, and by the time I'd got him to the top of the steps he realised what was happening, but he couldn't do anything about it. I bundled him through the opening, trying to hold onto him as long as possible to minimise the drop. It wasn't far to fall, and he flopped down the remaining length of the steps – about eight feet – relatively unharmed, I thought. I saw him look up at me just as I closed the trapdoor. I rolled a large steel beer barrel onto the top of it, collected the cleaver from where I'd left it on the floor in the middle of the room, and went into the kitchen. The cabinet containing the satellite radio rig was open but the rig wasn't switched on. I smashed at it with the cleaver until I was satisfied it was unusable and irreparable.

By now I'd made a lot of noise, and somehow it didn't surprise me when I saw Penny standing in the doorway.

What did surprise me was the shotgun she was holding. What surprised *her* was my speed. I flung myself forward as she was still raising the gun, and brought her down with sheer bulk and momentum. I heard the wind being knocked out of her as she landed on her back with me on top of her. She lost her grip on the shotgun in the same instant that she pulled the trigger. The gun exploded a foot away from my head and took a big, splintering chunk out of a wooden beam in the ceiling. With my ears ringing, I pushed myself up from Penny's fleshy body, not worrying about where I put my hands, and shoved the gun away with my foot. It was a single-barrelled weapon, and I didn't have time to search for more shells. I wasn't inclined to take it anyway. I kicked Penny in the head. I didn't do it very hard, and she'd get over it. I ran out of the front door and kept running until I reached Finn's van.

I started the van, rammed it into gear, and spun it around. I floored the throttle and took the road back down into town with the wheels spinning.

I drove as fast as I could. I didn't spare the van's bodywork, and I fishtailed on a few of the tighter corners, getting jolted around in my seat as the rear of the vehicle walloped against the banks on the sides of the road. I wasn't so much driving the van as steering it through a long, controlled skid. God knows what would have happened if I'd met a vehicle coming the other way.

I sped through Creedish without seeing anyone. Just as I accelerated up the hill, out of the other side of town, a car began to nose out of a side-road ahead of me. I didn't slow down, and the driver slammed on his brakes. The van missed the front of his car by an inch and I glimpsed a pale, surprised face I didn't recognise. But I had no doubt the driver recognised me – or

Finn's van, at least.

I followed the winding uphill road out of the town until I reached the place where Druce had stopped his car on my first day, and had questioned me about my intentions while we'd gazed out over the spectacular view. I stopped and took a look around, checking the landscape behind me. There didn't seem to be any vehicles on the roads, or – as far as I could tell – any activity down in Creedish, nestled in its hollow below me. Beyond the town and the distant coast, far out to sea, heavy black clouds were massing.

I drove on, downhill again now, exercising just enough restraint to prevent me from slamming the van into a ditch and overturning it. After ten minutes I passed the stone circle, brooding on its hilltop, and knew I was getting close to the final series of curves on the steep descent to the harbour at Tallog Bay. I slowed down and stopped just before I reached the last corner, beyond which I would be visible from the quayside. I parked the van on a patch of grass in front of a rusty farm gate, tucking it at as far off the road as I could, and got out.

I walked to the final bend in the road, staying close to the hedgerows. When I reached the corner I edged around it, scanning the vista that opened up below me – the roofs of the cottages that backed onto the hillside, the cobbled quayside in front of them, the jetty, and beyond it the wide, endless sea. There was no sign of movement down on the quayside, but Archie's boat was bobbing gently at the end of the jetty. I checked my watch. Nine fifty. He'd made good time, and with luck, if Harriet and Logan arrived at ten, as planned, we'd be able to leave straight away. I couldn't see Archie on the deck, or anywhere else, but I assumed he was in the wheelhouse. I moved out into the open and began to jog down the final stretch of road.

I expected Archie to emerge at any moment, but he still hadn't appeared when I reached the top end of the jetty. I squinted at the boat, trying to see through the front windows of the wheelhouse, but the reflection from the water was making them opaque. The storm clouds I'd seen earlier weren't visible from this side of the island, but the air was clammy with anticipation. I trotted down the jetty to the boat, and when I was still several yards away I could see the wheelhouse was empty. I stopped and looked back at the road, straining to hear the sound of Harriet's car approaching. Everything seemed eerily still, and the only sound I heard was the creaking of the boat as it bobbed against its mooring. I checked my watch. It was just after ten.

I stepped onto the boat, and as my weight caused it to rock I caught sight of something bobbing up in water between the side of the boat and the harbour wall. I peered down over the rail and found myself looking into Archie's open, bulging eyes. His hair and beard floated around his face like the tendrils of a wispy sea creature, and a thick rope was wound tightly around his neck.

I leaped back onto the jetty and sprinted up to the quayside. My intention was to get back to the van, but as I ran past the row of cottages I saw the door to Ogden's place was ajar. I stopped. The idea that there might be a satellite rig in there flashed through my mind, along with the thought that a man was dead and maybe it was time to try and get help from the outside world. I looked for a dish or antenna, but the angle was too steep for me to see anything that might have been mounted on the far side of the roof, or the back of the building, where the cottages huddled into the steep hillside behind them.

I stepped forward and flattened myself against the wall beside the doorway.

Carefully, I reached out and pushed the open door wider. I waited a moment then took a quick look inside. It was dark in there. I withdrew my head and waited for another moment before slipping around the doorway and into the front room, hugging the wall.

I remembered the dog about a quarter of a second before it went for my throat. I raised my left arm just as its front legs thudded into my chest and its teeth snapped shut on my forearm, ripping through the fabric of my jacket and puncturing my skin. I grabbed the dog's collar with my right hand and twisted as hard as I could. The dog took its teeth out of my arm and gave a gurgling, throaty yelp as it scrabbled against me. I got my other hand around the collar and twisted some more, holding the clawing, thrashing animal as far away from my body as possible. With my arms still extended I whirled around like a shot-putter, flung the dog across the room, and dived out of the doorway. As I slammed the door shut behind me it shook under the impact of the dog inside hurling itself against the thick wood.

I took off at a fast run with my right hand clutching my left forearm, pressing against the wound, hoping to hell it wasn't too deep and the bleeding would stop soon.

I opened the van door and paused. Could there be another route between Creedish and the harbour? I hadn't seen one, but it would have been easy to miss a narrow turn-off, tucked into a curve somewhere on the winding road between the harbour and the town. I weighed up the odds, and figured there was nothing I could do if Harriet and Logan were coming a different way, other than keep my eyes open. I turned the van around and began driving back to Creedish, fighting the impulse to go as fast as I could. It was still possible that Harriet and Logan were simply running late, and were heading towards me on the route I was taking. However, the later it got, and the more I thought about Archie lying dead in the water, the less likely I thought it was.

My resolution to keep my speed down probably saved my life. I reached the tight bend where Ogden's car had hit Mary on my first day, and as I rounded it I found myself facing what looked, for a disorienting moment, like a wall. But it was moving. It was the massive tractor I'd seen the previous night and it was reversing out of a gate, directly into my path. I made a fast calculation, shifted down a gear, hit the throttle, and drove up onto the bank, tilting the van at such a steep angle it was touch-and-go whether it would topple over. The tractor revved up and lurched backwards, trying to ram me. There was a massive jolt and a grinding of metal as the back of the tractor snagged onto the van's rear bumper. I shifted down into first and pressed my foot to the floor. For a moment the wheels spun and the engine whined, then the van shot forward as the bumper ripped away. I gripped the steering wheel, trying to keep the van under control as I forced it back down onto the road. I made it, and accelerated away. In the rear-view mirror I saw the tractor stop. High up in the cab, the driver didn't even look around. From the glimpse I got of his silhouette I was sure it was Barty.

By the time I reached Creedish my arm had stopped bleeding.

I didn't see anyone as I drove up the main street, and there seemed to be fewer cars parked along it than usual. I stopped outside Harriet's house and got out of the van, and waited for a moment, looking around. There was no sign of life anywhere.

As I raised my hand to knock on Harriet's front door I saw it wasn't closed. I pushed it open slowly and waited. After a

169

few seconds I stepped into the hallway and called Harriet's name, then I called out for Logan. I checked the downstairs rooms. Nobody was there, and when I ran upstairs and looked in the bedrooms I found them empty. There were no signs of disturbance, and nothing seemed out of place. I stood in the hallway, trying to think clearly, running through my options.

The front door was still open, and I noticed a change in the quality of light. I stepped to the doorway and looked out. Massed banks of tall grey clouds filled half the sky, and as I watched, I saw them rolling closer.

I scanned the empty street. I knew the entire town was deserted. It wasn't simply that I couldn't see any people around, or any movement anywhere; there was a palpable quality of absence in the air: a feeling of subtraction. Whatever was running through my mind, my body knew the truth, and could detect – perhaps at a molecular level – the lack of living energy behind the walls and windows of the houses. Which left the question of where everybody had gone.

I was halfway down the steps when I changed my mind and ran back into the house. I opened the mahogany bureau in Harriet's office and switched on the satellite phone rig. A small screen lit up and I used the keypad to run the through the display until I found the call log. I put on the headset, punched a number, and waited. After a few seconds I heard a burst of static, then the voice of Lars Hansen:

'Harriet? What is it?'

'It's not Harriet,' I said. 'Where is she, Lars?'

'Adam? Is that you?'

'Yes. Where is she?'

'I don't know where Harriet is. Why ask me?'

'You're lying. Tell me where she and Logan are.'

'What are you talking about, Adam?'

'Just tell me what's happening.'

'What do you mean, what is happening? I don't understand. I simply asked Harriet to draw up a formal contract for my offer to you, and told her I would appreciate it if she would persuade you to sign it. To do the best thing, you know? Are you saying you haven't signed it? Why not, what is the problem?'

'Hold on,' I said, 'didn't she call you?'

'No, not yet. I was waiting. I assumed this was her call.'

I thought for a moment. 'Lars, I think there has been a misunderstanding.'

'It's my final offer, Adam. That's it.'

'No, I mean a miscommunication. Harriet must have thought... Never mind, it's too complicated. But I want to accept the offer, Lars. I'm happy to sign.'

'You are? That's great. OK, we can do it electronically. It will still be good.'

'No, I want to do it in person. You have to come over here now. To the island.'

There was a pause, then Lars said, 'No, it's not necessary Adam.'

'It's necessary to me. And it has to be now, this morning.'

'It's not possible, Adam. The weather is turning very bad. If you insist on closing this deal in person with me, then we will do it later, or tomorrow, whenever the storm has cleared. OK?'

'No, not OK. Come over here in the next hour, or the deal's off.'

'That's crazy. Why do you put these conditions on it?'

'That's my business. You had your conditions, remember? Well, these are mine.'

After a long silence Lars said, 'I don't think so, Adam. It's really not necessary.'

'Lars,' I said, 'listen to me carefully. You get in an aircraft, and you get over here right now. I'll meet you outside the pub, where you land. If you don't come, I won't sell.'

My earpiece was filled with static for so long I began to wonder if we'd lost the connection. Finally I heard his voice: 'Thirty minutes, Adam.'

The line went dead and I took off the headset. Outside the window the sky was getting darker.

FOURTEEN

The storm still hadn't broken when I parked at the edge of the grassy plateau, but now the entire sky was filled with massive clouds, looming above the island like the pelt of a gigantic animal that was poised to smother its prey. A couple of times, bursts of rain had spattered the windscreen of the van, but had stopped again, increasing the sense of tension in the air. I positioned the van so it couldn't be seen from the pub, a few hundred yards away.

After fifteen minutes, I spotted the helicopter: a tiny black speck emerging from the banks of cloud. Even from this distance I could tell it was a smaller aircraft than the one that shuttled workers to and from the rig. That was a relief. It looked like a four-seater. I got out of the van and walked to the edge of the grass. If there was anyone in the pub, and they saw me, I knew I could reach the helicopter before them. It came in fast and began its descent. I ran out onto the grass.

As the aircraft made a bumpy landing I fought against the downdraft and ran in under the blades, head hunched into my shoulders, until I was next to the pilot's door. The pilot stared down at me impassively. Lars, sitting beside him, leaned forward and raised a hand in a tentative greeting, looking puzzled. I ignored him, and waved frantically at the pilot, then I extended one arm and made a wide, unsteady circling motion with the flat of my hand, and pointed towards the small rotor on the aircraft's tail. I knew the pilot wouldn't have a clear view of it, and I saw him craning around in his seat, then frowning at me. I repeated the gesture. He shook his head, jerked his thumb at the rotor behind him, and held up both hands in a sign of incomprehension, assuming I was giving him some kind of technical signal which he didn't understand – exactly as I intended. He unstrapped his safety harness, pushed his door open, and leaned down towards me, his mouth open as he began to yell something to me, straining to be heard above the thudding whomp of the helicopter's blades.

I reached up and grabbed him by the front of his flying jacket, and pulled as hard as I could. He scrabbled at the fuselage on either side of his door for a moment, then lost his balance. As he fell out and down, I sidestepped and he hit the ground hard at a bad angle, taking the impact in his shoulder and hip. I got a grip on the doorway, and as I pulled myself up I saw him from the corner of my eye, rolling over and wincing as he tried to struggle to his feet. Then I was inside the cockpit, in his seat. I slammed the door and turned to Lars Hansen, who was staring at me, frozen and white-faced.

'Hello Lars,' I said with manic cheerfulness, 'let's take a ride!'

The pilot was on his feet, staggering towards the door, but

at the last moment he seemed to think better of it. Perhaps he was influenced by the insane grin on my face when I turned to eyeball him. He swayed for a moment, then crouched down and backed away. I dismissed him from my mind and ran my eyes over the controls. I wasn't familiar with this aircraft, but most of what I saw made sense to me. I recognised the basics, or I hoped I did. The engine was still running, so I increased the power. I pulled up on the collective stick, and got ready to use the anti-torque pedals. Nothing happened. I gave her more power. The aircraft leaped up abruptly like a startled deer, and as I tried to get it under control the nose swung violently to one side. I righted us just before I was about to lose control, and swung the aircraft around in a jerky, ascending turn. I was starting to get a better feel for the ratio between stick and pedals, and how sensitive the setup was.

'Whoops,' I said to Lars, 'I'm a little rusty.' It was true, and I had no idea if I could fly the thing safely, let alone pull off what I had in mind, which was to scare the shit out of Lars. First, however, I needed to stop scaring myself quite so much. While fear was a useful way to give myself a bracing shot of adrenaline that could help me keep my head clear, it was important to get the dosage right. I put a smile on my face and glanced over at Lars. He was gripping the sides of his seat, rigid with fear and confusion.

He didn't look at me as he yelled, 'What are you doing?'

He started to say something else but his voice was drowned by the whine of the engine as I took us up violently in a steep turn, directly into the roiling storm clouds. The machine bucked and shivered, and I was aware I might be approaching the limits of what it would do. As I levelled her out again I heard Lars making a coughing, panting sound. I saw he was loosening his tie and undoing his collar. He turned to me, his rimless glasses catching a glint of reflection from the sea as we approached the clifftops.

The engine settled down. 'Adam, please stop this!' Lars said. 'Just take me back and land. There won't be trouble for you, and I'll make everything OK with the pilot, and nobody else will know. Adam! I promise!'

I gave him another grin. 'Hey,' I said, 'let's take the scenic route!'

I turned the helicopter in another tight, fast arc and pointed her at the ridge of hills that ran inland from the clifftops. There was a narrow gap in the middle of them, like a notch at the top of a wall. I increased our speed and the hills rushed towards us.

'Oh my god,' Lars said in a low, shaky voice.

'Damn,' I said, 'those hills are in the way. But I think I can see a shortcut.' I aimed for the gap, but I deliberately yawed the aircraft erratically from side to side, pretending I couldn't control her. I stopped pretending when we were a hundred yards from the gap, and I realised I might have overdone it. The gap was very narrow. I concentrated hard.

Lars yelled, 'Shit, shit, shit, shit, shit!'

I took us through the gap with a few yards to spare on either side. I glanced at Lars. His eyes were shut, and when he opened them I said, 'That was exciting, wasn't it?'

'Please Adam, don't do this,' he said.

'We made it, Lars! And now we've got a lovely view of the sea. Look!' I swung us into another turn and we cleared the cliffs. 'Let's take a closer look,' I said, and began a descent, pointing the nose down at the sea. It wasn't a particularly steep or dangerous dive, but it probably looked and felt that way to Lars.

'Oh Jesus Christ, just tell me what I must do, Adam!'

'What you must do, Lars, is tell me what the fuck is happening around here.'

'What can I tell you?' His eyes were wide and his voice rose. 'There is nothing! I don't know anything! Pull up, Adam, we're going into the sea, pull up!'

'Good point! You mean like this?' I yanked the nose back up and we levelled out momentarily. I heard him trying to control his breathing. Slowly I pushed the nose down again, and he began to hyperventilate. I kept my expression impassive, trying to mask the intensity of my focus on the calculations I was making, and the extent to which I was less in command of the helicopter than I hoped I appeared to be. 'No,' I said casually, 'I don't think so. Let's see how close we can get to the water without going in! How about that?' I put us into a sudden downward plunge.

'No! Stop, we will crash!'

'Tell me the truth, Lars.'

'About what? Your crazy theory about some kind of pollution scandal?'

'I'm not crazy, Lars. If I was crazy I'd do something like this...'

I took us down even lower, until we were only yards above the sea, with the downdraft chopping the water, raising angry waves. I began to spin us around, making the turns sharper and faster until I had to ease off and unflex my fingers and shake the perspiration from them while momentarily swapping hands to grip the stick.

'Stop!' he yelled. 'I will tell you! Anything you want to know!'

I took us up about thirty feet, but continued to circle, slower and more lazily, but still enough to keep Lars feeling queasy. I hoped he wouldn't vomit.

'OK,' I said, 'yes or no – are you dumping toxic waste out there?'

'No! No, nothing like that. You're wrong about all that, I swear it.'

'Very well. Answer me this – and tell me the truth, Lars, or this ride is going to end very badly – what happens to the children on that island?'

Lars tried to moisten his lips. 'I don't know. It's nothing to do with us.'

I stopped circling, and turned the aircraft back towards the land, staying low over the water. We were heading for the cliffs.

I turned in my seat to face him. 'I warned you.'

Lars started at the approaching cliffs, his face drained of colour. He gasped, 'Look out! We will hit the cliffs!'

I remained facing him. 'I was lying, Lars. I *am* crazy. And I don't give a shit what happens. Now,' I said, assuming a patient, fatherly tone of voice, as if I were talking to a petulant teenager, 'I've explained to you that you must tell me the truth, haven't I? So, tell me what you're doing to those children.'

'Nothing! We do nothing, I swear on my mother, oh Jesus fucking Christ, we're going to crash!'

I kept my eyes on him. I didn't look at the approaching cliffs but I knew how close they were. I guessed I had a couple of seconds left before it would be too late to pull up and clear the top of them. Even then, it would be touch and go. I told myself I didn't care.

Lars screamed again, and began gibbering in Norwegian. I caught the words 'gud i himmelen.'

I wondered what would happen next. I figured that if I acted now, this instant, my chances of avoiding the cliffs altogether were about fifty-fifty. The chances of clearing them, but damaging the underside of the helicopter, were perhaps slightly better: say, sixty-forty, with another set of odds to consider as to whether the damage would be lethal or not, which were probably at about fifty-fifty again, if the first outcome – of clearing the cliffs – was favourable.

I was outside my body, watching myself. It wasn't so much that time stood still, as that my mind was moving very fast, and consequently slowing down my perception of how time was passing. That's not to say my mind was racing; it was simply travelling at great speed, but without haste, like a distant Japanese bullet train that seems, as you watch it flash past, to be purposeful but unhurried. The abiding impression is of serenity.

It wasn't the first time I'd had this experience. The first time was when I was a little kid, jumping off the roof of our garage. Below me there was a small patch of grass, off to one side, but the ground directly beneath me was concrete. I was aiming to land on the grass, but I realised my chances of getting there weren't great. I knew that what I was doing was dangerous, and I could hurt myself badly, but I wanted to do it. I leaped in the air, and then I left my body. I watched myself with interest as the realisation grew that I might just reach the grass, but not all of my body would be cushioned. As it turned out, it wasn't much of a cushion anyway. I broke my arm, twisted an ankle, and collected several cuts and bruises. My mother thought it was all a dreadful nuisance.

The same thing happened several years later, at a moment when I was about to engage in a serious conflict. In the instant when I need to choose between fight or flight, I stepped out of my body and watched myself make the ill-advised choice to fight. I barely survived the ensuing carnage. But I'd wanted to do it.

And there was an occasion, two days after my eighteenth

birthday, when I found myself in a filthy derelict house, and I paused with my finger on the plunger of a syringe of heroin I'd just inserted into my arm. There was a strong chance it was part of a bad batch that users on the street had been talking about, and that it was contaminated, probably with rat poison. I knew one person who'd died, and heard of two others. But there was also a chance it wasn't part of that batch. Once again, I watched from outside myself as I slowly pressed the plunger, drew back the swirling bloom of blood, pressed again. Admittedly, in those circumstances, my choices were more limited. I was an addict, and, like every addict, I wanted to get high, and I wanted it more than anything else in the world at that moment. More than life itself.

These memories occupied my mind for no more than a second. We were about to smash into the cliffs. I hauled the helicopter up, and further up, and up to the point of stalling, forcing her up and over, clearing the edge of the clifftop by inches. Lars was still screaming, and before he stopped I yelled: 'Tell me what happens to the children!'

'It's them!' he gasped. 'It's the islanders; it's not us. They do it! It's them, it's them, for the love of god, Adam, please!'

I kept the aircraft hovering just above the cliff edge. 'What do you mean, they do it? What do they do?'

'I don't know! It's something secret!'

I executed a tight turn and took us back out over the cliff. 'Lars,' I said, 'I don't like these secrets between us.' I released a heavy sigh and allowed us to plummet down towards the rocks at the edge of the sea. Lars tried to scream again but his throat was constricted. At the last possible moment I gave the helicopter some lift, and pulled us up. We circled over the rocky shoreline, passing dangerously close to the side of the cliff with each circuit, although I was pretty confident we wouldn't actually hit it, as long as I could stave off the cramp in my hands and legs.

Lars slumped in his seat. 'I'll tell you,' he whispered. 'I'll tell you what I know.'

I could see he was ready. It wasn't the fear that had finished him, it was the hope, as always. The crucial moment was when we'd cleared the top of the cliff, and he relaxed fractionally as he believed the worst of the ordeal was nearly over, only for me to drop us down like a stone again, back over the edge and down towards the rocks.

'The people here,' he said between deep breaths, 'you've seen them. The way they act. They display exceptionally low emotional response. What a psychologist would call a lack of affect. Flat. Dead. You must have seen it, yes?'

'I've seen it. What about it?'

'It's for real! No feelings; nothing. They are cold. Nothing gets to them. They are like ice; nerves of ice, you know what I mean? I've never seen it before.'

'And that's why you employ them?'

'They are very valuable for our work.'

'Why? Because the work is dirty? Is that it? Toxic shit, right?'

Lars shook his head. 'No. That's not it. Yes OK, it's potentially toxic, if there was a mistake. An error. But they don't make mistakes! So, we pay them well, and they do the work efficiently, and they don't make problems with Health and Safety, you know what I mean? They save us a large amount of money. Amazing. They are like machines. Better than machines.'

I thought for a moment. 'But what makes them that way? What happens?'

'I don't know. It's just how they are. I don't ask questions.'

'You're lying again.'

181

'No, I swear.'

I made a slow, exaggerated tutting sound. 'I'm disappointed, Lars. I thought you'd stopped playing games with me. And now you're making me do this...'

I wrenched the aircraft out of the lazy circling pattern I'd been holding, and sped out over the sea for a few seconds, flat-out, then I made an abrupt turn and pointed us back at the cliffs, full speed ahead.

Lars went rigid, then he flailed his arms around like a rag doll being shaken. He tried to grab the controls but I smacked his arm away viciously.

'It's the game!' he screamed, 'in the Summer School!'

I kept us on course for the cliffs. 'The game? What happens in the game? Tell me Lars, or I swear to god I will send us both to hell!'

He began to weep. 'I don't know. It's part of how they get the way they are. It's some kind of selection process. It's the way they turn them into the people I pay for, here and at other places. They become cold. That's all I know! Believe me, please!'

I glanced at him. He was empty, with no lies left. I swerved away from the cliffs and took us up slowly. 'When is the game?' I said. 'It's happening soon, right?'

'It's today.'

I didn't know if I'd misheard him. 'What?'

'It's today. Now. They do it today.'

'Jesus. Where? Where does it happen?'

He shut his eyes. 'Stone Heart Deep,' he whispered. 'At the house.'

'Oh god. The house?'

'Yes. Stone Heart House. Your house.'

'Oh fuck,' I said, and took us up over the cliff edge. It was

182

nearly dusk and the entire sky seemed to be churning with dark, towering storm clouds. I began to fly inland, skirting the hills and heading in the direction of the lake, and the house.

I glanced at Lars. He didn't look good. I said, 'That's where the children go?'

He nodded, barely moving his head. 'Yes, for the game at Summer School.'

'All of them? All the children on the island?'

'Yes. At the age of six, for the game. The others to…watch. Everyone.'

'But what do they do to them?'

A feeble spark of energy seemed to animate him. 'I don't know! The details are hidden from me. But whatever happens to them, whatever makes them into who they are, that is where it begins. There at the house.'

I caught sight of the lake in the distance. Stone Heart Deep. In less than a minute we were at its edge. The water was placid and black, eerily calm beneath the gathering storm. We skimmed across it and I took us down low, nosing along the shoreline on the approach to the huge old house that brooded at the water's edge.

Lars understood what I was doing. 'Adam!' he cried, 'there's no landing place!'

'Not yet,' I said. I coaxed the helicopter down towards a patch of rocky scrub on an outcrop about two hundred yards from the house. From the corner of my eye I saw Lars gripping the edges of his seat. He was shaking. I took us down as slowly and carefully as I could. We hit the ground with a massive, bone-rattling jolt, then another. I cut the engine. We were still for an instant, but we were on a slope, and the aircraft began to slide down it in a series of thudding skips, dislodging scree and cascades of pebbles. For a moment I thought it might topple over, but finally it came to rest, tilting at a dangerous angle. I got my door open and struggled out of my seat.

'Adam, wait!' Lars said.

I pushed myself out and jumped to the ground, managing to land squarely on both feet, and started half-scrambling, half-sliding down to the shoreline, trying to keep my balance.

Behind me I heard Lars's plaintive wail. 'What about me? Adam! What will I do?'

I ignored him. As I sprinted towards the house the entire landscape was abruptly lit up by a huge burst of lightning. Everything was pin-sharp and blindingly bright for an instant, as if illuminated by countless fluorescent lamps; then the storm burst with a deafening crash of thunder and rain fell down in sheets.

The front doors were locked. I huddled under the portico as the storm raged at my back, twisting and shoving at the big iron handles, but they didn't budge. I recalled my previous visit to the house, when I'd explored it with Harriet and Logan, and tried to remember if I'd seen any other entrances, but nothing came to mind. I considered trying to make a circuit of the building, but the fierceness of the storm discouraged me.

I decided to smash the nearest window on the ground floor. I was just beginning to struggle out of my coat, with the intention of wrapping it around my fist, when I saw something I hadn't noticed before. Tucked into the angle between the door frame and the brickwork, on the right-hand side, was a rusty iron bell-pull. It descended from an aperture just above the door and ended in a handle at waist height. What the hell, I thought, and pulled it. Maybe an ancient butler would materialise, and usher me silently inside, then inform me the Count would see me as soon as he woke up in his coffin. That didn't happen, and neither did anything else. I figured the mechanism was probably broken long ago, although the storm was so loud the bells of hell could have been ringing inside the house and I wouldn't have heard anything. For no particular reason, I pulled it again, twice, in quick succession.

Very slowly the doors began to open. I prepared myself to face whoever was opening them, but after a moment I realised it was happening mechanically. I watched and waited until both doors were wide open, and edged forward. It was dark inside. I slipped through the doorway and swerved to one side: the light behind me was dim and grey, but the inside of the house was darker, and I didn't want to be silhouetted for longer than I needed to be. As I stood with my back to the wall, straining to detect any movement, I heard a creaking noise. The front doors were closing. I waited until they shut with a soft, heavy thud, and the noise of the storm outside diminished abruptly. The only sound I could hear now was the patter of water coming through leaks in the roof. Slowly my eyes adjusted to the darkness.

The house felt deserted. I walked slowly and carefully to the foot of the massive, curving staircase and peered up into the gloom. I waited for a full minute, then I took the stairs quickly, one hand brushing the wall. I was thinking about the huge ballroom on the first floor – where I'd danced with Harriet and Logan – and trying to imagine it full of people, silently waiting for me. It seemed unlikely, and as soon as I reached the doorway I saw the room was empty. In the dim grey light coming through the windows I could make out the traces of the footsteps we'd left in the dust, and they were undisturbed. No one had been in there since then.

I felt a sudden ache of longing. I allowed myself to taste the happiness I'd felt when the three of us had danced, and recalled the playfulness that overtook us. Was it only two days ago? There had a been a moment, just after we stopped dancing, when my eyes met Harriet's and we both knew we were going to sleep together, and the sensation was delicious. Part of me wanted to stop time at that moment, and live in it for ever.

My eye was caught by something outside one of the tall windows – barely even a movement, more a shift within overlaid textures of greyness, with the grime of the window obscuring the sheets of rain, which in turn veiled the landscape. As I walked to the window a bolt of lightning split the sky, and I saw the figure of Lars Hansen on the crest of an outcrop a hundred yards from the helicopter, momentarily immobilised in the brilliant flash of light like a figure in a tableau staged to depict a thief, caught in the act, fleeing the scene of the crime.

The image vanished in an instant, with the lightning. I thought about Lars. Had he lied to me? I'd been certain that the terror of our helicopter ride had drained him of all deceit, and yet there was nobody here in the house. I felt a sudden impulse to rush out and catch him, and subject him to further pressure, but I didn't move. It was just a spasm of frustration. Yes, he may have held some information back, but I was sure he'd essentially told me the truth, and the key to everything was here, in the house. The certainty I experienced wasn't an intuition or instinct, or any kind of feeling – no sudden prickling of the skin, or that type of bullshit – but a deep knowledge. It's the same when you're faced with an important choice, and you think you're weighing up your options, and taking the most logical path, but the reality is that you've already made the decision, and all you need to do is get yourself out of your own way. So, I didn't rush outside and follow Lars. I knew I was in the right place.

I left the ballroom and walked down the staircase, able

to see my way more clearly now. I made my way along the passage leading to the rear of the house, and I didn't pause to check the rooms I passed on either side. When I reached the huge kitchen I didn't stop. I crossed the tiled floor to the far side of the room, and there it was – the door at the far end, where the back of the house pressed against the hillside behind it. The door that had been locked on my last visit. And was now, very slightly, ajar.

FIFTEEN

I pushed the door, expecting it to creak on its iron hinges, but it opened smoothly without a sound. I glanced behind me to confirm what I already knew – that I was alone, and no one had followed me – and was about to step through the doorway when I stopped.

Something had glinted in the corner of my eye. I took a step back and peered around, searching the gloom. I couldn't see anything. Then a tiny reddish light winked, and was gone. I waited. There! It winked again. I counted five seconds and it happened again, then again after five more seconds. Finally I made out where it was coming from, and what it was. A small CCTV camera was tucked into a corner of the high ceiling. I would never have noticed it without that tiny pulse of light. I thought back to my earlier visit, and wondered why I hadn't spotted it, given the amount of time Harriet and I had spent exploring the kitchen. It was very unlikely that the camera hadn't been there, and had been installed since then. The only explanation was that it hadn't been switched on during my first visit. But it was now.

I turned back to the open doorway, and stepped through it. I found myself at the top of a dozen stone steps. They led down to a passageway that stretched ahead for as far as I could see, dimly illuminated by lightbulbs recessed behind cradles of wire mesh in the low ceiling. I descended the steps and paused at the bottom. I half expected the door at the top of the steps to slam shut behind me, but everything remained still and silent. I began to walk slowly along the passage.

Beads of water trickled down the walls, and droplets plopped onto my head from the ceiling, a few inches above me. After fifteen yards, the tunnel began curving to the left. Another twenty paces brought me to a wall that appeared to block my way, but when I reached it, I saw it was a corner where the passage turned sharply to the right. I turned the corner and nearly fell headlong down another set of steps. They were steeper and narrower than the steps that led down from the kitchen, and I took them carefully, with one hand on the clammy stone wall. There were four flights of six steps, descending in a zigzag. At the bottom, the tunnel continued, curving to the left once again. When it straightened out, I knew I'd lost my bearings, although I had a strong feeling I'd doubled back on myself and I was now directly beneath the house again. But wherever I was, it was deep under the ground.

I saw a dull gleam ahead of me. After a few steps, the gleam resolved itself into a metal door that reflected a pair of recessed spotlights trained on it. As I got closer, I saw the door was similar to the one that led to the passage at the back of

189

189

the kitchen, but this one wasn't so rusted. There was a sturdy horizontal handle at one side. I positioned myself in front of the door, grasped the handle, and pushed it downwards. There was no resistance. I let go of the handle and the door swung open.

A silhouetted figure was facing me. It stepped forward, into the light directed at the doorway. It was Doctor Caleb Druce.

'Hello Adam,' he said, 'it's good to see you.'

He thrust out his hand, and I took it. Even as I was thinking that it was an odd gesture in these strange circumstances, I felt him tighten his grip. He pulled himself towards me. As his face loomed closer to mine I was overwhelmed by confusion, even wondering for a fleeting moment if perhaps he were trying to kiss me. From the corner of my eye and a fraction of a second too late, I saw the sudden upward movement of his left arm and felt a sharp pricking sensation in the side of my neck. He released my hand and stepped back. He was holding up a syringe. Reflexively I clapped my hand on my neck where he'd punctured it.

I stared at him stupidly. 'Have you just poisoned me?' I said. My tongue felt thick.

Druce smiled. 'No, I haven't poisoned you, Adam.'

'What have you given me?'

He extracted a plastic pouch of some kind from his pocket, dropped the syringe into it, and slipped it back into his jacket. 'It's a little mixture of my own,' he said. 'There's a modified hypnotic sedative in the dose, and a couple of things I synthesised myself, including a mild hallucinogen, and an opioid similar to fentanyl but even more powerfully concentrated, if you will.'

At the precise moment he said the word opioid, I felt it. Ah, there it was. A pulse streaked through my mind and in an instant the neural pathways that had sprung to life the first time I took heroin, all those years ago, were juiced again, like a system of desiccated gulches suddenly flowing with nourishing syrup. I thought I'd buried that network for good, but it had simply been dormant, and now I was flooded with warmth and clarity as I slipped my moorings and turned a gorgeous somersault inside myself.

There's nothing like it. If you could distil the feeling of coming home from a hard day's work, and having a perfect martini and a relaxing bath, then another martini, followed by great sex, after discovering you've won the lottery and will never need to work again, and condense all that into a single experience rushing into you all at once, it still wouldn't come close. Nothing matters; everything's clear; all is well.

The other drugs began to kick in behind the opioid. I thought I detected a stimulant somewhere in the cocktail, and figured it was probably intended to prevent me from getting too groggy. I wondered why Druce had drugged me. It didn't bother me at all, but I was curious.

'Why?' I said. I knew he'd understand what I was asking.

Druce nodded judiciously. 'I wasn't quite sure of you, Adam. I didn't want to take the risk that you might decide to leave before you've seen what I want to show you, or cause some kind of problem in respect of what we're doing here, so I've given you something that should make you a little more compliant than you might otherwise be.'

I found what he said amusing. I knew that ordinarily I would have reacted against the idea of compliance, but now it didn't seem unreasonable. I wasn't thinking the way I did usually, and at the same time, I was fully aware of the fact. I felt that I was now sharing myself between two distinct frames of mind, but there appeared to be no friction between them, and

I could occupy both of them at once; no problem.

Druce had been studying me keenly, and now he seemed satisfied. 'Please follow me, Adam,' he said, and turned to lead the way.

I had no intention of disobeying his request. It wasn't so much that I'd lost the will to resist, more that when I considered, in a spirit of idle experiment, the possibility of rousing the part of me that might have refused to do what he asked, it simply rolled over in its sleep and muttered, 'Leave me alone'.

I followed the doctor. After a few steps, I stopped and looked around me, and tried to make sense of where I was and what I was seeing. I was still in a passageway, but this one was wider than the stone tunnel I'd been in before, and much brighter. When I looked up, I couldn't see a ceiling. The top of the passage appeared to be open, and powerful lamps shone down into it from somewhere high above me. I squinted up at them, trying to make out where they were mounted, but it was impossible to tell, and my eyes began to hurt. I turned my attention to the walls of the passage on either side of me, and saw they were lined with metal doors. At eye level on each door there was a hinged flap, obviously intended for the purpose of observation. One of the doors was nearly adjacent to me. I took a step towards it, then I checked myself as I remembered I was meant to be following the doctor.

'Take a look,' Druce said, and I turned to see him standing a few yards ahead of me, watching me with no hint of impatience. 'Open the hatch, if you like,' he said. 'We don't use them much these days, for reasons you'll understand soon enough. But if you're curious, don't let me stop you.'

I stepped up to the door and released the catch that held the flap in place. It swung down, revealing an aperture roughly the dimensions of a letterbox in the front door of an average house. I brought my eyes close to it. I was looking into a room about eight feet square. A small girl I didn't recognise was sitting on a wooden chair next to a table, looking nervously down at the floor. A candle was burning on the table, beside a plate of cookies. There was a large rectangular window in the far wall of the room, with a desk in front of it. Behind the window there appeared to be another, identical room.

I don't know whether the girl had heard me opening the hatch, or if some instinct told her she was being watched, but she looked up suddenly and our eyes met. I recoiled, and closed the hatch. The child's wide-eyed gaze had conveyed an odd mixture of fear, defiance, and resignation. I stared at the closed door. I was aware the encounter had evoked an emotional response in me, but I found I couldn't identify it properly. My feelings moved through me fleetingly, like the headlamp beams from a passing car sweeping across the ceiling of a bedroom in which you're half asleep. All I could say with any certainty was that I felt vaguely unsettled. I knew the drugs were making me emotionally inert, and I wondered if I should try to struggle against their effects.

'If you're ready, Adam, perhaps we may continue.'

As I turned back to Druce, a figure crossed the passageway several yards beyond him. Druce saw me react, and smiled. 'It's a busy time for us here.' He turned away and continued along the passageway. I followed him.

We reached the point where I'd seen the figure crossing our route, and I stopped again. It was an intersection with a passage that crossed our path diagonally, and stretched away on both sides. More doors were visible. As I peered along the corridor to my left, I saw a woman stride briskly across it, at another intersection. I realised we were in a kind of maze, and as soon as the thought crossed my mind, I recalled the disorienting layout of the house. I was sure we were directly beneath it, in a system of passages that replicated the pattern of those inside the house. As above, so below.

Ahead of me, Druce had come to a halt again and was waiting for me. For a moment, I thought he was standing in front of a wall, but as I got closer I saw it was a smooth stone pillar, ten feet in diameter, that stood in the centre of another intersection. I ran my eyes up the pillar, tilting my head back to try and see the top of it, but it disappeared up into a darkness that was made all the more impenetrable by the lights blazing down from somewhere high above us. A skeletal metal ladder ran vertically up the side of the pillar, secured to it with bolts. There was a thin handrail on one side. It reminded me of something, and it came to me after a moment: the ladder to the wheelhouse in Archie's ferry. Something inside me seemed to spin smoothly, like a revolving door, and I remembered Archie was dead.

How much time had elapsed since I'd seen his bulging eyes staring up at me from the water? It couldn't have been more than a few hours, but that didn't feel right. My mind wanted to push his death further back in time, allowing me to see it from a distance of weeks or even months, and to respond to it as an event that belonged in the distant past. I tried to pull it forward, into its proper temporal perspective, and as I did so, a train of connections snaked through my thoughts. Archie. The harbour. The harbour where I'd gone to wait for Harriet and Logan, who didn't arrive, and who weren't at home when I went to find them, in a town that was deserted, so where were they?

They were here. Of course they were here.

'How are you doing, Adam?' Druce said. I struggled to focus on him. His features seemed to be distorted, moving oddly, as if his face were in a state of flux, and I marvelled at the rubbery contortions it underwent. Slowly, my vision stabilised. I guessed that the effect of the drugs in my system had just hit a peak – particularly the hallucinogen, which I estimated to be far from mild – but now they seemed to be settling down. For a moment I wondered if I could expect more peaks and troughs to hit me, and how long the waves would keep coming, and if there was anything I could do about it, but I decided not to be concerned.

I joined Druce at the foot of the ladder. He patted my shoulder. 'Perhaps you'd better go first,' he said, and stood back.

I gripped the handrail and climbed up. After a few rungs, I paused and craned my head back. I saw that I was heading for a platform about thirty feet above me. I climbed up towards it, gripping the handrail firmly and taking care of my footing on the narrow rungs of the ladder. I noticed that my basic motor skills seemed unimpaired by the drugs in my system, but nonetheless I kept my focus firmly on the task of ascending the thin vertical ladder, which eventually took me up through a gap in the platform, then ended. I stepped off it, and onto a metal surface. I moved away from the top of the ladder, to make room for Druce to emerge. He was right behind me. I gazed around, and at first my brain was incapable of assembling what I was seeing into a coherent picture, but gradually I began to understand where I was.

SIXTEEN

The platform was about six feet wide, with a safety rail at waist height. It encircled the central pillar I'd just ascended, which extended upwards for another fifteen feet above my head, where it met the stone roof of a vaulted cavern. A dozen more pillars supported the groined roof at other points in the chamber. My vantage point on the platform made it seem as if I were stationed high in the gallery of a church, and when I ran my eyes around the roof, the style of its architecture reinforced the church-like impression. I marvelled at all the work that must have gone into creating it.

'It's strange to think,' Druce said from beside me, 'that we're underneath the house, isn't it? As you can see, that roof is a wonderful construction. There's ten feet of solid rock above it, and originally it covered a chapel, a crypt, and a system of cellars – the floor of which used to be roughly where we're standing now.'

I continued to gaze at up at the vaulted stone edifice. I visualised the massive bulk of the house above it, and felt an oppressive force bearing down on me.

'The house is a lot older than it might seem,' Druce said. 'There's been a building on the site, with a crypt beneath it, since the fourteenth century. Over the years, both the building and the underground chambers were rebuilt and extended many times, and the roof that's now above us dates from the early fifteen-hundreds. Then, in eighteen-sixty, everything below us was constructed. They built downwards, extending the pillars as they went. Remarkable work.'

He stepped to the rail. 'Come and look.'

I edged forward to join him, and looked down. What I saw was astonishing.

The platform was perched above a system of rooms and corridors that were interconnected in a kind of labyrinth. It was like looking down into an archaeological excavation in which everything had been carefully restored, then populated by animated figures who re-enacted various tasks in the network of exposed chambers. But the people below me were real, and what they were doing wasn't a re-enactment. I wondered if they would be able to see me if they looked up, and stepped back instinctively.

'It's all right,' Druce said. 'They can't see us. The light coming from up here is too powerful. There's relatively little illumination inside the chambers themselves. It's all directed downwards from the roof. Look.'

He pointed to the top of a nearby pillar, and I saw a nest of spot lamps around its crown with their beams trained downwards. There was an identical set of lights at the top of each pillar, including the central pillar where we stood.

'In the days before electric lighting,' Druce continued, 'there was no overhead illumination, and everything relied on a system of gas lamps down there. As you can imagine, there were various drawbacks. For one thing, it was dangerous, and ventilation was a constant problem. It was a great improvement when the first electric spot lamps were installed up here in the roof.'

'When was that?' My voice came out in a croak and I had to clear my throat.

'Just before the Great War. They weren't terribly efficient to begin with, but they've been updated several times over the years, naturally, and the latest ones are superb lighting devices, as you can see.' He glanced around at the nests of lamps. 'I'm told they're the absolute state of the art when it comes to LED lighting.'

'I guess they would cost a lot of money,' I said.

Druce smiled. 'I expect they would. As it happens, they were a gift from Lars and the boys out at the rig. They installed them for us about five years ago. Skandiflow runs various types of mining operation around the world – some of them with very deep excavations – and they developed a special diode for these lamps in their own labs. We're very fortunate to enjoy the benefit of their work.' He gazed around the chamber. 'There's much more we can do. And soon there will be less need for secrecy, as I believe the political climate is becoming more amenable to the kind of progress we're making here.' He paused, and allowed himself the trace of a smile. 'We no longer require the façade of quaintness. I was fond of Archie, but Skandiflow will set up an efficient modern ferry service. I anticipate us achieving a lot together.'

'And what do they get in return?'

He cocked his head. For all I knew, it was possible Lars had somehow contacted him by now, and informed him about our joyride. Druce twisted one corner of his mouth up. 'Let's just say there's a *quid pro quo*, and leave it at that, shall we? We're of use to each other. But until they put in this latest lighting system, I wasn't able to get such a clear overview, which can sometimes be very useful. It enables me to sense the currents flowing down there. What you might call the deep ambience.'

I peered down over the railing again. It was hard to believe the people down there wouldn't see us if they happened to look up. I scanned the labyrinth. There were about twenty rooms, connected by myriad corridors. Adults and children were moving between the rooms, and engaged in activities inside them that I couldn't exactly comprehend, although it seemed that some type of test was taking place. I estimated there were more than a dozen children down there, and maybe thirty adults. Looking down at them from my vantage point, I was inescapably reminded of rats in a laboratory maze. Perhaps that was the intention.

I was aware that Druce was standing close behind me. 'Of course,' he said, 'I don't need to get the big picture all the time. Especially now we have the cameras.'

I turned around to face him, and for the first time I saw the screens. Six surveillance monitors were mounted on a panel that curved part of the way around the pillar, above a narrow desk. The screens were blank, showing nothing but a dull, grey glow. Druce spun on his heel and strode to the desk. He picked up a remote control handset and pressed a button, and the screens flickered to life. At first each screen showed a different image, then he operated the control again, and all the screens switched to the same view. Two steps brought me close enough to the monitor bank to see it clearly. I stared at the screen nearest to me.

I was seeing a child who looked about six years old, from a shallow overhead camera angle. The picture zoomed in slightly and I realised it was the little girl I'd seen when I looked through the inspection hatch. She had freckles and was frowning, and was taking slow, deep breaths. In front of her, the candle on the table flickered in its brass holder. The plate of cookies was next to it. Slowly the girl extended her hand, palm downwards, towards the candle flame. At the last moment she hesitated. She glanced at the plate of cookies, then looked around the room. She seemed frightened.

'Interesting,' Druce said. He operated the device in his hand again. The image changed, and the view split between alternating screens: one showed the girl in a big close-up, and the other was a wide shot of the whole room. In the close-up, the girl looked very upset. Her lip was trembling and she seemed on the verge of tears.

Druce glanced at me, then he began to write something on a pad that lay on the desk. 'This could go either way,' he murmured. He finished writing, pressed a button on the desk, and watched the screens again. After a moment, a door opened and a woman walked into the room. She crouched beside the little girl and spoke to her coaxingly.

I turned to Druce. 'What is this?'

'It's what you've been looking for all this time, Adam.'

'What do you mean?'

'It's the game,' he said, and dimmed the images on the screens.

I waited for a moment before replying, trying to collect myself. 'It looks to me,' I said, 'like an experiment. Is that what you're doing here? Experimenting with human lives? Experimenting on children?'

'Not an experiment, Adam. Not any longer. Not now that we know how to do it.'

'How to do what, exactly?' I said. I felt a sensation that it took me a moment to identify – to distinguish as a signal amid the narcotic noise – and I realised it was fear, gripping me as I understood the implications of his words.

He walked towards me and stood in front of me, very close. I tensed. He reached out and put a hand on my shoulder. His hawkish features, inches from my face, remained inscrutable but his eyes gleamed. 'Do you remember,' he said, 'our fascinating conversation about human nature?'

'I remember it.'

He nodded slowly then took a step back. He gestured at the screens. 'Natural selection is a very beautiful process,' he said. 'It's perfect. Inexorable. The only criticism one might make of it is that it's slow. Very slow. But we're an ingenious species, and there's no reason why we shouldn't apply our ingenuity – which itself is the outcome of natural selection – to improving the process in this respect. To make it a little more effective in its timescale. We need to intervene, Adam, in the most gentle and compassionate way we can, to control and optimise the functions of human nature, as they mould us into the creatures we become, both individually and collectively.'

He operated his handset again, restoring the views on the TV monitors. The little girl with freckles was now seated at the desk on the far side of the room. The desktop was an angled surface containing what looked like a basic set of controls: a dial, a couple of switches and buttons. A microphone on a swan-necked armature was close to her mouth. The woman I'd seen earlier was standing beside the girl, speaking to her. The girl still looked scared.

'For fuck's sake,' I said, 'tell me what's going on.'

Druce shook his head. 'I'll show you. It's easier.' He used the handset to scroll through a series of shots and angles. They settled into two different views, displayed on alternate screens. One shot was a wide view of the girl, showing the window beyond her desk. It reminded me of a window in an interrogation room. In the room behind the glass, I saw that a figure was strapped to a chair. The other camera view, displayed on the alternate screens, showed the interior of that room. The figure in the chair was a small boy. Electrodes were attached to his wrists, ankles and scalp.

'Jesus,' I said, 'tell me this isn't what I think it is.'

'What do you think it is?'

I gazed at him. His expression betrayed interest, but nothing else. I edged past him and looked at the screens. 'With kids?' I said. 'The fucking Milgram test?'

'Not exactly, no. If you remember, in the original Milgram Obedience Study, the role of the learners was faked. They used actors. And when the subjects thought they were administering electric shocks as punishment, the actors pretended to react to pain, which they didn't actually feel. The purpose of the study was to test the obedience of the subjects, and the degree to which they'd overstep perceived societal and moral restraints at the behest of authority figures who ordered them to punish their counterparts.'

'I know,' I said, 'but the subjects were adults, not children! And even then, the ethics were questionable.'

Druce tapped a fingernail thoughtfully on the control panel. 'What's your real concern, Adam?' he said. 'No one has ever proved that the results Milgram obtained were invalid. And they've been replicated. Some of the conditions were changed, admittedly, but only because there was some squeamishness expressed in certain quarters about the degree of deception involved. Mostly performative, in my opinion. But as I've just mentioned, what we're doing here isn't a precise replication of that study and its methods. We've made one or two significant changes, and I would argue that what we're doing here – the way we proceed with the tests – is actually more ethical, because there's less deception involved. Certainly no acting or pretence on the part of the learner.'

I stared at the little girl on-screen, who was listening intently to the woman, then switched my attention to the boy strapped in the chair. I was playing for time, to erect a defence against the reality of what he was telling me. 'No acting at all?' I said eventually.

'None. I won't be party to that kind of thing. All responses are authentic.'

'You can't mean it,' I said, although I knew he did.

'Let's have the audio on, shall we?' Druce flipped a switch on his handset.

I heard the woman's voice, startlingly close and clear:

'I'm afraid Jack is being very naughty,' the woman was saying. 'I'm sorry, Tara, but you'll have to punish him, otherwise he won't learn his lesson, will he?'

The little girl looked up at her. 'But I don't think he can hear me!' she said. 'He can't hear what I'm saying to him! That's why he's not doing it! I'm sure that's why!'

'Oh yes, he can hear you,' the woman said. 'He can, Tara, really. He's just being very disobedient, and he's pretending he can't hear you, and that's just naughty, isn't it?'

Druce smiled at me. 'Watch this,' he said, and flipped another switch. Now we could hear the audio from the room where the boy was strapped in his chair. He was breathing heavily, with a rasping catch in his breath. From his side of the glass he could see the little girl and the woman speaking, but the sound wasn't audible to him. They were mouthing like fish in a bowl. Suddenly he began to yell. 'I can't hear you!' he shouted. In the adjoining room, the woman and the girl continued to talk. They couldn't hear him, any more than he could know what they were saying. 'Tara!' he yelled, 'I can't hear you! Tell me what you want me to do! Please, just tell me!' He began to sob.

'This way, you see,' Druce said, 'we get valuable data on all three subjects.'

The woman put her hand gently on the freckled girl's shoulder. 'I know,' she said sympathetically, 'it's very difficult for you, isn't it? But you'll have to punish him, Tara. There's no other way, my darling.'

'Oh god,' I said, 'is that her mother?'

'Yes, it's one of the most important bonds we deal with. Perhaps *the* most important, in the early years, although it's instructive to investigate the degree to which it can be moderated by peer group pressure. It's a very complex set of relationships.' Druce peered closely at the screens and nodded with satisfaction. 'I think we're getting there,' he said. 'Pay attention now, Adam, I'm pretty sure we're going to see a breakthrough here very shortly.'

The girl, Tara, slowly reached out and touched the dial in the control panel in front of her, then recoiled. Her mother carefully took her hand and guided it back to the dial. This time Tara didn't remove it.

'That's a good girl,' her mother said. 'Now darling, you have to turn it up. It's for his own good, you know.'

Tara looked up at her mother. 'But it's nearly in the red part,' she said.

'He's got to learn,' the woman said.

'But you said that if the needle goes into the red bit, it'll really hurt him.'

Her mother squeezed her shoulder encouragingly. 'It's the only way. Go on, Tara, do it now. Please do as I say.'

I moved closer to the screen in front of me. My body felt as heavy as lead. 'Oh god, no,' I whispered. I was aware that Druce was watching me, but I couldn't tear my eyes away from the screen.

Tara turned the dial on the panel in front of her. Behind the glass the little boy was jolted upright, arching his body, struggling in the straps that restrained him. He didn't cry out, but he squeezed his eyes shut and bit his lip.

'More!' the woman said. 'Turn it more, Tara!'

The little girl stifled a sob and turned the dial again. This time Jack let out a desperate, animal howl of pain.

From the corner of my eye I saw Druce flip a switch. Suddenly Tara and her mother were able to hear Jack's cries of pain. The little girl snatched her hand from the dial, but her mother grasped her wrist and guided her hand back to the dial. As she touched the dial, the screens went blank and the sound cut out.

I turned to see Druce watching me intently. He was holding the handset, with his thumb on one of the buttons. He raised an eyebrow. 'Fascinating, isn't it?'

After a moment I said, 'No. It's insane.'

'I don't think so, Adam.' He placed the handset carefully down on the control desk. 'What's insane is the rage and violence of the life we've both witnessed out there, in the world at large. The rage and violence we both despise. Remember?'

'I remember the conversation we had, yes. That doesn't mean this isn't insane. I don't think anything we talked about gives you the right to be playing god.'

'But you couldn't tear your eyes away, could you? And even

205

now, there's a part of you that wants to know what's happening down there, isn't there? You'd love me to switch the monitors on again, and see how far that girl will go. Admit it.'

'Leave me out of this.'

Druce chuckled. 'That's not possible, Adam. You're deep in this already, in ways you may not quite realise.' He walked to the edge of the platform, and leaned against the rail, and looked down at the labyrinth below us.

Somewhere down there, the drama I'd been observing continued to unfold, as a little girl made a decision about whether to inflict pain on another child. What happened in that room would determine the course of their lives. These were people, I told myself, not animals. And yet I couldn't deny that I wanted to know what happened next. I wanted to know how the story ended. Was that what Druce meant when he said I was in deep? Or was he threatening me? I wondered what would happen if I simply turned and walked away from all this. But even as the possibility crossed my mind, I knew I wouldn't do it.

Again, it wasn't that I felt incapable of leaving; it was that the will to do so was weaker than the compulsion to remain. I came to this conclusion dispassionately, observing the unequal battle within myself as if from a great height. I wondered if the cocktail of drugs was peaking again, but on reflection I decided the feeling wasn't quite the same. Earlier, a wave had lifted me, crested, and set me down, whereas now I was observing my own experience from an unchanging elevation, in stasis, at a fixed point.

A flutter of curiosity prompted my next question. 'Are you telling me,' I said, 'that you'll try to prevent me from leaving?'

Druce straightened up and gripped the rail with both hands, but he continued to gaze down into the maze. 'I advise you not to act,' he said quietly, 'before you hear what I'm about to say. I need to give you some background. Are you prepared to hear it?' He looked grave. There'd been a certain levity – almost a jauntiness – in his manner up until now, but it had left him.

'All right,' I said, 'go ahead.'

'More than a hundred and fifty years ago,' he said, 'an extraordinary man arrived on this island. He was a colleague of Darwin's. Or perhaps it would be more accurate to say he was a rival. He had a brilliant mind. In some ways, his gifts were greater than Darwin's, because he was able to see further, and to take the other man's ideas to their logical conclusion.'

'Right,' I said. 'I've heard this story before.'

He shot me a keen look. 'I don't think so, Adam. Not this particular one.'

'Maybe not, but nearly every apology I've heard for eugenics has begun with the argument that it's where you arrive if you take Darwin's ideas about natural selection to their logical conclusion.'

Druce made a dismissive gesture. 'I suggest you hear me out before making assumptions about what I'm going to tell you. Yes, the man I'm talking about found himself at odds with the scientific establishment, but so did Darwin, to begin with. And with the church, and with society at large. But unlike Darwin, this man was shunned, and hounded out of his job, and out of society. That's one reason why he came here. He was persecuted by the very people who should have been his allies – I'd go so far as to say they should have been his disciples – and all because he had a vision, and they couldn't accept it. They were cowards. They were too small-minded and too unimaginative, and too scared to follow him. His vision was too big for them.'

'I don't trust vision,' I said. 'It's what politicians have instead of eyesight.'

Druce turned and gazed at me impassively, but I saw a muscle tense in his jaw. I realised he was angry. It was the nearest to a display of emotion I'd seen in him since we'd met, and it lasted only a moment. He gave me a sardonic smile. 'That remark is beneath you, Adam. It's a glib soundbite. You know perfectly well what I mean by vision. And when it comes to eyesight, this man was able to see what was going on around him very clearly. More clearly and dispassionately than his colleagues, and that's why they hated him. He saw their weaknesses and their self-deceptions, and his only crime was that he told them the truth about themselves. And you know what else he saw? He saw the potential of human evolution. He recognised the necessity of eliminating the primitive behaviour patterns that thwart our development as rational beings. And he found the perfect place to do it: here, on this island, in an isolated community where he could take control of the gene pool, and begin the task of breeding that contamination out of the bloodline. Here, he could do the work that was needed, and achieve the goal he was born to attain.'

'No, wait,' I said. I felt clear-headed and grounded now. 'You're talking about human feelings. The idea that you can create some kind of utopia by destroying emotions isn't just grandiose and dangerous, it's bad science. You must know that as well as I do.'

'But I don't. And neither do you, in fact. Bad science? No. There's only one kind of science, and it's forged through experiment, testing, and replication of results. In other words, proof. You haven't done the work, Adam. We have. For a hundred and fifty years, we've done the work here. And do you know what we've proved? We've proved that those tired old emotional responses are redundant. They're like the appendix.

Given time, they'll shrivel away, and we shall no longer be slaves to the destructive passions that cripple human progress. We'll be free.'

'Really? When will that be?' I shook my head. 'I can't believe what I'm hearing here. The kind of evolutionary changes you're talking about take thousands of years. Altering the genetic composition of a population? Longer. Millions of years?'

'Not necessarily. Not at all. I'm working very closely with the latest thinking on the inheritance of acquired characteristics.'

'What, old Lamarck and his fucking frogs? Give me a break!'

'Toads, not frogs. The midwife toad. But that wasn't Lamarck; he experimented on mice, in the nineteenth century. The midwife toad experiments were conducted by Paul Kammerer in the 1920s, to develop Lamarck's ideas.'

'Oh sorry,' I said sarcastically, 'my knowledge of the history of blatant scientific frauds is a bit sketchy. But I know one thing: all of that bullshit was disproved and discredited, along with the Missing Link theory.'

Druce smiled. 'You're behind the times, Adam. The conventional scepticism is being revised. Ideas about natural selection and genetic adaptation, and inheritance, are far less rigid these days, and we're beginning to understand that these processes – like everything else in nature – take place along a continuum. I'll admit that we're still nowhere near the goal of acquired characteristics and behaviours being inherited within a single generation, or even several generations. But we're closer now than anyone ever thought possible. Much closer!'

'You're the one who's out of date,' I said. 'There are people out there now who are modifying the genomes of living organisms, and having all kinds of fun with gene editing, and DNA, and god knows what else. Molecular biology is the way to go for the discerning modern Frankenstein, surely, not crude behavioural torture in a bloody cellar?'

He gave me a deadpan stare, then raised one eyebrow fractionally.

A dead weight sank inside me, like an anchor plunging into black water. 'Jesus Christ,' I whispered, 'don't tell me you're doing that as well? Gene editing?'

He smiled with what could have been seen as modest pride in less horrible circumstances. 'Early days yet, Adam. Early days.'

I didn't want to believe what he was saying. I shook my head, trying to clear it.

'Don't worry,' he said, 'the biology is only a small part of it. There's a limit to what can be achieved by manipulation at that level. Physiology, yes, and intelligence, to a certain extent. You can select for physical and mental health. But you can't replicate the impact of lived experience, and learned behaviour. That can only be achieved in the context of socialisation. In other words, what's happening here, at this moment.'

I had nothing left. 'It won't work,' I said.

Druce chuckled and leaned back. 'It's working already! Why won't you believe the evidence of your own eyes, Adam? You told me yourself you thought there was something strange, something different, about the people on this island, didn't you? How do you think that happened?'

'I don't fucking know. Training. Conditioning. Culture.'

'Exactly!' Druce threw his arms wide. His eyes gleamed. 'Culture, Adam! The other half of the equation. And we work on both at the same time.' He took a step towards me and studied me with an air of appraisal. 'You'd be the first to admit,' he said, 'that we are more than our genes. Far more. And now we're learning that all the barriers we erected in our thinking, for so many years, are artificial: mind and body, nature and nurture, ideas and feelings, structure and agency – none of these are separate. Everything is interdependent. We live in an age of memes as well as genes, yes? And what we do here is multidisciplinary.

'The different factors you just mentioned – training, conditioning, culture – are developed in tandem with genetic modifications, in terms of both breeding and biological intervention. The different areas of experiment modulate and shape each other, to produce real results, in the real world. We live here in a constantly evolving feedback loop that transcends all preconceived boundaries. It's truly beautiful when you understand it.'

He looked at me expectantly, like a kindly teacher encouraging a dim pupil to see what's in front of his nose. Finally I said, 'I don't care how you dress it up. What you're trying to do is manufacture a certain type of human being, to behave in a certain way. It's eugenics, plain and simple.'

'And I,' Druce said, 'don't care what you call it. It's a process, and it's one we can accelerate, by using the gifts nature herself has given us, as we have always done. Face the facts, Adam. We've always manipulated the development of all manner of species, from apples to bacteria to carthorses. Selective breeding. Encouraging and enhancing what's useful to us, and discarding what's not. Nothing more or less, and we are simply applying those principles to ourselves. That, in essence, was the work begun here in eighteen-fifty-five by Leo Druce.'

It took a moment to hit me. 'He was called Druce?'

'That's right.'

'He was your ancestor?'

Druce nodded slowly. He took a step towards me. 'And yours.'

I was aware of a buzzing in my head. 'Mine?'

'Your great-great-grandfather.'

When I finally spoke my throat was constricted. 'That's not true,' I croaked.

Druce folded his arms and leaned back against the railing. 'Your mother was a capricious woman, Adam. In some ways she was a fantasist. She found it difficult to face the truth, and for that reason she also had a problem *telling* the truth. She was a liar. She lied to you about your father being dead. But I think you knew that, didn't you?'

I had a sensation of settling, and stillness. It was as if a series of heavy, well-made objects had fallen into place inside me, after being misaligned for a long time. I felt both satisfaction and despair, if such a thing is possible. My mind was a blank.

Druce was watching me. 'At the very least,' he said, 'you've suspected the truth since you arrived here on the island and met me, haven't you?'

I thought back. He was right. 'Yes,' I said, 'I think so.'

He nodded. 'Good. You're old enough now. You should know everything, now you've come back to us.'

At first I didn't understand what he meant. When I'd figured it out, I said, 'When was I here before?'

'You were born here. Your mother took you away when you were two. Just after your second birthday, in fact.'

'Why did she take me away?'

'She believed, as far as I could tell, that she was saving you. That was what she said, anyway. She may have been sincere, or convinced herself she was, although I suspect her motives were at least partly selfish. They usually were.'

Druce tilted his head back and observed me from beneath heavy-lidded eyes. I got the impression he was testing me, or even goading me – which may have been the same thing in his mind. I wasn't going to play that game.

'Saving me?' I said. 'From what? From you?'

'From this,' Druce said, sweeping an outstretched arm around. The gesture was consciously theatrical, and the corners of his mouth twitched. 'From the game.'

'Did she think I'd fail? Or was she afraid I'd succeed?'

He made a wavering motion with one hand. 'She couldn't make up her mind. On the whole, I think she was probably afraid you might fail, and that was enough for her, or enough of an excuse. Just before she took you away she told me she wasn't going to risk it, because she was convinced you'd fail. But you wouldn't have failed.'

'How do you know?'

'I know my son.'

I felt a pain in my chest. 'You don't know me,' I spat, as if the words were poison in my mouth.

'I do, Adam. I know everything about you. And I know you're a true islander. Like me. You're a winner.'

'But not like my mother?'

'She came from island stock,' Druce said, 'but she was an outsider at heart. I found her desirable and I told myself we'd breed fine offspring. That was a mistake I've never forgotten. I allowed my desire to blind me, and I convinced myself of something that was untrue. I wanted her, and that made me wrong about her. But I was right about you.'

'Is that what I am? Good stock?'

'Yes. That's why you belong here. Some of the others had doubts, and wanted you to leave, or to get rid of you in one way or another, but I see things more clearly than them. Many of them have good instincts, but they're not entirely free from prejudice.' Druce shrugged. 'Why should they be? It's not necessary. They can function perfectly well in this

213

society without overcoming everything that's irrational in them; in fact it's an advantage – a competitive advantage for the culture as a whole – if many of them remain ignorant, to a certain extent. Every group needs its drones, and its more malleable material, as it were. But it needs leaders, too. This work we're doing won't continue by itself. It requires dynamic stewardship. A strong will, and a clear mind.'

I tried to audit my thoughts and feelings. The truth about my parenthood was like a wall in front of me. I knew there was a door in the wall, but not where it was. I was in shock. And all the time there was a tingling urgency running through me like a taut wire being plucked, and it was my desire to know what was happening with the little freckled girl, and her mother, and the boy behind the glass. I hated myself for it, and Druce knew it, just as he knew about the compulsion that made me want to witness the experiment.

I shook my head. 'This work, as you call it. I don't want to do it. I want no part of it. What you're trying to do is wrong, no matter how you try to justify it. What kind of people are you trying to create, for god's sake?'

'People like you, Adam. Like us.'

'No. Not like me.'

'Yes,' he said fiercely, and pointed at me, as if in denunciation. 'Like you! Be honest! Don't hide from it, don't be a coward! Think, Adam! What is it about you that makes you so good at what you do? When you were in the military, and now, the work you do? What gives you the strength to resist the fears and passions that enslave other men, and to control those feelings? Why do you succeed where others might fail? You know the answer. You know why you succeed.' He lowered his arm and the fierceness left him. He'd made his point.

After several moments I said, 'What happens here, to the

ones who fail?'

'They're cared for. We don't allow them to breed, but they're looked after.'

'Looked after? What does that mean?'

'It means they're cared for, as I said. Cared for very well.'

'Where?'

'In a special place.'

'Where is it?'

'I'll explain that later. But there's something else I want to show you. I think you'll find it interesting. Just for a moment, come and watch this, exactly as Leo Druce would have watched, all those years ago, with no cameras or screens. Which he would have loved, by the way. The new technology. The game evolves, Adam, like everything else. Developments in psychology, genetics, neurology – we've absorbed them all, because they work. Successful adaptation. Now, take a look at that room down there, will you?'

He pointed to a chamber just to one side of the central pillar. I craned over the rail and looked down into it. A boy was sitting on the floor, and an adult was standing just outside the door of the room, unseen by the boy. It was her I recognised first, as I could only see the top of the boy's head. It was Harriet Baird. The child in the room was Logan.

SEVENTEEN

I felt a terrible coldness spreading through me as I gazed down at Harriet and Logan. A few minutes earlier, I imagined I'd shaken off the effects of the drugs, and that my thoughts and feelings had returned to normal, but I was wrong. Nothing had truly dissipated the fog – until now. Something inside me drained away, and the reality of what was happening pierced through everything like a needle. I turned on Druce, possessed by an anger I knew I needed to control. 'Hold on,' I said. 'Just wait.'

'Why?'

'Listen to me,' I said, thinking furiously and trying to sound reasonable. 'You want me to join you, and help you in this... these...experiments, right?'

Druce gave me a long stare. 'I let the wrong one go, perhaps.'

'What do you mean by that?'

He smiled. 'Never mind. It will become clear, no doubt. But the answer to your question is yes, I want you to join me, and help me.'

'If I'm going to do that, I need time to think. I want you to put this on hold. Not for long, but just so I can get a couple of things straight. But stop it for now, all right?'

Druce knew I had no leverage. 'Not possible, Adam,' he said. 'To stop now, even to pause, would be entirely futile. Possibly even harmful.'

'Harmful? You think it's not already harmful? To that child down there?'

I pointed at Logan. Druce glanced down at the chamber, then he took two swift strides towards me and grasped my shoulders. His face was close to mine. 'You're asking the wrong question, Adam. It's not a matter of whether what we do is harmful or beneficial to one particular individual in this process. I know you've just had a shock, and some of this must be difficult for you to process, but try to think clearly. This entire series of tests is part of a collective destiny, and in that sense, any decisions we make based on the perceived wellbeing of one particular child is completely counterproductive. Surely you can see that. Don't allow your judgment to be clouded by an attachment that didn't even exist a week ago. It's absurd. You know that, don't you?'

'A lot can happen in a week. That's what's so strange about feelings. Mine, Harriet's, Logan's. Who knows? Maybe even yours.'

He gazed into my eyes. 'My feelings,' he said, 'aren't going to change, believe me, Adam. Now, are you ready to continue? I don't have time for any more procrastination.'

I lowered my eyes in a kind of gesture of submission, and

nodded. 'All right,' I said. 'I understand what you're saying.'

He released my shoulders. 'Good,' he said, turning to the screens. 'Now, let's see what's up with our friends, shall we?'

Druce adjusted the cameras. On three of the screens, views of Logan appeared. The other three displayed wide shots of the room. Logan was playing with a toy helicopter. It looked elaborate – and probably expensive – with a lot of detail. It was similar to the transport aircraft in which Logan, a couple of days before, had begged Lars Hansen to let him take a ride. The boy was utterly absorbed in his play. Druce toggled a lever on the handset, and one of the cameras zoomed in until Logan's face filled the screen. His expression of total, happy absorption made something inside me lurch.

'Now,' Druce said, 'it's time to move to the next stage.'

The door to the room opened. Harriet stood in the doorway, looking down at her son. He didn't notice her for a few moments, and when he saw her he looked up at her with a smile that had something tentative about it.

Harriet didn't return his smile. She walked up to him, and before she realised what was happening she swooped on the toy and plucked it from his hands. He reached for it, but she held it beyond his grasp.

'That's mine!' Logan said.

'No, it's not, Logan.'

'But you gave it to me.'

'I gave it to you to play with. I didn't say you could have it for ever. And now I'm taking it away.'

'But that's not fair!'

'Logan!' Harriet said sharply. The camera zoomed in to show her in close-up. I could see she was trying to keep her expression impassive, but her eyes were pleading with him not to say any more. He didn't. She turned and left the room, shutting the door behind her.

Logan looked both indignant and bereft, and he was fighting back tears. His lips seemed to be trembling, but when the camera zoomed in, I realised the boy was whispering to himself. Druce adjusted the audio and I heard what Logan was saying:

'They gave it to him,' he murmured, 'and then they took it away, even though it wasn't fair, because Logan didn't do anything bad, but he didn't cry, because it happened to Logan, and that was someone else, and he was a good soldier...'

Druce turned the audio down and looked at me with a smile. 'Well done, Adam. It's a good technique, especially for children, working on the basis that they're already hardwired for narrative. You've taught him a lot in a relatively short time.'

'I think you're giving me too much credit,' I said. 'He's a bright boy, and I just suggested a trick that might help him take a step back; that's all.'

'Exactly so. A step back from his emotions. That's the starting point of all our work here, so I'm very encouraged. The boy has absorbed what you've taught him, and is using it as a way to distance himself from what I refer to as a hot stimulus. However, I must tell you that Logan is still very much a borderline case.'

I tried to sound neutral. 'What will happen,' I said, 'if he fails?'

'I told you. He'll be looked after.'

'Where? Where is the "special place" you mentioned?'

'Later, Adam.' Druce turned back to the screens. 'It's time for the next step.'

I watched as Harriet walked back into the room. Logan stood up. The flicker of hope in his expression faded as he saw that she wasn't holding the toy helicopter.

'Logan, I'm afraid I have some bad news for you,' Harriet said. The odd stiffness in her tone reminded me of the way she'd treated me when I saw her the morning after we'd first slept together – the mask of formality she'd adopted, to defend our secret from other people, or perhaps from herself.

'What bad news?' Logan said. He went up to her and tried to hug her, but she pushed him away gently.

'I gave the helicopter to Alice.'

Logan stepped back and looked up at her, bewildered. 'Why? That's not fair!'

'That's not all,' Harriet said. 'I'm afraid Alice has broken it.'

Logan took a moment to absorb this. 'Really?' he said. 'But is it really broken badly? Can't I try to mend it?'

Harriet shook her head. 'No, it's completely broken. And she did it on purpose.'

'Why? Why did she break it?'

Harriet leaned down and brought her face close to Logan's. 'Because she's very, very naughty. She's a bad girl. And she needs to be taught a lesson, so she doesn't do anything like that again. You can help to do that, Logan.' She straightened up.

I knew what was coming next, and a spasm of dread clutched me. Harriet guided Logan to a chair that faced a control panel, just like the one in the room where we'd seen Tara, the little girl with freckles, being encouraged by her mother to inflict pain on another child. As I watched Harriet showing Logan the controls, something happened to the screen I was looking at. It was becoming cloudy. I realised I was peering at it so closely that my breath was misting it. As I leaned back and rolled my shoulders, trying to loosen the tension from my neck, I saw Druce observing me intently.

'It must be a familiar feeling for you,' he said.

'What are you talking about?'

220

'The moment before it all begins. I expect you're still hoping she won't go through with it. But she will, believe me.'

'If you mean Harriet,' I said, 'what does that prove? She's not happy about it. She's as unhappy as the boy is.'

'You didn't tell her everything, did you Adam?'

'Like what?'

'You didn't tell her about being an interrogator.'

'That was only part of my work in Afghanistan.'

'Yes, the part you didn't tell her about.'

In my mind, I saw the sweltering rooms, darkened against the sun, and other rooms, freezing at night in the mountains. Humans experiencing agonising pain will say anything they think you want to hear. Torture is counterproductive, and not just because it yields unreliable intelligence. It degrades those who use it, to the extent that they themselves become unreliable assets, compromised by what they discover about themselves. I recalled the sense of shame that soured any feeling of triumph whenever I broke a man's resolve, and extracted information. His shame, and mine.

As time went on, I came to detest my co-dependency, until I couldn't do the job any longer, despite the insistence of my superiors that I was good at it. I came close to disobeying a direct order, but I made them believe I was burning out, and they relented. I couldn't have continued. I hated what I was becoming, and I was repelled by a process that reduced humans to a collection of impulses. That was what I told myself. But the truth was that I didn't trust myself any longer. Because a part of me enjoyed it.

And the man now at my side, my father, knew that. Damn his soul.

As these thoughts flashed through my mind, my attention was drawn back to the screens by a sudden movement.

Logan stood up abruptly from his chair. I understood that Harriet had just opened a shutter that had been obscuring the partition between Logan and Alice, who was strapped into a chair in the adjoining chamber. Harriet had explained everything to him, but the actual sight of his friend, helpless and terrified, and the knowledge of what he was being told to do, was too much for him. His mother placed her hands on his shoulders and gently pressed him back into his seat.

'It won't take long,' she said.

'I don't like it,' Logan whispered.

'But you liked the helicopter, didn't you?'

Logan bit his lip and nodded. 'Yes.'

'And Alice broke it, on purpose, just to spite you.'

'She might have been...cross. Perhaps?'

Harriet squatted down beside him. 'Logie, what if I told you I've talked to Lars Hansen? And he says that if you're a good boy, and do as we say, he might let you ride in the real helicopter after all?'

I must have gasped audibly. I felt Druce's hand on my shoulder. I brushed it off and took a step away from him. 'Did you tell her to say that? I can't believe she came up with it herself. It's too...it's evil.'

'I'm sure you don't *want* to believe it, Adam. But are you sure you can't?'

I didn't reply. How well did I know her? Everything I felt about her told me she wasn't doing any of this willingly, but those feelings didn't make anything true. The feelings themselves may not have been true. I no longer knew what was true.

'I'll be honest with you,' Druce said, 'because I respect honesty. This is a collaborative process. A community project, you might say. Our preparations for it are thorough, and there is input from various sources. From me, and from others. Harriet didn't concoct that particular inducement on her own, but she accepted its necessity. I won't pretend she's a wholehearted participant in all this. She, like her son, was a borderline subject. But she knows how important it is for Logan to succeed, and I'm confident she'll do whatever is necessary.'

'What do you mean, she was a borderline subject?'

'Many years ago,' Druce said, 'when she herself underwent this process, I was required to make a judgement on her success or failure. In the event, I gave her the benefit of the doubt.'

'Why?'

'The simple answer is that I wanted to do her mother a favour.'

'Harriet's mother?'

'Yes. Her gratitude was useful to me, and to this community.'

I remembered what Harriet had said about her mother's loyalty to the island, and how she'd kept the truth about her illness a secret, and used it as means to ensure that her daughter made the choices required of her.

'Then it's all bullshit,' I said to Druce. 'It's got nothing to do with the kind of experimental objectivity you're claiming to be guided by, has it? It's all about you manipulating them to get your own way, just like any other cheap charlatan who wants to control people.'

A huge grin spread across his face. It chilled me to the bone. 'Adam,' he shouted, 'I never said I was a fucking saint!' He threw back his head and laughed as if he were possessed. I don't know how long he would have continued if we hadn't both heard, above his laughter, the sound of Harriet's voice issuing a sharp command:

'Do it now, Logan!'

We both turned quickly to look at the screens. Harriet was holding Logan's wrist, having guided his hand to the dial on the control panel. Slowly she let go of his wrist and withdrew her hand. I understood it would be necessary for Logan to take the action himself, without her assisting him. 'Do it now,' she repeated.

Logan was motionless for several moments. Harriet gazed down at him intently. I could see how hard she was trying to control herself. His hand twitched, then he turned the dial a little.

On the other side of the screen, Alice yelped. Her eyes widened and her mouth hung open, as if she were unable to believe what had happened. Logan gazed at her, his face a mess of misery and confusion. It was clear he wasn't receiving the audio feed from the other chamber – not yet. Druce and I, however, could hear audio from both.

'More,' Harriet commanded. 'Turn it more, Logan.'

Logan gave the dial another turn. Alice screamed. Again, Logan saw her reaction but didn't hear it. I wondered if she was able to hear the audio from Logan's side, and I was about to ask Druce, when I saw Harriet abruptly move closer to Logan. She took a deep breath and pointed at the dial. 'More,' she said. 'Turn it until the needle goes into the red part. There, look!'

Logan swung around, his eyes searching her face. 'But...but you said it would really hurt her if I did that. You said!'

Harriet gripped his shoulder. 'But she has to learn her lesson. She broke the helicopter, remember, but she's not sorry. Not yet.'

'How do you know, Mummy? How do you know she's not sorry?'

'Look at her. She's saying she doesn't care.' Harriet pointed at Alice, who was saying something on the other side of the partition.

Druce and I could hear she was saying 'Stop, please stop!' But from Logan's point of view, without the audio, she could have been mouthing almost anything, such was his confusion, and her distress.

'You'll have to do it,' Harriet said. Her voice was steady, but she was still gripping Logan's shoulder, and her knuckles were white. He squirmed, and Harriet realised she was hurting him. She released her grip. 'The sooner you do it,' she said, 'the sooner we can go home.'

Logan was trembling. Harriet leaned down close again. 'Just once,' she whispered to him, 'just get the needle into the red part. It's very important, darling.' She straightened up, and stood stiffly beside him, her hands clenched at her sides. I could see she was fighting to keep it together.

Logan frowned fiercely. His lips began to move. Beside me, Druce operated the handset to move the cameras in to close-up, and adjusted the audio. The boy was whispering to himself: 'Left, right, left, right. Halt. That's an order. Good soldier.' Logan had stopped shaking, and his face settled into an expression of determination. 'Left, right, left, right...'

Beside me, I heard Druce give a satisfied grunt. 'Good job, Adam. That's another effective little trick you've taught him. He seems an eager pupil. What do you think?'

I gazed at Logan, mesmerised. He lifted his hand from the dial, flexed his fingers, and grasped it again firmly. I spun around to Druce.

'Stop it. Stop the game. Now.'

'Out of the question.'

'I'm warning you. Just stop it.'

'Keep your nerve, Adam. That's what you do. It's who you are.'

'If you won't stop it, I will.'

Druce frowned at me. 'What are you going to do? If you intend to assault me, I assure you that would be very foolish. Pull yourself together.'

I said nothing. My back was to the railing. I gripped it behind me with both hands, spun around, and vaulted over it.

EIGHTEEN

The fall can't have lasted more than a second – the drop was thirty feet – but it felt longer. I had to jump at a slight angle to be sure of landing inside the right chamber, and to avoid hitting any of the dividing walls. As I fell, I tried to twist myself into the optimal shape to absorb the impact of landing, and be ready to go into a roll: I kept my body upright, with my legs together, knees unlocked, chin down. I hit the floor of the chamber on the balls of my feet, but they didn't land at the same time, and my weight was distributed unequally. As I went into a roll, I was aware of a sharp pain in my ankle. I came out of the roll and pulled myself up onto one knee, hands splayed down onto the floor, ready to spring up.

Slowly I toppled over. I'd misjudged the injury to my ankle, and I was still full of drugs. It probably would have looked comical in other circumstances. I scrambled up onto one knee again, hoping the ankle wasn't fractured, and looked up.

Harriet's face, white with shock, loomed over me. Logan was frozen in his chair, staring at me with his mouth open. I saw the figure of Druce far above me, leaning over the railing and gazing down at me. His expression was inscrutable. I got to my feet. The ankle was painful, but I was able to stand on it.

'Let's go!' I said.

Harriet gazed at me in astonishment. Logan jumped down from his chair and grabbed her hand. 'Can we, Mummy?' Without waiting for a reply he began to drag her towards the door. 'Let's rescue Alice too!' he said.

Harriet snapped out of it. 'No. Wait,' she said to Logan. 'We don't have time.' She looked at me doubtfully. 'Do we?' I shook my head. She bent down and kissed Logan's cheek quickly. 'We'll get her later, Logie.'

I ran to the door and flung it open, ignoring a hot flash of pain in my leg. I stepped out into a passageway that stretched away on either side. Opposite me was a blank wall. As I tried to figure out which way to go, I heard a door open somewhere to my right and saw two figures emerge into the passage, about a hundred yards away: Barty and Sim. They spotted me and broke into a run, their bulk almost filling the narrow corridor as they came charging towards me.

'This way,' I called to Harriet and Logan, and took off to my left, making sure they followed me. We'd only gone a few yards when Ogden and a man I didn't recognise rounded a corner in the distance up ahead of us, blocking our route, with Meg close behind them.

I paused. Logan and Harriet crowded in behind me, breathing hard. I saw we'd nearly reached an intersection, with a passageway leading off to the left. We ran to the intersection, took the turning, and pounded along the corridor. I looked for adjoining passages, but there weren't any. For all I knew, the only way out of the labyrinth was via the doorway through which I'd entered it, where Druce had met me. As I ran, I tried to force my sense of direction into action, and to see the rooms and passageways around us from above, and to superimpose a map on the maze. We took another turning, and ahead of us I saw the pillar with the ladder bolted to its side. We'd doubled back on ourselves, and were nearly at the point we'd set off from, but at least I knew we could get directly to the entrance from the central pillar. I ran to the pillar, and when I reached it I positioned myself with my back against the ladder. The metal door was at the end of the passage stretching away in front of me. I turned to check on Harriet and Logan, and my heart sank when I saw how distant they were. Barty and Sim were gaining on them.

'Come on!' I yelled to Harriet. When she and Logan had nearly caught up with me, I headed along the passage towards the door. It was only a hundred yards away.

'Adam!' Harriet shouted.

I whirled around to see her struggling to free herself from Sim's grasp, but she had no chance against his massive bulk and strong arms. Behind them, Meg was bearing down on Logan. He made a creditable attempt to kick her shins, but she evaded his flailing feet, spun him around, and secured his arms behind him, pulling him aside to make way for Ogden, Barty, and the other man, who squeezed past her and Sim, and barrelled towards me. I assumed a fighting posture. I knew my chances weren't good, but I was determined to inflict some damage before I went down. When Ogden and Barty were within a few feet of striking distance, I crouched low, preparing to leap upwards at them, and to get under their guard to catch them in the throat. With luck, I thought, I might crush someone's fucking windpipe. I caught a movement at the very edge of my field of vision and someone emerged from a room beside me. I spun around fractionally too late, and a hard object walloped me on the side of the head. As I fell, I saw it was an old-fashioned police baton of solid, polished wood, wielded by sergeant David Glynn.

I must have blacked out for a moment, then I was being carried away, towards the door I'd been trying to reach. Ogden held my arms, clamping my wrists together, and Glynn and Barty had a leg each. In the receding distance, Logan watched me with opened-mouthed horror. Beside him, Harriet kept her eyes on Glynn, looking at him with an expression of weary contempt.

I drifted in and out of consciousness over the next few minutes, which was probably lucky, given the way Glynn, Ogden and Barty manhandled me. I realised they were taking me back up to the house, and they hauled me like a sack of coal along the narrow passageways and up the flights of steps, without troubling themselves to prevent various parts of my anatomy from bouncing off the hard stone.

Their tempers grew even more ugly as they dragged me up what seemed like endless staircases inside the house itself. They were pretty strong, and there were three of them, but I'm not a small man, and I was a dead weight. Eventually they got me up a staircase that was considerably narrower than those below it, and I figured we'd reached the top of the house, where the low ceilings and cramped corridors suggested we were in what must have once been servants' quarters.

They unlocked a door and I was thrown into a room. I tumbled to the floor, and lay there for a moment, trying to get my eyes to focus on Glynn's shiny boots, inches from my face. I didn't like them being so close. I struggled up onto one knee and looked up at him. Ogden and Barty were beside him, and the way the three of them were looking down at me gave me the impression they had a powerful desire to kick the shit out of me, and perhaps to put me to sleep for good. The reason they didn't act upon this impulse became apparent a moment later when they stood aside and Caleb Druce walked in.

He looked at me in silence for a second, then said, 'That was foolish, Adam.'

There was a low, narrow cot along one wall of the room, which had been made into a kind of prison cell. I reached out and grabbed the edge of the cot, and pulled myself up and slumped onto it. 'It depends,' I said, 'who you think the fools are around here.'

'Don't be childish,' Druce said. 'What you did was utterly futile. As well as being foolish, it was destructive and costly.'

'Oh, good,' I muttered. I was finding it difficult to speak, and I felt nauseous. I looked down and tried to breathe evenly. I didn't want to throw up in front of them.

I heard Glynn say something quietly and I looked up to see him standing close to Druce, who was frowning at him. 'No,' Druce said sharply.

'Why not? There's no good reason,' Glynn said.

Druce gripped him by the shoulder. 'I'll be the judge of that, thank you.'

Glynn nodded curtly. Druce released his grip. 'I want him at the graduation,' he said to Glynn, nodding towards me. 'Bring him half an hour before we begin.'

I tried to sit up straight, but the cot was so low that my knees nearly touched my chin. 'I want some water,' I said.

'There's a tap behind the partition,' Druce said. 'And a toilet.

There's an extra blanket under the bed. You'll find none of the bedding can be put to any use other than that for which it's intended, so don't get any ideas. Not that I believe you would. Just make yourself comfortable.' He glanced around the cell. 'This is where we bring children who haven't quite decided how they wish to proceed with the tests. Borderline cases. We bring them here to give them a chance to think things over. I suggest you take the opportunity to do the same, Adam.'

Without waiting for me to reply, he turned to the others. 'I need you all back at your posts. This has cost us too much already.'

He turned on his heel and strode away without looking at me again. Ogden and Barty shuffled out. Glynn gave me a deadpan stare, held it for a few seconds, then walked out. He slammed the door shut and I heard a heavy key turn in the lock.

I felt like shit. I knew I was concussed, and my ankle hurt like hell. In addition, the drugs were starting to wear off.

The partition Druce had referred to was only three paces away, and I wanted to vomit, but I didn't know if I could make it. Instead I collapsed back onto the cot, and darkness fell on me.

NINETEEN

I woke up and crawled to the toilet and vomited, then I drank some water.

I felt a little better, but not much. I had a blinding headache and my ankle was throbbing. I took a look at it, and it was swollen, but I didn't think it was badly damaged. I'd fallen awkwardly on it and twisted it, that was all.

The basin and the toilet behind the partition were made of stainless steel, and were of the type you'd find in any prison: no removable parts, no sharp edges, everything solidly fixed. There was nothing else in the cell except the cot, which was narrower and shorter than a bed would be in an adult prison. There was a small window high up in one wall, and as I looked up at it I caught a glint of light. By flattening myself against the wall and craning my neck back until I damn nearly snapped it,

I could just see the edge of the moon, which at least gave me a rough idea of my orientation. I checked my watch and found I'd been asleep for nearly an hour. That was bad news if I was concussed, but there was nothing I could do about it.

I considered the window again. It was beyond my reach, and would certainly have been beyond the reach of a child, even if they'd stood on the low bed – which wouldn't have helped anyway, because it was bolted to the adjacent wall, well away from the window. They'd thought of everything.

Or nearly everything. I examined the bolts holding the cot to the wall. They seemed secure, but when I shook the bed frame, and tested its rigidity in every direction, I sensed the possibility of movement. I took off my jacket. The cell had been designed to hold children, and if any adults had spent time in there, it was unlikely they would have attempted what I had in mind. I squatted down, as if I were about to do some serious weightlifting, and gripped the edge of the bed frame with my hands wide. I began to tug rhythmically at the frame while twisting it from side to side, gently at first, then building up momentum. After a few moments I heard a faint crunching sound. The plaster around one bolt was beginning to crack. I focused all my efforts on that spot, twisting and tugging until I felt something give, and the corner I'd been working on came away from the wall by about half an inch, bringing brick dust with it. I stopped to take off my shirt and wipe off some of the sweat that slicked me, then got back to work.

It took nearly twenty minutes to get the frame completely clear of the wall. After that I lay down on the bed, trying to reduce the pounding in my head. It didn't work. I got up and dragged the cot into position under the window, with the raised bedhead directly beneath it. I stepped up onto the narrow metal piping of the bedhead and balanced on the balls of my feet. I could reach the window, but I wasn't high enough to get much weight behind any pressure I put on it. I looked more closely at how it was made, and noted the thick glass, reinforced with wire, in a sturdy metal frame. Then I saw something that surprised me. The window had a catch on it, with a short handle. It had been painted over, but it was still there. I looked closer and saw a groove that was designed to allow the window to open, but only by a few inches. But a few inches was a start.

I got down and worked on one of the bolts that had been holding the bed to the wall, and freed it from the frame. Then I got back up onto the bedhead and chipped at the thick paint covering the window catch until I'd got most of it off and could see the brass beneath it. I twisted the handle with all my strength, alternately pulling and shoving it, and finally I got it to move so I was able to push the window open to the end of the groove which restrained it. I rested for a moment and breathed in the cold night air.

Using the bolt as a lever, I began to prise the window out of its frame. The grinding of metal on metal made a lot of noise, and I paused a couple of times to listen for any sign that someone had heard what I was doing, but all I heard was silence, broken by the very distant plashing of water a long way below me.

I stopped worrying about the noise I was making. If anyone had been standing guard outside my cell they would have been alerted by now. After another ten minutes of sweating and heaving, I'd forced most of the metal frame away from the wall, and the window was hanging by one corner. I used the bolt to hammer at the final segment of the frame, then I pushed the window and it fell outwards, clattering against the outside wall as it tumbled down for what seemed a very long time. I heard it smash against something and there was a faint splash as it fell into the water, far below.

There was now a hole in the wall where the window had been. It was roughly two feet square, and I figured I could squeeze through it. But getting through it was the least of my problems, as I discovered when I hoisted myself up and stuck my head and shoulders through the gap. I was peering out of an aperture in a wall of smooth, solid stone. At the bottom of the wall there were rocks, and below them was dark water.

Holy shit, I thought, that's a long way down. It looked like at least fifty feet.

I tried to figure out where I was in relation the rest of the house, and why there was water directly below me. I realised the window overlooked a kind of inlet or fjord that snaked past the back of the mansion, and joined the lake further along the shore. From the outside of the building, you wouldn't have found it until you'd walked all the way around the bulky wing that thrust out awkwardly on its eastern side, and even then, you'd probably have to clamber up the rocky outcrop that enfolded it before it became visible. The inlet was narrow – about twenty feet wide – and it looked deep, but there was no way of knowing that for sure. From up here, a person wouldn't be able to gauge its true depth until they'd dived into it, which seemed like a foolish way to find out if it was shallower than it looked. But if that person had no choice, they'd just have to risk it.

I'd never been much of a diver. I was a keen swimmer as a kid, and I was still good at it, but the prospect of jumping into water from a height had always struck me as a mug's game. I didn't like the way the water went up your nose, and I loathed being submerged for any length of time. And I didn't like heights. That was a challenge I'd faced and overcome as a helicopter pilot, but that was part of the job. Falling into the water just for the hell of it – which was what I considered diving to be – held no appeal for me. But there was only one way out of the cell, and it was through the window, and down into the water; jumping, diving, falling – whatever it took.

To be certain of landing in the water, I needed to propel myself outwards, and get clear of the wall by at least a few feet. If I simply wriggled out of the hole and allowed gravity to take its course, it wouldn't matter how deep the water was, because I'd smash into the rocks before I even got there, maybe head-first. I needed to find other options.

At this point, I felt an absurd pang of self-pity. It was only a couple of hours since I'd swallowed my fear, and leaped over the handrail, and it didn't seem fair that I was facing the prospect of another swift downward trajectory, from an even greater height. It was as if a malevolent spirit had decreed that my first jump hadn't quite been challenging enough, and now the stakes were raised, and I was required to confront not only my fear of heights, but also my prejudice against falling into the water, and if I'd thought thirty feet was bad, try sixty for size, my friend.

I allowed myself a mirthless laugh, and turned around – still balancing on the bedhead – so that my back was to the wall. By standing on tiptoe and arching my back I was able to reach up and out of the aperture, and touch the upper edge of the hole on the outside of the wall. I launched myself upwards – carefully – and landed in a sitting position on the inside windowsill, with my head inside the cell and my backside hanging out of the window. If you've ever been shown around an old Scottish castle, and your guide has gleefully pointed out a tiny chamber, poking from the wall precipitously, at a great height, and described it as 'the lang drap', that, unfortunately, was the image that flashed through my mind. When it had gone, I drew my arms back in and hooked my fingers under the top edge of the opening on the inside. Slowly I drew my knees up, then I manoeuvred myself through the hole, arse-first, until I was bent double, squatting with my feet on the bottom edge of the opening. All that now prevented me from toppling backwards was the grip of my fingertips, pressing against the inside wall.

I didn't look down. It wouldn't have helped. I took as much of a breath as I could, and let go with my fingers, simultaneously pushing myself up and away from the aperture with my feet. I twisted around as I fell, and tried to get myself into an upright position, and to get another breath before I hit the water, but I wasn't quick enough, and my lungs were half empty when my feet broke the surface.

Down, down, down. I knew I should conserve my breath, and not attempt to get back to the surface until I'd finished sinking, but it was difficult to resist the urge to fight my way upwards, especially as the water was so dark, and seemed unnaturally dense.

Finally I felt the momentum of my fall was over, and I began to kick. Nothing happened. I spun myself around, trying to see through the churning, viscous water. One of my ankles was constrained by something thin and white. I panicked, shaking my leg and trying desperately to pull it free. Suddenly it was released. The water cleared momentarily, displaced by my thrashing, and I found myself peering down at what looked like a large sea anemone of some kind, with thick tendrils waving lazily in the peaty water. Abruptly, the swirling water obscured everything around me again.

My lungs were empty now. I stretched my arms out above

me, then drove them back down to my sides as I thrashed with my legs to propel me to the surface. Arms up again, and down. Up...and down. Again, again. It seemed as if I'd stopped moving, and would never get there, then suddenly my head was above the water.

I swallowed great gulps of air. My teeth were chattering, and I knew I needed to get onto dry land quickly. I was cold, I was weakened by the effects of the drugs and their aftermath, and it was possible I'd been concussed. But I didn't get out. I'd glimpsed something down there in the water, and I needed to know what it was. I told myself I was still drugged, and the swirling water could have combined with my own imagination to produce a hallucination. But part of me knew what I'd seen was real. A terrible dread seized me, and I prayed I was wrong.

I took several deep breaths, held the final one, and upended myself. I swam down, and further down. I saw nothing. Just as I began to believe that my own mind had conjured up what I thought I'd seen, I found myself directly above the softly waving tendrils again.

But they weren't tendrils.

They were arms. Small, pale human arms reaching towards me, as if begging me for help. Further down, a face was gazing up at me, its mouth a gaping hole. I recoiled, stiff with shock, and was borne upwards by the buoyancy of the water. After a couple of seconds I forced myself back into action, doubling myself over with a jerk, and fought my way downwards again through the cloudy water.

Then I saw it. A forest of white arms, waving gently. Hundreds of them. And beneath the arms were the ghost-white bodies and the faces – dear God, the upturned, eyeless, howling faces – of countless children, preserved in the peaty water, like specimens in formaldehyde.

This was the special place. This was where the children who failed the tests, and didn't finish the game were 'taken care of' – here, in this terrible liquid mausoleum that entombed them.

I had no air left. I raised my face and kicked desperately, my lungs burning and my throat collapsing on itself in the effort to hold my breath. I saw the surface above me, but it seemed too distant to reach. I raised my arms, and pumped them down through the dense water, pushing myself upwards, but fluid began to flow in through my nose. I felt myself choking. I expelled everything from my lungs, resisting the agonising pressure to fill them. Just as I was about to open my mouth, unable to stop myself from taking a breath, my face broke the surface. I gasped, and took in air, along with liquid – too much liquid, and I felt it begin to fill me. But then the density of the water, which had clung at me when I was beneath the surface, began to work in my favour, and I was able to use its buoyancy to get my head completely clear. My lungs shuddered and water spewed out of me. I devoured the cold night air, coughing and spluttering.

I suppressed my instinct to strike out for the shore, and instead I waited, treading water, while I got my breathing under control. All the time I was horribly aware of what was beneath me. The pale, drifting arms, the open mouths. The bodies, so small.

Eventually I felt strong enough to swim towards the shore, about thirty yards away.

I hauled myself up onto the rocks. I wanted to rest, but I needed to get warm, and although it was late summer, the night was cold. I knew I should keep moving, and keep my blood circulating, until I found a place where I could at least wring the water out of my clothes, if nothing else. I was shivering violently. I looked around. Behind me was the sheer wall and the window I'd jumped from, a small square of light high above me. I needed to get well away from there, wherever I went. I scanned the terrain. The mouth of the inlet, where it opened into the main part of the lake, was about four hundred yards away to my right. In the opposite direction, where the inlet narrowed, it curved as it made its way inland, and I couldn't tell where it went, and whether I'd end up being trapped if I went that way. It looked as though it snaked up into the hills, and I couldn't face a climb even if I'd wanted to take that route.

I headed for the lake, scrambling across the rocks. In some places they were steep and jagged, and I made slow progress, especially as I was being careful with my ankle. It hadn't got any worse, but it was still painful, which was reassuring, in a way: if it had been broken or fractured I probably wouldn't have been able to feel it by now, and that would have meant serious problems. As I got closer to the mouth of the inlet, I saw it was tucked away behind an outcrop, which was why you couldn't see it from the lake until you got close. At a point just before the inlet met the lake, the rocks fell away and the ground flattened out into a kind of low plateau, like a flat stone platform abutting the water. It was a wide area, but it was still concealed from a frontal view if you were looking from almost any point around the shore of the lake. There must have been a track leading to it, and a dozen vehicles were parked along the edge of the stone platform, Finn's van among them. I thought about checking to see if any of the vehicles had their keys in them, but decided against it. My shivering was becoming more extreme, and I was starting to shake spasmodically. I knew I'd be in trouble if I didn't find cover soon.

I made my way to the mouth of the inlet, moving at a crouch, and emerged onto the shore of the lake itself. The front of the house was now about a quarter of a mile away, to my left, across pretty rough terrain. But behind the shoreline, as the ground sloped up into the hills, there was some thick woodland, and I began to tack towards it, moving crab-wise up and along the rocks. I hoped the trees would at least give me a certain amount of protection, and I wondered if I'd have the strength to build a shelter. Even thinking about the prospect made me weary.

As I reached the treeline, I saw a clearing at the edge of it, and a small wooden building. I recognised it as the hunting lodge from the old photographs I'd looked at with Harriet and Logan when we were inside the house. I skirted the edge of the clearing, trying not to get my hopes up. The lodge – more of a cabin, really – was dark, and it looked unoccupied. I approached it from the back, and found a dusty window, but I couldn't see through it. The window was reinforced, and set very securely into the wall. The same had been true of the window in my cell, and I'd managed to bust through that, but I'd expended a lot of time and energy in the process, and now I was short of both commodities. I circled the lodge, but the windows in the side walls were as thick and secure as the one at the back. Far from being discouraged, I began to feel increasingly optimistic: I figured that if someone had taken so much trouble to prevent people breaking in through the windows, maybe there was something valuable inside, and I hoped I was right about what that might be. It was a hunting lodge, after all. Strangely enough, when I'd worked my way around to the front of the building, I found that the door was the most vulnerable point. It was secured by a big, beefy padlock, but a padlock is only as strong as the loop that the pin goes through, and the metal plate securing it, and the hasp that hinges over the plate – all of which, in this case, were screwed to a wooden wall and a wooden door. It took me less than a minute to find a suitable rock, and not much more than another minute to bash the hell out of the metal plate, and prise it out of the splintered wood to which it had been screwed.

I kicked the door open and edged in. There was a light switch at my shoulder but I didn't use it. Moonlight was seeping through the window on one side and when my eyes had adjusted I looked around, still pressing myself against the wall, and I saw what I was looking for. A tall, narrow cabinet, bolted to the wall. It was secured by two padlocks, and while they weren't as hefty as the one I'd dislodged from the front door, they looked pretty solid. The rock was still in my hand, but I scanned the room, hoping to find something more useful. One corner served as a rudimentary kitchen area, with a sink and a two-ring camping stove on a table beside it, but no sign of a gas bottle. There were a couple of drawers in the table. I crossed the room and pulled open the drawers. Among the assorted cutlery and implements I found a carving knife, and a long, thick sharpening steel. I crossed back to the cabinet on the wall and used the sharpening steel as a spike to lever open the top padlock, bashing the handle with my rock to force it into the lock until it popped, then I did the same with the bottom one.

Holding my breath, I opened the cabinet. Four shotguns. There was a small wooden case beneath them that was locked, and which I simply smashed at with the rock until I could rip the lid off, and saw what I'd hoped to find in there, namely several boxes of shells. I opened one of the boxes. The shells, with their fresh red plastic bodies and gleaming brass bases, possessed unsurpassable beauty to me at that moment.

As I took one of the shotguns from the rack I began to

shudder and almost dropped the weapon. With shaking hands I replaced it in the rack and began to rub myself frantically, slapping at my arms and legs, trying to get my circulation going.

There was a stove in the middle of the opposite wall, and a big basket of logs beside it, but there was no way I could risk starting a fire, and it would take too much time. I peered around the room again. It held nothing but a faded old couch, a couple of rickety armchairs, a card table, a dining table, and a glass-fronted cabinet containing an assortment of mismatched plates and cups. Then I saw it. Tucked under the table where I'd found the cutlery, right back against the wall, was an old two-bar electric fire. I dived under the table, fished it out, and plugged it into a socket in the back wall. I felt the blood pounding in my head as I prayed it would work, and switched on the socket. Nothing. Then I examined the back of the fire – and saw two switches, one for each bar. I flipped one of them, and immediately one of the bars glowed red. I felt like a man at the bottom of a well who sees a ladder being lowered down to him. I pulled the fire as far away from the window as I could, and closed the front door, then I dragged one of the armchairs over and placed it in front of the fire. I decided to risk the second bar. It worked, and nothing popped or fizzled.

I stripped off my clothes and draped them over the chair, wringing out my socks and underwear before I positioned them carefully to get maximum heat without scorching them. As I'd expected, I felt warmer naked than I had with my wet clothes on. I went back to the cabinet and examined the guns. There was a lovely Purdey over-and-under, with a lot of fine engraving, that would probably fetch at least twenty grand on the open market. Two of the other guns were also quite fancy, but I selected the simplest and plainest gun, which was an old

Charles Lancaster, in excellent condition, with twin barrels whose chambers had been extended to take modern loads. I found the right shells, loaded the gun, and hefted it, and I felt very comfortable with it.

My socks and underwear were getting dry, and although the rest of my clothes were still damp, they'd warmed up a little, and I got dressed. I tipped a handful of shotgun shells into the pocket of my coat, and took the remaining boxes outside, and flung them into the undergrowth behind the cabin. I did the same with the three remaining shotguns. I knew they weren't the only guns on the island, but anything that improved my odds was worth doing. I returned to the cabin, turned off the fire, and stepped out into the night.

TWENTY

I began to weave my way down from the cabin to the shore, and almost immediately I saw a glow in the distance, coming from the inlet. I dropped to a crouch and moved along the edge of the treeline. After a couple of minutes the glow increased and I was able to see individual points of light. As I got closer, the lights rounded the mouth of the inlet. They were blazing torches, held aloft by a big crowd. At least fifty people. They were heading for the low plateau of rock at the edge of the lake where I'd found the parked vehicles. I moved further back into the trees and straightened up. I'd been carrying the shotgun in the crook of my arm, broken, and now I snapped the barrels back up into position with a satisfying click. I began to jog along just inside the treeline, parallel with the moving lights, keeping pace with them.

When I was about two hundred yards from the torchlit procession I saw it was coming to a halt. I loped down through the trees towards the shoreline, veering to my left so I could get myself behind an outcrop of rocks. I dropped down behind the rocks and crept closer to the gathering. Once I'd got nearly as far as I could, I lay down on my belly, crawled forward gingerly for a final few yards, and cautiously raised my head. I was close enough now to pick out individual faces, illuminated by the flickering light of the blazing torches, and I recognised many of the people I'd encountered on the island since my arrival. I couldn't see Harriet and Logan, but I was getting only a partial view through gaps in the rocks, and I couldn't risk getting closer, or trying for a better sightline, without becoming exposed. As I watched, the crowd formed itself into a semicircle around the flat rock, facing the water. When they were in position, everyone became very still, and an eerie silence descended.

Caleb Druce stepped forward. Then I saw that the silent crescent of torch-bearing islanders enclosed a cluster of about a dozen children, isolated in the middle of the platform. They were as still and silent as the adults, and it struck me that if any of them wanted to get away, the only way they could go was towards the water. Before I could get a better look at the children, and identify any of them, Druce moved forward again, blocking my view of the little group. He began to speak.

'My dear companions,' he said in a loud, clear voice, 'we are the true people of the island. We are strong and free, and we rejoice in our strength and freedom. I salute you, every one of you. My pride in you, and what we have accomplished together is immeasurable. Thank you. Thank you from the bottom of my heart.'

He turned to look down at the children. 'My dear young

friends,' he said, dropping his voice a little, forcing me to strain to catch what he was saying, 'each one of you is precious, and you are our future. We care for you, and we cherish you. We are glad when we see you are strong and healthy, and we are unhappy if we see that you are weak and sick. This is the way of the island, and the people of the island.'

Druce paused for a moment, and I saw one or two of the torches waver – just a fraction, but enough to confirm my sense that a ripple of tension was running through the assembly. Something was about to happen.

'Being weak,' he continued, 'is a sickness itself. Even if you don't feel unwell, it is a sickness. That is the sad truth. And we must protect ourselves from sickness. We don't want it to spread. That's only natural, isn't it?'

Druce stooped down a little and reached into the cluster of children. When he straightened up his hand was resting on a small shoulder. It belonged to Alice – Logan's friend – and he drew her gently forward, away from the other children.

'This child,' he said, 'is weak and sick. Our dear little friend, Alice, must leave us. We know it must be so, and she knows it too. Isn't that right, Alice?'

The child raised her head slowly to look at Druce. I saw that her eyes were blank and her face was expressionless. She was in some distant, empty place. Druce took her hand, and she allowed him to lead her to the end of the flat outcrop of rock. He moved into position behind her, and with his hands on her shoulders he manoeuvred her to within inches of the edge, where she stood, gazing out over the dark, moonlit water whose still surface reflected the flickering torches behind her. She remained perfectly immobile.

Druce stepped back and turned to survey the remaining children. 'There is someone among you,' he said, 'who can help

Alice. Who is it? Who will prove their strength and freedom? You know who you are. You know you have doubts. But by helping Alice, you can overcome your weakness, and stand proudly as a true islander. Face your fear. Do what is right. Come forward.'

The cluster of children parted, revealing Logan, who was standing in the centre of the group. He took a few tentative steps towards Druce, then stopped. He was trembling.

I caught a slight movement among the adults, and one of the torches appeared to dip for a moment, but everyone settled into stillness again before I could tell exactly where it had happened. Druce raised his head and looked around at them slowly. Nobody moved. He nodded briefly, satisfied. He returned his attention to Logan.

'Good boy, Logan,' he said. 'This is your chance. Your chance to put all doubts aside, and to prove you are worthy.'

He beckoned to Logan. The boy took another step forward, and paused. He glanced fearfully towards Alice. She was still gazing out at the lake, motionless, poised above the surface of the dark water.

'Don't worry,' Druce said to Logan, 'you won't hurt her. She knows she can't stay with us, and she wants you to help her. Come along. Be strong, Logan.'

Logan took a deep breath and began to walk forward again. Druce stood aside, and as Logan reached him, he placed a hand on the boy's shoulder and guided him the remaining few steps to the edge of the plateau, until Logan was standing directly behind Alice. Druce stepped away. Logan glanced at him, trying to control his expression, and Druce nodded. The boy turned again. His face was only a few inches from the back of Alice's head. A very slight breeze stirred her hair, but otherwise she remained utterly motionless, and gave no sign she was aware of Logan so close behind her – or of anything that was happening. Logan raised his arms.

A voice cried out. It was Harriet, calling her son's name. I saw her now, lurching forward. She was trying to break out of the semicircle of adults, but she was being restrained by the man beside her – David Glynn. As she tried to call out again he clamped his hand over her mouth and pulled her back roughly.

As Logan heard his mother's voice he spun around, but Druce stepped forward swiftly, blocking the boy's view of her. Logan tried to peer past Druce, but the doctor reached out and cupped the boy's chin in his hand, tilting his head up so their eyes met. Druce held his gaze. 'Do it now, Logan,' he said, and took his hand away.

Logan leaned forward and placed his hands against Alice's back. His legs were shaking. He closed his eyes and his lips began to move. After a moment I saw that he was bracing his feet. He was about to push her into the water.

'Stop,' I shouted, and stood up. I pointed the gun at Druce, and kept it trained on him as I clambered over the rocks that had been shielding me. Once I was on level ground, I strode to the limit of the stone ledge, where it overlooked the water, and positioned myself beside Logan and Alice.

'Logan,' I said, 'step back.'

Nothing happened for several seconds. Finally Logan lowered his hands and took two shuffling steps backwards, away from the girl.

'Alice,' I said softly, 'turn around.'

She didn't move, or give any indication she'd heard me. I lowered the gun for a moment and reached out to pluck at her shoulder, but as I did so, Druce took a step forward. I raised the gun again and gave him my full attention.

'Adam,' he said, 'I was hoping you would join us for the graduation, but I'm afraid you're interrupting us at an important moment. Please allow us to continue.'

'No,' I said, 'this stops now.'

'You're not thinking, Adam.'

'I've done enough thinking. Get back. Over there.' I gestured with the gun. Druce seemed to be considering his options. I pulled back one of the twin hammers and cocked it, and raised the weapon to point directly at his chest. He backed away, and I advanced on him, making him retreat until he was standing at one end of the semicircle. Keeping the gun trained on him, I walked diagonally towards Glynn, who still had one arm around Harriet's shoulder, holding her tightly, although he'd removed his hand from her mouth. I swivelled the gun in Glynn's direction. We locked eyes.

'Let her go,' I said.

He hesitated. His eyes flicked towards Druce, who was within my field of vision, and close range of the gun, but I didn't turn to look at him. I kept the gun on Glynn. I didn't see whatever passed between him and Druce, but he returned his gaze to mine and began to remove his arm slowly from around Harriet's shoulder, staring at me stonily all the time. Harriet shook herself free and ran to Logan, and dropped to her knees and hugged him. Beyond them, Alice was still standing at the plateau edge, facing the water. I walked backwards with the gun at waist-height, swinging it in a smooth arc between Glynn and Druce, taking in the arc of the crescent. I stopped when I was beside Alice again. Harriet was a few yards to my right, now standing behind Logan with her arms encircling him. She didn't look frightened, but she was breathing heavily. I turned my head slightly and spoke Alice's name. She didn't react.

'It's too late,' Druce called to me. 'She's heavily sedated. A drug is working its way through her system. All this has been precisely timed so she will feel nothing. She's gone, Adam.'

A careful sideways step brought me closer to the girl. I glanced at her profile. Her eyes were wide and unblinking. Slowly I reached out to touch her hand. It was cold. I grasped it more firmly, and pulled her gently towards me, away from the water. Alice seemed to crumple, and she fell to the ground as if she'd been made of paper and had been held upright by nothing but air. She was lying on her side, with her face towards me, and I could see it was deathly pale. She showed no more awareness than a waxwork.

Harriet clutched at Logan and swung him around, pressing his face against her body so he couldn't look at Alice.

I knelt down, still keeping the gun raised, and felt for a pulse in Alice's neck, but didn't find one. As I moved my fingers, hunting for any sign of life, I felt a tiny flutter in her throat, and heard a faint rattle, then a slow, exhausted gasp as her final breath left her.

I stood up and stared at Druce, searching for some acknowledgement that a small child had just died as a result of decisions he'd taken. He folded his hands in front of him, in a gesture that made him look monkish, and met my gaze impassively. I looked around at the other adults. They appeared solemn, but none of them betrayed any sign of being disturbed by what was taking place. They were more like a church congregation, participating in a service that evoked in them a sense of both awe and fulfilment.

I turned to Harriet. 'Let's go.'

She gazed at me expressionlessly. My stomach lurched. I had no idea what I'd do if she refused to leave with me. But after a couple of seconds she seemed to snap out of a trance. She grasped Logan's hand, and led him to where I was standing.

'Stay very close behind me,' I said, and stepped forward.

Caleb Druce spread his arms and moved towards me. I raised the gun to my shoulder and sighted down the barrel at him. He halted, and stood there, arms outspread, like a sacrifice. 'You're my son,' he said.

'I'm leaving.'

'You can go. But you can't leave.'

'I don't need any pseudo-mystical bullshit, thanks,' I said. 'Dad.'

He gave me a faint smile. I walked towards his end of the semicircle, with Harriet and Logan behind me. When I was a few yards from my father, he lowered his arms and stepped aside. The people next to him did the same, and parted to make way for us.

As we went through, I swivelled around so I could keep the gun pointed at them. I said to Harriet, 'We're taking one of those cars.' She put a hand on my shoulder, so she could help guide me backwards towards the parked vehicles, while I kept the assembly covered, although nobody showed any indication of trying to make a move.

'Logie,' I said, 'can you do something for me? See if any of those cars are open. If any of them have got the keys in, take them out and bring them to me. Will you do that?'

'OK,' Logan said, and trotted away.

'Guide me to the Land Rover,' I said to Harriet. I wanted a rugged vehicle, in preference to any of the saloon-type cars, and I knew I could start the Land Rover pretty easily if the keys weren't in it.

'It's at the end,' she said, and steered me to my left. After a few moments I decided we were far enough from the assembly – where everyone was watching us, but nobody was moving –

and turned my back on them, and ran to the old Land Rover, with Harriet beside me. Logan rejoined us as we reached the vehicle, and held out four sets of car keys, breathing heavily. 'The others didn't have keys and three were locked,' he gasped.

I took the keys. 'Good boy.'

Harriet opened the driver's door of the Land Rover. 'The keys are in the ignition,' she said. 'You drive.'

'Sure, but start it up for me, will you? And take this, and keep an eye on them.' I handed her the gun, and ran to the water's edge, where I flung the car keys Logan had given me into the lake. I heard the Land Rover starting up. When I got back, Harriet led Logan around to the passenger side, where she lifted him onto the bench-type seat and clambered in behind him, still holding the shotgun. I got into the driver's seat, shifted into gear, released the handbrake, and swung us in a tight arc, tyres spinning as we hit the track that ran along the shore of the lake.

Harriet broke the shotgun and folded it over her thighs. She leaned out of her window to check the track behind us, keeping one arm around Logan's shoulders as he nestled into her, his eyes fixed on the road ahead.

'The ferry is in the harbour,' I said.

'What about Archie?' Harriet said.

'He's...not there,' I said.

'Did you see him?'

I didn't reply. She glance at me enquiringly, and I cut my eyes at Logan, and let her see me do it, and shook my head. She understood that something was badly wrong, and took a deep breath. Logan saw that something was up.

'Are we going to see Archie?' he murmured.

'I'm not sure, darling,' Harriet said. 'Perhaps another time.'

'Why not now?'

254

'Harriet glanced at me. 'He had to go away,' she said to Logan, 'but he's lending us the ferry. Isn't that right, Adam?'

'That's right.'

'But how can we drive it without Archie?' Logan said.

'We'll manage,' I said. 'It will be fun. You can help.'

Logan nodded slowly, but didn't say anything.

We'd now driven half way around the lake, and reached the point where we could turn off the track and get onto the road. I took the turning without slowing down, shifting to a lower gear and accelerating up the incline. As soon as we were on the road, I drove as fast as the Land Rover would go without losing traction altogether on the corners.

'There's a turning,' Harriet said, 'coming up on the left. We can cut across the top of the valley and bypass Creedish, and get back on the main road as it goes down to the harbour. Coming up now. Here it is.' She braced herself and held onto Logan as I took the turn. The road was steep and twisting, and I changed up and down through the gears all the time, trying to maintain maximum possible speed.

I glanced at Logan. 'OK, Logie?'

He didn't reply. Harriet drew him closer. 'We're going away. With Adam.'

'Where to?'

'We don't know yet,' Harriet said. 'It's an adventure.'

Logan sat up in his seat, pulling away from his mother slightly. He looked around, suddenly appearing to be more alert. 'Am I an islander?' he said.

'Not for ever,' I said. 'You're just you, Logan.'

'I played the game.'

'That doesn't mean anything,' I said. 'The game isn't like real life, Logie. It's just an idea made up by doctor Druce, and he tries to get everyone to agree with it. You don't have to go along with it if you don't want to.'

'All my friends did it,' Logan said.

I didn't know what to say to that. I saw Harriet open her mouth to speak, but she thought better of it. Neither of us wanted to start talking about Logan's friends. We didn't want to say anything about Alice. But our silence didn't do any good.

'Alice was weak,' Logan said, 'and I was going to kill her.'

'But you didn't!' Harriet said. 'You didn't, darling, and that's what matters!'

'Why?' Logan said.

'Because it's not right. And I'm glad you didn't do it, because I love you.'

'But now I'll never know.'

Harriet leaned forward, and craned around to gaze into his eyes. 'What do you mean, darling?'

'I'll never know if I could do it. If I'm an islander.'

'I don't care if you're an islander, Logie. What I care about is that you're my son, and I love you. I love you so, so much.'

I heard the catch in her voice. She was on the verge of tears, trying to keep it together. I focused on my driving, and we were all silent.

Harriet cleared her throat. 'Here's the harbour road. Go right at the junction.'

I slowed down and took the turning, and we emerged onto the main road at almost its highest point, just below where I'd stopped with Druce – my father, I had to remind myself – on my first day. Beyond us in the distance, spread out like a vast sheet of grey slate infused with a dim, sullen glow, was the sea. We were only a couple of miles from the harbour now. Downhill all the way.

TWENTY-ONE

As we sped down the hill towards the harbour, I was aware we were approaching the blind corner where I'd been blocked by the tractor in the morning – it was hard to believe it was still the same day – but I simply assumed it would have been moved. The last time I'd seen it, Barty was using it as a battering ram, trying to crush me as I scraped past it, and in my mind's eye he wouldn't have just left it there blocking the road.

But that's exactly what he'd done.

I slammed the brakes on and the Land Rover went into a skid, and I flung out my arm, trying to protect Harriet and Logan. We hit the tractor's wheel, but my outstretched arm was too high to restrain Logan as he was thrown forward by the impact. His head struck the dashboard. Harriet grabbed his shoulders and pulled him upright. His eyes were closed and blood welled up in a diagonal streak on his forehead. I opened my door and jumped out, and ran around to the passenger door. 'Come on,' I said to Harriet, 'and I'll get him out.' I helped her down, then leaned into the cab, and got my hands under Logan's shoulders and pulled him gently out of the vehicle. I cradled him in my arms and looked closely at his face. 'I don't think it's too deep.'

'Give him to me,' Harriet said. As I transferred the boy to her arms, his eyelids fluttered. 'Logan,' she said, 'it's all right, darling.'

'Shit,' I said. Harriet glanced up and saw what I was looking at: headlamp beams slicing up into the sky, then dipping down as vehicles crested the hill a mile behind us.

'Oh god,' she said. She looked around and jerked her head at the tractor, and the Land Rover rammed up against its wheel. 'But they won't get past that lot in a hurry.'

'It's going to slow them up,' I said, 'but they'll move it. There's a lot of them.'

'We can still make it on foot.'

'OK, I'll carry Logan. Get the shotgun.' I held out my arms for the boy.

'We can cut across the fields,' she said, nodding at a gate fifty yards beyond the tractor. 'Here.' She passed Logan to me, and reached into the cab of the Land Rover for the gun. We edged around the front of the tractor, and jogged to the gate, which Harriet opened. It led into a field that rose up steeply ahead of us. I wished I could have carried Logan over my shoulder, but if I didn't keep his head up there was a risk of more bleeding – which had almost stopped – so I hoisted him higher in my arms and set off behind Harriet as she made her way up the steep hill. She glanced over her shoulder occasionally and raised an eyebrow, to which I responded with a nod to confirm I was

OK. Neither of us wanted to waste our breath on conversation.

After five minutes I wondered how much further uphill we'd have to go. Logan wasn't a big child, but he seemed to be gaining weight with every step I took. I was relieved when a few seconds later Harriet stopped and turned to me.

'This is the top,' she said, panting. 'Downhill from here.'

I joined her at the top of the rise. 'Give me a second,' I said, and lowered Logan to the ground, and sat down. I just needed to catch my breath.

Harriet knelt beside me. 'Want me to take him?'

'Nope, I'm good.'

'Look,' she said, pointing behind me, 'they can't have reached the tractor yet.'

I turned and saw that the beams of light from the headlamps of the vehicles pursuing us were still dipping and swinging. I glanced at Logan, then I grasped Harriet's arm. 'Quickly,' I said in a low voice, 'just tell me one thing. Did you set me up?'

Harriet's eyes widened. 'What do you mean?' she hissed.

'Did you seduce me because Druce told you to?'

'Fuck you. Do you really think I'd do something like that?'

'Sorry. I just needed to—'

'Druce doesn't care. Don't you understand that? It's all just an interesting experiment to him. Once he'd told me who you were, he just wanted to see what happened. That's all he ever wants. He—' she broke off, looking at something behind me. 'Shit,' she said, 'I spoke too soon.'

The lights from the road were no longer moving. The convoy had reached the tractor. I got to my feet and picked Logan up. He was still a dead weight, but as I looked down at him he opened his eyes fully and blinked. 'Hey there,' I said, 'just rest for a bit. We'll be fine.' Logan nodded and closed his eyes again.

Harriet led the way down through the field ahead of us, and the going was much easier than the uphill trek we'd just taken, although the muscles in my arms were still aching. It took us only a few minutes to reach the bottom of the field, where Harriet opened another gate. 'We need to get back on the road for the last bit,' she said.

We came out of the field and onto the road at the point where it took the final curve down into Tallog Bay. As we turned the corner, the sea came into view again. The light was changing and it would soon be dawn. I saw the ferry, still moored at the quay, bobbing serenely, and I felt a sickening drop in my stomach as I remembered it was concealing a corpse that floated between its hull and the harbour wall.

We hugged the side of the road as we made our way down to the harbour, glancing over our shoulders every few steps. When we reached the quayside, I lowered Logan to the ground and Harriet knelt down beside him as I bent over, standing with my hands resting on my knees, breathing deeply.

'Mummy,' Logan said, and Harriet helped him to sit up. She wiped his face gently, and I saw that the cut had stopped bleeding.

'OK,' I said, speaking between gulps of air, 'I'll...go. And start...the boat.'

Harriet looked up a me. 'Let's all go and get on it now.'

'No,' I said. 'Stay here with the gun. Keep it trained on the road. In case there's a problem with the boat.' It was true that I was concerned about getting the boat started, but I also wanted to ensure that Harriet and Logan came on board at the last possible moment, so there was less chance of Logan catching sight of Archie's body. Harriet nodded, and stood up. She positioned herself between Logan and the approach to the quayside, pointing the gun back up towards the road.

I caught Logan's eye and winked at him. 'Look after your mother for me. I'll just get the boat started and we'll be off. Not long now, Logie. Good boy.' I straightened up and jogged along the jetty. I jumped onto the boat without looking down into the water beside it. Either Archie's body had worked its way free, and wasn't there, or it was still trapped between the hull and the wall, in which case I didn't need to see it.

Once I was in the wheelhouse I ran my eye over the controls. They looked pretty basic. I located the ignition button and pressed down on it. The engine turned over, coughed twice, and died. I wondered if I needed to open some kind of feed for the fuel, but I couldn't locate anything that looked like it did that job. I tried the ignition again, but the same thing happened as before. I studied the controls, and found something that looked like the choke in an old-fashioned car. I pulled it out about halfway and tried the ignition again. This time the engine nearly fired, so I pushed the choke back in a little, tried once more – and it caught. I felt the boat pulling at the mooring rope and realised the engine was already engaged in its drive setting. Rather than spend any time trying to figure out how to disengage it, I set the throttle to idle at the lowest possible revs, and hoped the ropes would hold the boat back.

I climbed down from the wheelhouse, ran to the side – and froze.

On the quayside, all the islanders who had been at the graduation ceremony were now facing Harriet in a silent, curved line – an eerie re-enactment of the semicircle they'd formed at the lakeside. Logan was crouched behind Harriet, who had the shotgun levelled at Druce. He was standing in front of the others, and now he began to walk slowly towards her.

I sprang onto the jetty and sprinted along it. When Druce

saw me, he paused as if he was happy to wait for me to join him, and glad I could make it. As soon as I reached the cobbled surface of the quay, two big men stepped forward – Ogden and Sim. Behind them was David Glynn. I came to a halt and glanced at Harriet. She seemed paralysed, but I saw that her finger was curled around the gun's triggers, and both hammers were cocked. It would take only the slightest pressure to fire the gun.

'Harriet,' I said, but she didn't respond, or even look at me. He eyes were wide. I was aware that Ogden and Sim had separated and were circling me, one on either side. I didn't move. Glynn walked up to me, and stood for a moment, gazing at me with narrowed eyes. He stepped back and nodded to the two men, who moved in and took an arm each. I allowed them to pinion me, and they probably imagined they were gripping me tightly enough to immobilise me. They weren't, but I didn't intend to prove it at that particular moment.

Druce shot me a thoughtful look, and I got the impression he knew as well as I did that I could have freed myself if I'd wanted to. He turned back to Harriet.

'Put down the gun,' he said.

I said, 'Don't listen to him, Harriet.' Finally she looked at me and her face was as white as chalk. I tried to keep my tone calm. 'Harriet,' I said, 'tell Logan to go to the boat.' I raised my voice a little and said, 'You hear that Logie? Go to the boat. Your mother wants you to.'

Glynn moved into my eyeline again. 'You,' he said, pointing at me, 'leave my son alone.' He moved past me and raised his voice. 'Stay there, Logan,' he said, 'and Harriet, put that gun down. I'm warning you.'

I looked at Harriet. Her jaw was clamped and her gaze was fierce, but there was an odd movement in the muscles of her face, almost as if another, different face were beneath it, whose expression of anguish was trying to break through to the surface. I turned on Glynn. 'You stood by, and let all this happen to your own son?'

'I did,' Glynn said, 'as my father did before me.'

Druce walked across the cobbles to us and stood at Glynn's side. He put a hand on his shoulder. 'And was I right, David?'

'You were.'

Druce patted Glynn's shoulder and turned to me. 'You see, Adam? This is who we are. Your family. David is your brother, and I'm Logan's grandfather. We are your family, and Harriet's family, too.' He nodded to Harriet. She was still keeping the gun trained on him, but now her hands were trembling.

I felt curiously lightheaded, as if something in my mind was being released, like a bird or a tethered balloon. I recalled what Druce said, back in that dreamlike, cavernous space when the experiments were underway – that perhaps he'd let the wrong one go. He'd been referring to me and David. I searched his face, trying to find something in his expression beyond calculation – some sign of warmth or compassion – but all I saw was his perfect self-control, and I had a chilling sense he knew exactly what was going through my mind.

'I came to an agreement with your mother,' he said. 'I allowed her to take you away, and in return David was to stay. It was easier than opposing her, and perhaps getting rid of her, which could have entailed a risk. She was an islander, but not entirely pure-bred. Of course, we're all immigrants of one kind or another, if you go back far enough, but there was a relatively recent branch of her family still on the mainland, a great-uncle and his wife and son, and they could have made trouble. They're gone now. But I don't regret anything. I'm proud of David. We don't always see eye to eye, but I know he's loyal. To me, and to us. That's what families are about, Adam: loyalty, and sacrifice, and an individual's willingness to do what is necessary for the greater good. That's what everyone here understands.' He looked around at the semi-circle of silent islanders, and returned his gaze to me. 'We are all a family here, you see.'

'What kind of family,' I said, 'kills its own children?'

'The kind that cares about our future. The kind that's prepared to take tough decisions for the sake of everyone, not just themselves. That's what makes us who we are, Adam. We all know that. All of us here, including Harriet. Which is why she's going to give me the gun.' He turned and took a step towards her. 'Isn't that right, Harriet? You don't have to fight us any longer. You and Logan are safe with us. We care about you. You can give me the gun now.' He reached out and took another step closer to her.

'Harriet!' I called out, 'Don't trust him! They don't care for you!'

She turned her face slowly to me. 'Do you?'

I forced myself to speak. 'Yes,' I said. 'I love you.' I knew she'd seen my hesitation. 'Please believe me,' I said.

'Oh yes,' Druce said. 'Our old friend love. I was waiting for that.' He looked from me to Harriet, and shook his head as if he pitied us. 'Of all the ways that people find to hurt each other, love is probably the cruellest.'

'That's not true,' I said, 'There's more to love than heartbreak.'

'That must be hard for you to believe, Adam, after all you've been through.'

'What are you talking about?'

'Your mother, of course.'

'She loved me.'

'Exactly.'

I felt a bitter taste in my mouth, and my heart was pounding. 'You think you know everything about people, don't you? But no matter how clever you are, you'll never know as much as she did.'

'What did she know? All she knew was how to hurt you. And all your life you've been trying to struggle out of that web of pain she trapped you in.'

'She knew what love is, which is more than you do.'

'You disappoint me, Adam.'

'I don't care. I don't care about you, or what you think. I care about Harriet, and Logan. I'm taking them with me.'

Druce turned his back on me and walked up to Harriet and stood directly in front of her. The gun barrels were shaking. He reached out and grasped them, and placed the muzzles against his chest. He looked Harriet in the eye calmly, released his grip on the gun barrels, and pressed himself against them, spreading his arms. 'You'll have to kill me if you want to leave with him, Harriet. And you'll have to kill David, your child's father. Would you really do something so brutal and insane for the idea of love? That's all it is, you know – an idea. A notion. It has no substance, no reality. Not like you, and me, and Logan, and his father. Shooting me would be real. The cartridges in this gun would tear a gaping, bloody hole in my chest, and kill me. And then you'd have to turn the gun – the real gun – on David, and do the same to him, if you had the presence of mind to fire only one barrel at me, and save the other for the purpose of annihilating your child's father. Destroying him. An eruption of blood and bone and flesh. That's real.'

Even before he finished speaking I saw Harriet's hand tremble momentarily as she took her finger off the triggers. Her body seemed to sag, and very slowly she lowered the gun. I turned my attention to Glynn. He was edging cautiously towards Harriet and Druce. The two men holding my arms were so intent on watching his progress that I could have freed myself from their grasp easily, if I'd wanted to. But there was still a loaded gun at the heart of what was unfolding only a few yards away, and any sudden movement could have had unpredictable and terrible consequences.

From the corner of his eye, Caleb Druce saw Glynn approaching, and took a step back, clearly calculating – correctly – that it would be safer for Glynn to creep up beside Harriet and take the gun from her than for him to attempt it while he was still standing directly in front of her. She'd lowered the weapon, but not completely, and it would take less than a second for her to raise it again and fire it. I waited, running through alternative scenarios in my mind.

Then something utterly unexpected happened. Logan, who'd been crouching behind his mother, noticed that Glynn was edging towards them. In a single movement he sprang to his feet, slipped around his mother like an eel, and pulled the gun from her grasp. He did it so quickly, and Harriet was so unprepared for the possibility, that the gun was out of her hands before she even registered what was happening.

Logan staggered forward as he tried to hold the weapon up. It was much heavier than he'd expected, and it nearly overbalanced him, and the gun barrels swung around wildly for a moment until he steadied himself. He raised the gun with difficulty, and pointed it at his grandfather. Harriet's hands flew to her mouth, stifling a cry, and she reached towards Logan, but he backed away, swinging the gun around again as he tried to prevent the barrels from dipping to the ground. Harriet got down on one knee and held out her hands to him.

'Logan,' she said, 'please give Mummy the gun. Or just put it down. Please, darling, it's very dangerous. We can sort all this

266

out, I promise. Please. Come on, Logie.'

Logan shook his head. He jabbed the gun towards Druce, who flinched very slightly, but controlled his reaction and smiled at the boy. Logan took a small, tottering step towards him. 'We want to go with Adam,' he said.

Druce nodded. 'All right, but perhaps we should wait a moment, Logan. Let's just think about this, shall we?'

'No!' Logan said furiously, the gun almost slipping from his hands before he managed to get it under control again. 'We want to go!' He glanced at me, and I tensed my muscles, then twisted myself free from the hands of the two men holding my arms. They hardly seemed to notice; like all the other islanders, they were gazing at Logan and the gun he was pointing at Druce, mesmerised by the scene, and especially by what Logan was no longer noticing – the stealthy approach towards him of David Glynn.

I moved into Logan's eyeline as I walked towards him. 'Hey Logie,' I said, 'let me come and help you. We can make it a story.'

Logan glanced at me, and his eyes were wild. It wasn't a story, and he was within a hair's breadth of firing the gun. I stopped in my tracks.

At that moment, Glynn launched himself forward and made a grab for the gun. Logan saw him and sprang backwards, jerking the gun out of his reach, and as Glynn lost his balance and toppled over, his outstretched hands knocked against the gun's barrels. Logan staggered, and in his effort to right himself, and keep his grip on the shotgun as he swung it away from Glynn's grasp, his fingers tightened on the triggers.

Druce took both barrels in the middle of his body from a distance of six feet, and the blast nearly cut him in half. His torso erupted in gobbets of pink and purple as he was flung backwards, and slammed into the wall of islanders behind him. He remained upright for a moment, as most of what was left of his insides fell out, then he slid slowly to the ground. He didn't take his eyes off Logan, even as the light within them faded, and they began to glaze.

Logan dropped the gun, and Harriet got her arms around him, and tried to turn his head away. Glynn was still on the ground, where he'd fallen, lying on his side, gazing at the dying man. I ran to the gun, dropped into a roll as I dived for it, and by the time I came out of the roll I was already reloading it. I got to my feet and pointed the gun at Glynn. He knew I was there, but he didn't look up at me until the islanders began to cluster around Druce's corpse. He raised his eyes slowly.

'Kill me,' he said.

'I'm not going to kill you.'

'You know what I've done. To her and to that boy.'

'Whatever you've done, you have to live with it.'

'You too, Adam. All that anger you've got. You hate me, don't you? So do it. Let it all out, and kill me.'

'No.'

He gave a strange, barking laugh and got to his feet. I took a step back, keeping him covered. 'You see?' he said. 'You can control it. You're just like us. Like him.' He turned to look at his dead father – our father – and I saw that the islanders had laid him out on the cobbles. They'd folded his arms together over what remained of his torso, and placed something – a rolled up coat, it looked like – beneath his head, to prop it up. As I watched, I saw Ogden leave the group and walk towards his garage.

Glynn turned back to me. 'It's true, isn't it? You're one of us, brother.'

'I don't think so, David.'

'No? Look at everything you've done since you've been here. You've been in control of yourself all the time. Even with them.' He nodded towards Harriet and Logan, a few yards from us. She was still on her knees, with Logan's head cradled against her. She was looking at me. She seemed completely calm now.

'I love them,' I said, loudly enough for Harriet to hear me.

'Do you, now?' Glynn said. 'Very well, if that's what you want to tell yourself. But I know you better than you know yourself, and you're just like us.'

'No, I'm not. I'm like people who think and feel, and have to deal with the reality that sometimes those two things may be in conflict. It's not perfect, but it's human. It's all part of who we are.'

'It's not who we could be.'

'I don't want to be whoever you think that is.'

'You've got no choice, Adam. And in a week, or a month, or a year, or whenever the time comes, you'll remember this conversation, and you'll ask yourself about those feelings you profess to have, and you'll know I'm right.'

'Get back,' I said, and motioned with the gun.

'No, I don't think I will. I think I'll stay here.' He planted himself squarely in front of me. 'Unless you want to shoot me.'

I faced him in silence for a moment, then I called over my shoulder, 'Harriet, take Logan down to the boat. We're leaving.'

Harriet stood up. 'Come on, darling,' she said, 'this way, eyes front, look where we're going, not behind you, that's a good boy.' She took Logan's hand and led him to the jetty. I began to back away in the same direction.

Glynn folded his arms. 'You know they'll come and destroy us, don't you?'

'You're dead already.'

'Goodbye, Adam.'

As I backed away from him to the top of the jetty, I saw movement among the group of islanders behind him. They'd been clustered around Druce's corpse, and now they stepped back to reveal they'd placed it on a large wooden pallet, that had presumably come from Ogden's garage, the doors of which were now open. Ogden himself was in the process of handing out thick wooden sticks with rags tied around one end. Torches. I spotted Finn, emerging from the garage with two jerry cans. I realised what was about to happen, and I turned and ran.

I caught up with Harriet and Logan as they reached the boat, and I lifted Logan up and swung him onto the deck, then I helped Harriet jump aboard, and whispered, 'Don't let him see what they're doing back there. Take him to the prow.' I unhitched the mooring rope, and as the boat began to move I raced up into the wheelhouse and took the wheel, nosing the boat away from the jetty. I opened the throttle a little and began to swing us around, heading towards a glow of light on the horizon where the sun was just rising. Harriet and Logan were standing at the rail, watching it.

As the boat turned, I caught a sudden flare from the corner of my eye. I looked back to see a column of flame rising from the quayside. They were burning my father's corpse. As the flames rose, the islanders dipped their torches into the blaze then raised them aloft in a spreading circle of light surrounding the funeral pyre. The figure of David Glynn was silhouetted against the flames, standing exactly where I'd left him, arms folded and legs apart, like a sentinel gazing out to sea – and at me.

At that moment I experienced a strange sensation. Suddenly it was me standing there on the quayside. I was inside Glynn, looking out through his eyes at another me, on the boat. It was like being in two places – or two people – at once.

I became aware of Harriet and Logan, squeezing through the doorway of the wheelhouse. Harriet was blowing on her hands. 'Too cold out there,' she said.

I kept my eyes on the horizon, checking that we were heading in the right general direction, which was about the extent of my navigational skills. I expected to see the mainland before too long, and I was reasonably confident I could find the little port from which the ferry sailed. It was the only one along that stretch of coast.

Logan came to stand beside me, and watched my hands on the wheel. After a moment he said, 'Are we dead?'

Harriet whirled around from the window and tried to conceal her shock. She reached out to stroke Logan's cheek. He took her hand, and looked up at me. 'But are we dead, Adam?'

'Hey Logie,' I said, trying to make it seem like he'd asked a perfectly ordinary question, 'why do you say that?'

'Because we're sailing away, aren't we? You said so in the car the other day. You said we're all on an island, and when we die, we sail away on a boat.'

His expression was grave. As I tried to think of how to respond, I saw a low, dark line on the horizon – the mainland. 'Maybe I did,' I said, 'but right now we're not really sailing away. We're just taking a short trip, and we know where we're going. You can even see it from here.'

'That's right, darling,' Harriet said. She hoisted Logan up so he could kneel on the ledge below the wheelhouse window. 'There's the mainland, you see? And you can help Adam by looking out for the harbour, so he can steer us there.'

'Absolutely,' I said. 'That would be great, Logan. Keep your eyes peeled, and as soon as you spot the harbour, give me a shout, OK?'

Logan nodded and put his arms around his mother's neck. I looked at the back of his head, trying to imagine what was in his mind. What would he do with the memory of his grandfather's body disintegrating in front of him, and his eyes clouding in death as they stared at him? I thought about my own buried memories, and the pain of excavating them. I'd made my choices, but Logan had his life ahead of him. I tried to visualise Harriet and Logan and me together, as a family, but I couldn't conjure up a fixed image in my mind. Everything seemed fragmentary and fragile.

I was acutely aware of the island behind me all this time, like a physical force exerting pressure on me. I looked over my shoulder. It was a long way off now, and all I could see of the funeral pyre was a wisp of smoke rising into the clear morning sky. But in my mind's eye I still saw the figure of my brother, David, gazing at me from the quayside, and again I experienced the feeling it was I who was standing there, and my feet that were planted on the cobbles.

I turned back to see Logan looking at me. I smiled, and nodded at the approaching coastline. 'Not long now. Have you spotted the harbour, Logan?'

'I think so.' He twisted around and pointed ahead and slightly to our left. 'That's it over there, I think.'

'I think you're right,' I said, and spun the wheel. I looked at Logan's small, thin arm, still outstretched, as if he were pointing at his own future. He was so young.

No matter how hard I tried to focus on what lay ahead, I couldn't stop thinking about the island. I'd been born there. My father had just died there. My brother was there. I owned the house that brooded at the edge of the lake called Stone Heart Deep. I thought of what David had said, about everything coming to an end. What if I didn't alert the authorities to what had happened? I couldn't imagine anyone else doing it. Certainly not Lars Hansen, unless he decided it was in his best interests. I was pretty sure he would continue to work with the islanders, and that David Glynn would take on his father's role, if I did nothing and left them alone. Everything was down to me, and I could decide the fate of the island and everyone on it.

I cast my mind back to my arrival, and the strange, shocking event that had taken place when I'd been on the island less than an hour. Suddenly I understood what the old woman, Mary, had been trying to say to me just before she died. Until now, I'd assumed that when she said 'Mother,' she'd been asking for her own mother, but she hadn't. It was my mother she was talking about. 'She was right,' Mary said, and I saw her fierce, blue eyes. She'd wanted to tell me that my mother had done the right thing. For my entire life, I'd nursed the belief that she'd neglected me, and that she hadn't really cared about me. But now I understood what she'd done.

I found myself recalling something that had happened in Afghanistan, after I'd been there for about a year. When I first began to undertake intelligence work, my interpreter was a quiet, humorous man called Farzad. One day he seemed very downcast, and eventually he told me that a cousin of his, a young woman who'd been married for two years, had lost her only child in a bomb attack. The boy had been eleven months old, and she was almost mad with grief. Her husband – himself shattered by their loss – couldn't comfort her. It was a very sad story. About a year later, when I happened to be back in the UK for a while, I heard from Farzad that his cousin and her husband now had a new baby – a little girl. I was very glad to hear the news, and that there might be at least some light in the darkness for the young couple. But eight months later, when I was back in Afghanistan, I was stunned to hear from Farzad that his cousin had walked out on her husband and their child. Apparently, she'd become increasingly distant and unhappy, until finally she refused to have anything to do with the little girl. It was an unusual thing to do, and everyone knew how difficult life would be for a single woman who'd left her family like that. Her husband went to find her, and he succeeded, but he returned home without her, and made no further efforts to coax her back. I said to Farzad that perhaps his cousin was still traumatised by the loss of her first child, and she'd found it hard to give enough love to the new baby. 'No,' he said, 'it was the exact opposite. She loved the girl too much.' I said I didn't understand. He explained that his cousin was afraid of the love she felt for the baby. What if she lost her? What if there was another bomb, or the baby fell ill and died? The woman would have been unable to bear the pain of such a loss for a second time, and had been trying to protect herself from it.

Now, as I thought about the story, I felt that I began to understand my mother's behaviour. In effect, she'd lost her first son, David, by leaving him with Druce. Now I knew why she'd seemed so distant from me.

And I knew I would return to the island.

I'd need to get the timing right. Ideally, I would arrive with a camera crew just ahead of the authorities. I'd want to get everything in place before I raised the alarm, and I'd need a few security people with me if I was going to be there for even a short time before the police arrived. There was no point in risking my neck, or anyone else's.

My view of the approaching mainland was framed between Harriet and Logan's heads. I wondered if they would come back with me. It would have to be done sensitively, of course, but the presence of Logan on camera in my report would make a stunning impact. I imagined him on the quayside, describing what had happened, and in the cavernous laboratory – or what was left of it, if Glynn and the others suspected I was returning, and tried to destroy it – and then I visualised him trembling beside the eerie stillness of the lake, perhaps at twilight. That would be immensely powerful, and I could see the shot already.

Harriet turned to me. 'Nearly there,' she said. She frowned. I must have been gazing at her blankly. 'Adam,' she said, 'what are you thinking about?'

I summoned up a smile. 'I don't know. The future. What to do next.'

She nodded. 'Me too. I can't seem to think beyond the next half hour. I'll be able to see things more clearly when we get there, and we're safe.' She jerked her head towards the mainland. 'One step at a time; that's what it feels like to me.'

She turned away and drew Logan towards her. I couldn't believe I'd just been thinking so cynically about using them to help me make a good story. I tried to let go of the idea. It had been a long time since I hadn't lived my life without being caught up in some kind of scripting process: planning the next stage of my career, my next project, my speech at the next award ceremony. I wanted that to end. I didn't want to be at war with myself any longer, and I truly believed I could change. I would make a new life with Harriet and Logan.

We were nearly in the harbour now. I made an effort to bring myself fully into the present moment, and to feel grateful for what I had.

But all the time I felt the island behind me, pulling me back.

THANKS

I would like to thank my editor, Scott Pack, for his invaluable advice and support. I'm also grateful to Wendy Lee, Sara Davies, and Iain Farmer for their feedback and suggestions as I developed the book, and to Adrian Bleese for taking the time to set me straight about helicopters.

If you have enjoyed *Stone Heart Deep*, do please help us spread the word – by posting a review on Amazon (you don't need to have bought the book there) or Goodreads; by posting something on social media; or in the old-fashioned way by simply telling your friends or family about it.

Book publishing is a very competitive business these days, in a saturated market, and small independent publishers such as ourselves are often crowded out by the big houses. Support from readers like you can make all the difference to a book's success.

Many thanks.

Dan Hiscocks
Publisher
Lightning Books

You might also enjoy Paul Bassett Davies' previous novel, published by Lightning Books in 2020. Here's the opening chapter as a taster:

PLEASE DO NOT ASK FOR MERCY AS A REFUSAL OFTEN OFFENDS

Paul Bassett Davies

KILROY

Manfred faced his execution in high spirits. He sang snatches of unrecognisable songs with great gusto, and recited peculiar stories that he seemed to be inventing on the spot. It was all nonsense and gibberish, of course. His mind was deranged, and everything was scrambled up. The crowd couldn't have asked for a better show.

But then there was some unpleasantness. Manfred began to blaspheme in the most appalling way, even repeating the odious words and phrases that had brought him to this regrettable termination. Parents covered their children's ears, and Manfred was silenced swiftly. The remainder of the ceremony was conducted in a more restrained atmosphere, and after it was over there were the usual grumbles from some among the dispersing crowd, deploring the outdated custom that allowed the condemned man to say a few words. They asked each other why the courtesy of a final speech should be extended to scoundrels who exploited it as an opportunity to scandalise decent families. There was no excuse for that kind of exhibition, they said, even if the man was bonkers.

People also complained, as they always did, about how long it took to get out of Shadbold Square, owing to the narrowness of the surrounding streets, and the failure of the authorities to lay on extra trams for these occasions, which were always well-attended despite everyone assuring each other, after every execution, that they certainly wouldn't be coming again and things were very much better in the old days.

Manfred's shoes were presented to his family the next day. His son, Roland, was proud of the memento, but Sheba, his older sister, made a mime of vomiting every time she passed the mantelpiece on which the stained footwear was displayed. The children's mother, Wanda, was a practical woman, and a few days later, when the kids were at school, she put her late husband's shoes in the garbage grinder. When the children came home Roland kicked up a fuss, but his mother mollified him with the promise of a visit to the fish museum. As for Sheba, she seemed indifferent to the loss. However, the very next morning young Roland was confronted by a dreadful scene in the kitchen when he came down for breakfast. Blood was spattered on the walls, and was congealing into a sticky pool beneath the body of his mother, which lay on the floor. Her throat had been cut, and a large kitchen knife was sticking out of her eye socket. There was no sign of Sheba, some of whose clothes and belongings were discovered to be missing, along with a backpack.

It seemed like an open-and-shut case of Abrupt Matricide Syndrome with an absconding culprit, but the authorities naturally asked the police to investigate.

Detective Kilroy was given the job. He was a handsome fellow, and a professional from the brim of his hat to the soles of his shoes. He lived for his police work, and for Creek, the parrot who shared his austere bachelor quarters. It was a gorgeous specimen of the Freakin Grey species, and Kilroy was very fond of it.

Occasionally he wondered if perhaps he should have risen higher in the force by the age of thirty-nine, but he never let the thought linger in his mind for too long. Regret was a useless indulgence, and he wished he'd known that when he was younger.

Kilroy's first task was to talk to the son. Roland was eleven years old, and Kilroy expected him to be flustered. He'd recently lost his father in unfortunate circumstances, and then, before he could catch his breath, came the additional surprise of his mother's death. No boy could be unaffected by seeing his dad executed, then stumbling across the bloody corpse of his mother in the family kitchen on his way to school.

Beneath his gruff exterior Kilroy was a decent man, and he was surprised to learn that Roland had been taken into custody. When he tried to find out who had given the order to arrest the boy, nobody seemed to know. Kilroy didn't claim to be an expert in child psychology, but he figured that being locked up would do nothing to improve the youngster's frame of mind.

His own plan had been to adopt a friendly approach, and perhaps take the boy out to tea, which he imagined a person of his age might appreciate. But now, the best he could do was to bring a glass of spood juice into Roland's cell, and ask the custodian to remove the shackles. He was determined to treat the boy like his own son, if he'd had a son, and assuming he had a good relationship with the hypothetical child.

Kilroy sat down opposite Roland, handed him the juice, and smiled at him. He wanted to show he wasn't a beast, and he began the interrogation by asking the boy how he was feeling. That was a mistake.

To Kilroy's surprise and embarrassment, the youth began to speak, not just of his feelings at the present moment, as Kilroy had intended, but of his emotions in general. It seemed that Roland's tender young heart was a cornucopia of conflicted passions, which he promptly disgorged.

Sometimes, he said, I feel that life's plentiful syrup is erupting through my pipes, and I am almost overwhelmed by a sense of pure, unbounded joy; I fear that I must swoon at the sheer beauty of the world, in every particular, both great and small, and oh, I am undone.

I see, Kilroy said, playing for time, and at others?

At other times, Roland said in his clear, high-pitched voice, I feel the aching sadness of life pervading my weary existence like an eldritch fog, engulfing me in a haunting melancholy that is nigh on unbearable.

Kilroy checked the notes in his file. Was the kid really only eleven? Yes, according to the notes. Kilroy wondered what the hell they taught them in school these days. As it happened, the file contained copies of Roland's school reports. Kilroy glanced at the most recent one and noticed that the boy had expressed an interest in training to enter the priesthood.

Eventually he managed to get the interview back on track, and questioned Roland about the events leading up to his mother's presumed murder, and the disappearance of his sister, Sheba. That was when the mystery deepened.

The forensic specialists had established the time of Wanda's death as between five and eight-thirty in the morning. That fitted with Roland's account, of coming down to breakfast at nine to find his mother's corpse still warm, her blood in the process of congealing, and the onset of rigor mortis only just beginning. It appeared that Roland was gifted, in addition to his eloquence, with an advanced understanding of human biology. But he was adamant that he'd heard his sister packing her things and leaving the house just after midnight. He was absolutely certain of that.

And later, Kilroy asked, did you hear her come back in?

No, replied Roland, but I sleep very heavily between the hours of one and seven. My nocturnal rhythms are rigid to the point of despotism. If Sheba had returned to the house later, I would have heard nothing.

Kilroy asked if Sheba's behaviour had seemed unusual in the days between her father's execution and her mother's death.

The lad furrowed his brow. Hmmm, he ventured, I didn't see much of her, to tell you the truth. I remember she said she'd been reading a lot.

And that was unusual?

What?

Her reading a lot.

Not really. She was always a keen reader.

Kilroy tried to keep the irritation out of his voice. You just implied, he said slowly, that it was unusual for her to be reading a lot.

No, Roland said with a shake of his head, I didn't. That may be what you inferred, but you asked me if her behaviour had been unusual, and I mentioned that I hadn't seen much of her. That was the unusual part. Normally, I'd see her reading. She would sprawl about the place, engrossed in the trashy girls' stuff she liked. But during the period about which you enquired she spent most of her time in her room, and when I asked her what she'd been doing in there she told me she'd been reading. And before you ask, she didn't tell me what. I suspect she didn't want me to know.

I see, Kilroy said once again. But he saw nothing. He was stumped.

Kilroy excused himself and went outside the cell to collect his thoughts. It didn't make sense. Why would the girl leave the house in the early hours of the morning, taking her backpack with her, and then return a few hours later in order to murder her mother? Unless…unless…what?

Kilroy was aware that an alternative hypothesis was lurking just beyond his mental field of vision, like a distant road sign that was unreadable to a man who'd left his glasses at home. Only by approaching closer could Kilroy decipher the message, but for every step he took in its direction, it receded by an equal distance, remaining tantalisingly fuzzy. Experience had taught him that he needed to relax, unclench the mental fist that constrained him, and allow the message to present itself to him in its own good time, perhaps when he was asleep, which sometimes happened.

But sleep would have to wait. Right now he had a precocious eleven-year-old boy locked up in a cell, and limited time in which to question him. At any moment a social advocate could arrive and pester him to either release the boy, or charge him, or put him to the itching test and have done with it. Even if Kilroy let him go, Roland would have to be rehoused with foster parents, and Kilroy needed to put himself out of the picture before he got entangled in the process, thank you very much. The red tape was a nightmare, and Kilroy didn't need that shit in his life.

But something told Kilroy the boy had useful information, if only he could get it out of him. He refused to consider the itching test. He had never knowingly hurt a child, and despised anyone who would do so. Anyhow, Kilroy didn't generally go in for that type of thing. No rough stuff, unless it was strictly unavoidable.

Back in the cell he was about to resume his questioning when Roland forestalled him by bursting into tears. Kilroy wondered if it was just another tactic, like the eloquence and the emotional disclosure, but nonetheless he handed the snivelling boy a handkerchief that he kept in his breast pocket for occasions like this. The storm of tears began to abate, and Kilroy was thinking that perhaps he might try a new approach, based on jovial, man-to-man camaraderie, when the custodian entered the cell, and told Kilroy he was wanted on the telephone.

Kilroy took the call in the custodian's office. It was the Chief's secretary, telling Kilroy to release the boy and come to see the Chief immediately.

He handed the receiver back to the custodian with a sigh.

The man raised his eyebrows. Trouble?

My middle name, Kilroy said.

The Chief was a big woman, as large as a house. Not literally, but whenever Kilroy thought about her he pictured her as an imposing municipal building, inside which he was not welcome. He found it impossible to imagine any type of intimacy with her.

In reality she was a medium-sized woman with an air of competence and efficiency that often made Kilroy feel like he needed a shower. She had a habit of communicating in a series of questions, some of them rhetorical. In this instance, the questions were as follows:

Why had Kilroy taken a juvenile witness into custody?

Was he aware that this could look bad for the department?

As a matter of interest, was Kilroy a fucking idiot?

When was Kilroy going to focus the investigation on finding the girl?

How far away did he think she could have got by now?

Why wasn't he out there right now, tracking her down?

What was he waiting for?

Kilroy decided not to point out that the order to arrest Roland hadn't come from him. He didn't want to appear defensive or whiny. Besides, if the Chief herself had given the order, Kilroy judged it unwise to confront her about it. And if she hadn't, that meant it must have come from further up the chain, or from a special services unit, operating under separate authority, and Kilroy had no desire to open that particular can of worms. It was a sizeable can, into which it was surprisingly easy to fall.

He simply nodded, stood up, and walked to the door. As he opened it, the Chief spoke again. Kilroy, she said, wait.

He waited.

You're a good cop, she said. One of our best. I'm under pressure to find this girl and get the case wrapped up. Certain people are nervous about it, and these are turbulent times, what with social unrest, people going wrong, people dropping dead for no reason, and so on. So, please proceed swiftly, but with caution. I don't want to lose you, and this girl could be extremely dangerous. Look what she did to her own mother. If you find your safety threatened in any way, slay her without hesitation. Shoot first. I know you can be sensitive – no, don't try to deny it – and you're not as jaded as you like to think. Keep your pistol handy. I know you'll do your best. Thank you, Kilroy.

Kilroy closed the door gently behind him.